The SeaOx

Book 1

Terrence (T) Mault

Strategic Book Publishing and Rights Co.

Copyright © 2014 Terrence Mault. All rights reserved.

No part of this book may be reproduced or transmitted in any form or by any means, graphic, electronic, or mechanical, including photocopying, recording, taping, or by any information storage retrieval system, without the permission, in writing, of the publisher.

Strategic Book Publishing and Rights Co.
12620 FM 1960, Suite A4-507
Houston, TX 77065

www.sbpra.com

ISBN: 978-1-62857-439-5

Design: Dedicated Book Services, (www.netdbs.com)

Dedication

For Patricia, a beautiful lady of infinite principle, my inspiration, my best friend, and my life mate.

Table of Contents

Acknowledgement vii
Introduction viii
Chapter 1 Hans Christian Pilot House Sailboat 1
Chapter 2 Hijacked 6
Chapter 3 Marta and the Lake A-4 11
Chapter 4 The Utrecht Chateau 20
Chapter 5 The Twins' Guests and the Country Hustle 31
Chapter 6 The Paris Broker and Attempted Escape 40
Chapter 7 Widow Kidnapped 48
Chapter 8 Basque Assassin in Control 60
Chapter 9 Suspects 74
Chapter 10 Revenge of the Basque Assassin 82
Chapter 11 New Ransom Demand 91
Chapter 12 UPS Driver Killed, Ransom Missing 98
Chapter 13 Chateau Love, Lust, and Other
    Arrangements 106
Chapter 14 Ruth and Her Basque Clients 118
Chapter 15 Basque Money and Capture 124
Chapter 16 Andre, the Broker, and the Basque
    Assassin 130
Chapter 17 Andre Cleared, Ruth, and Assassin at
    Large 137

Chapter 18 Andre, Ava, and Frosted Beer Mugs 149

Chapter 19 Andre and Ava Sail to Portugal, Ruth
and Pelling Plan Their Escape.. 164

Chapter 20 Lisbon Marina, Where Old Enemies
Meet 177

Chapter 21 Trapping the Assassin 200

Acknowledgements

This book began many years ago while I was sailing with a good friend, Don Cranston. I asked myself, *what if a successful single guy chucked the rat race, bought a great sailboat, and started on an idyllic adventure, only to have disaster strike when his boat is hijacked and he is about to die*? The finished manuscript took too long and was too long. One of my first readers, John D. Hansen, suggested it could be two books. The author in residence at the University of Alberta suggested the same, or even a trilogy. So, the *SeaOx* became book one of a trilogy.

    I would like to thank the special friends I have sailed with over the years: My first mate, Patricia, and John Fleming, Don Cranston, and Percy Ross Bradford. I would also like to thank the Long Ridge Writers Group for the knowledge I gained when taking their courses, and especially my mentor, Kris Franklin.

Introduction

I spent many years working in the Investment Industry as a stock and commodities broker for Richardson Securities and Merrill Lynch. Prior to Patricia and me taking sailing lessons, I took flying lessons and earned my pilot license. The boat of my dreams has always been a Hans Christian Pilot House model and the airplane is, of course, a Lake A-4 Amphibian, wonderful machines both. They are prominent throughout the story.

Chapter 1

Hans Christian Pilot House Sailboat

The Radi Abri Marina
Brest, France

From his stool at the bar, the stranger sipped his beer and watched the green-hulled sailboat glide to a stop as her tall, tanned skipper stepped onto the dock holding the bowline. The skipper nodded to the marina employee helping with the lines, then entered the harbourmaster's office.

"Can I bring you another Beck's?" asked the cute, blonde bartender. She had delivered his first beer and introduced herself to the rugged, good-looking stranger, clearly hoping for a conversation, but he couldn't shift his focus from the arriving sailboat. He continued watching dockside.

"No, thanks. That's all for me," he said, eliminating conversation once again.

* * *

Inside the office, the skipper handed his sailboat's papers to the marina manager. "Welcome to Brest, Captain Laurent. We've reserved slip 210 for the *SeaOx* for this afternoon. Proceed straight ahead and our dockhand will be waiting to assist with your tie up."

Andre Laurent paid for the dockage with a credit card and said, "I'll be leaving as soon as I top up my fuel and water. Is there a post office in your chandlery?"

"Yes, Captain, it's located at the back of the grocery section."

Andre Laurent left the office, untied the bowline at the dock, and hopped aboard with it in hand. "Heave me the stern line, please," he said to the dockhand. He untied and heaved it aboard to the skipper, who then motored forward to his designated slip.

* * *

The stranger stepped outside the Chart Room lounge to watch the beautiful Hans Christian Pilot House cutter chug slowly away from the dock. He smiled at the name on the transom, *SeaOx*. The morning light bouncing off the water reflected a kaleidoscopic dance along the emerald hull as it moved slowly down the water lane and docked at a slip alongside the main jetty, two hundred yards from the Chart Room entrance. Returning to the dining room, the stranger sat at a table where he had a clear view of the *SeaOx*. He ordered the fresh catch and fries his way, and continued his surveillance.

He watched as the tall skipper secured his boat's lines, with the help of the dockhand, and connected the water to his boat. The skipper entered his boat, returned moments later with a small parcel, walked back up the jetty, and entered the chandlery.

The stranger's meal of fish and fries arrived exactly as ordered: fresh-caught snapper poached, not battered, sweet potato fries baked in the oven, not deep-fried, and a sprig of steamed broccoli. He caught a waft of the sea coming from his plate and imagined this morning's scene on the rolling and dipping boat that had produced this catch. His scene was complete with humming engines and the smell of fish and diesel fuel. His first taste of the snapper brought him back to the reality of this well-crafted meal.

While finishing his lunch, the stranger observed the tall sailor carrying a number of bags of groceries down the jetty to his boat. A teenaged boy carrying additional bags assisted him. The sailor tipped the boy and began taking the bags from the jetty onto his boat.

After paying for his meal, the stranger began moving up the jetty toward the busy sailor. When only two bags remained on the jetty, he was within two boat lengths. The unsuspecting sailor picked up the last two bags and carried them aboard. When the sailor reached the bottom of the stairs at the entrance to the boat's galley, the stranger made his move.

* * *

Andre Laurent's dream about falling down a stairway was so realistic and painful it awakened him. The ache at the back of his head sent tears streaming down his cheeks. He was hanging naked, feet dangling a foot off the floorboards. He couldn't feel for a cut or bruise on the back of his head as his hands were tied behind his back. Shaking his head didn't help it clear. He tried to concentrate, listening to his sailboat's familiar sounds. The steady dip and roll and the pitch of the whirring rigging indicated the boat was sailing at about six knots. His wrists, underarms, and ankles throbbed for attention. The continuing motion of the *SeaOx*, surging forward from the pull of her sails, tempted him back to unconsciousness. He fought to stay awake, bringing his head up abruptly when it lolled against his chest.

Who in the hell is at the wheel and why am I tied up naked like this? He blinked his eyes and shook his head again, forcing himself to concentrate. *I'm dangling by my safety harness. It leads up through the overhead hatch and is attached to something on deck. I'm suspended just off the floorboards, one ankle tethered to the settee leg, the other tied to a table leg.*

"What the hell?" Andre croaked, but nobody responded. Terror rushed up his spine like an electric current, enveloping his body in a drenching sweat. His head drooped against his chest as he tried to remain conscious.

Deep breaths seemed to hold his fear in check as he tried to focus. *My memory video shows me topping up the boat's fuel and water tanks at the Radi Abri Marina in Brest. I see myself with the envelope containing the audiotape I made for Ava, carrying it to the marina store, and mailing it to her in Hamburg. Then I buy a few provisions. Yeah, there's the young clerk bagging my groceries and helping me carry them to the SeaOx. We're setting the bags on the deck and I'm digging out a tip, thanking the kid. I see him moving up the jetty towards the chandlery as I start taking the bags down to the galley. I'm at the bottom of the stairs with the last of the groceries when everything goes black, and yet the SeaOx seems to be sailing well. If the attacker is at the wheel, he knows about sailboats, so why tie me up naked like this? Is he some kind of pervert? Why am I still alive? Stop it! Think! I'm not hurt that badly, but my wrists are so . . . numb. Where are we heading? Maybe it's just my boat he wants? Is he still on board? I'm losing it . . . gotta stay awake . . . try to think! My head is . . . soupy. Concussion? Or was I drugged?*

When the Seth Thomas clock on the port bulkhead chimed eight times, Andre calculated he was attacked just before he planned to cast off lines at 6:00 p.m. But was that yesterday? It was now eight in the morning. Could he really have been out of it for fourteen hours?

Who's at the wheel and where's he heading? Is there only one hijacker? Maybe there's more than one of them.

Andre heard someone coming down the steps from the pilothouse, and a man suddenly appeared before him wearing only a pair of Andre's white sailing shorts. He looked to be between thirty and thirty-five years old, built like a weightlifter. He appeared to be military, with his sun-bleached hair cut close to his scalp, and his face clean-shaven.

Andre's parched throat croaked, "Who are you, and what do you want?" No response.

"Can you get me some water, untie me, and let me put on some clothes? It's humiliating as hell hanging here naked, like a side of beef. I won't cause you any trouble. I just need to get some circulation back into my wrists and ankles." Silence. "My feet are numb . . ."

The attacker untied Andre's ankles, and then swung him so he was facing the bulkhead and no longer blocking the entry to the forward v-berth. The man put his hand on Andre's naked buttock to push him out of his way. This so startled Andre that anyone watching would have thought he'd been zapped by a cattle prod. His nerves yelled "battle stations" and he went on immediate alert.

"Whoa! Easy, Laurent, you're not my type." The stranger's voice sounded amused. "When I was going through your papers, I came across Polaroid photos of you and a yummy lady, plus your explicit notes about her and her family. Looks to me like you have a wealthy widow on the line. Shame on you, Laurent, leaving naughty pictures lying around for anyone to see; someone might get the idea that you're in the blackmail business. Those notes say you and the hot widow have a rendezvous set for June 3 at her Paris apartment. Well now, you just stay cool and I'll see that you get there as planned."

Chapter 2
Hijacked

"*SeaOx* calling Radi Abri Marina," the stranger said.

"Radi Abri to *SeaOx*. What can I do for you, Captain Laurent?"

"Please file float plan to Bassin De La Manche Marina at Le Havre, ETA 1400 hours on Thursday May 31."

"*SeaOx* float plan will be filed for Bassin De La Manche Marina at Le Havre ETA 1400 this Thursday. Radi Abri out."

"Thank you, Radi Abri. *SeaOx* out."

The stranger thought, *Good thing Laurent is forehanded. He has his nautical chart with his trip to Le Havre complete with waypoints, departure time 1800 hours, and ETA at Le Havre at 1800 hours on the thirty-first. I'll only have to adjust times on the way. I had to get the hell out of there; I couldn't chance someone dropping by the SeaOx to visit, so I left four hours early.*

The stranger decided not to put the sails up until he reached the Isle de Ouessant. He'd just chug along at a steady six knots out into the Bay of Biscay, then head north, keeping sight of the mainland on his right. "At this speed, I'll be making almost eleven kilometres each hour, so I ought to be hoisting sail six hours from now around 7:00 p.m.," he calculated out loud.

A sudden thought occurred to him and he checked the chart once more. Damn! He'd forgotten about the tides and currents. He was relieved when he saw Laurent had the arrows of current drawn in a northern direction. *Good, the currents will help us along. We'll be early.*

Isle de Ouessant, 1835 hours

After getting the sails up, the stranger turned off the diesel and changed his heading to forty degrees, sticking with Laurent's navigation. When the diesel tuned out, the apparent wind in the rigging hummed them forward toward the English Channel. He consulted the chart for the upcoming waypoints Laurent had noted and decided to take twenty-minute naps at the top of each hour when he would engage the automatic pilot. He set his wristwatch alarm and curled up on the bench seat. When he reached Alderney Island, he anchored offshore.

He could see the Cap de la Hague in sight to his right. He was right on course. He went below and checked on Laurent, who was unconscious but murmuring incoherently. The stranger listened, crouching over his captive, but could only make out the widow's name, Elspeth. Laurent was still secured to the bunk. *No need to give him another shot. He isn't going anywhere*, the stranger thought.

It was seven in the evening and he was dead tired after twenty-seven hours of sailing with only bits of sleep. He needed a good sleep, so he set his wristwatch alarm for midnight. Five hours would have to do.

When he awoke, he started the engine, motored over the anchor, brought it up using the electric windlass, and secured it. He raised the sails, cut the engine, and turned onto a heading of one-hundred-twenty degrees for the final ninety-two mile run into Le Havre.

He saw the lights of Cherbourg off to starboard by two in the morning, and could still see their faint glow until the looming Pointe de Barfleur blocked them out. He went below at 5:00 a.m. and made a snack. He checked on his hostage, who was sleeping soundly and went back up top. At the inside steering position, he consulted the chart and calculated he was still ten hours from Le Havre; his new ETA would be six thirty that evening. He decided he'd call the marina that afternoon to confirm their arrival.

The stranger recalled when he had untied Andre Laurent and handed him jeans to wear. He'd fashioned a hobble around his ankles, which forced him to shuffle rather than walk freely. He'd motioned him over to the chart table saying; "Go ahead, Laurent, check over the navigation if you can function."

Laurent had fumbled with the ruler and dividers with his bound hands, trying to take measurements. *He saw by my notations on the chart, we were sailing his original course to Le Havre. While I opened up some soup, I had a chance, unobserved, to drug Laurent's cup. While putting the cups into the microwave, I saw him shove the chart drawer closed. The look of defeat on his face told me he was probably after the flare gun, but was bummed out when he found the drawer empty.*

The stranger remembered catching him looking at him, peering over the edge of his cup. *Sizing me up, probably.* Laurent was fit enough—tall, maybe six four, and in his early forties. *You won't be making any kind of move against me just now, buddy, because you look like you are about to faint,* he remembered thinking. *The drug was kicking in. Laurent did come at me verbally after finishing his soup. He figured I was some opportunistic boat bum who had hijacked his boat and told me I lucked out by keeping it afloat. Bad tactic! I backhanded him in the jaw, which sent him reeling until his hobble tripped him and he crashed to the floorboards.*

"Jesus! What the hell . . .?" Laurent cursed in pain.

"Keep the sarcasm to yourself, or I'll slice you up proper and toss you to the sharks," the stranger said.

The look on Laurent's face told me that he'd gotten the message. I hoisted him to his feet, shoved him down the hallway into the forward berth face down, and tied him securely to the berth so even in a severe roll of the SeaOx he wouldn't move. I pulled the overhead hatch closed and went back up to the forward steering position.

Andre had laid motionless on the forward v-berth, his head buzzing from the snake-like backhand from his captor.

Soon, though, a warm flush crept over him and the ache in his neck and face went away. Before passing out, his thoughts were for Elspeth and the harm he may cause her.

* * *

Noon, May 31

The stranger reached for the ship-to-shore radio and tuned it to channel sixteen. "This is the *SeaOx* calling the Bassin De La Manche Marina at Le Havre. Come in, please."

"Hello, *SeaOx*, this is Bassin De La Manche. Good morning, Captain Laurent."

"Captain Laurent is very much under the weather, I'm afraid. I'm just calling to confirm our slip reservation and request directions when we're closer. ETA is 1830 hours. Captain Pelling, over."

"Captain Pelling, we have the *SeaOx* at slip 115. Call when you pass the red can buoy at the entrance to the marina. We'll direct you from there, over."

"Roger, will do, marina radio. *SeaOx*, over and out."

* * *

Bassin De La Manche Marina

"Is there a law office close by that would still be open?" Pelling asked the marina manager.

"In the next block there's a young lawyer, works late, stays open until 2100 hours during the week," answered the manager.

"I've purchased the *SeaOx* from Captain Laurent and we need to have a legal transfer drawn," Pelling offered.

"I see. Please get me a copy of that transfer. I'll need it together with the *SeaOx* papers while you're here, Captain Pelling," the manager said.

* * *

After forty-five minutes at the law office, Pelling was now the legal owner of the *SeaOx*. He had given a one-hundred-seventy-five-thousand-dollar cheque to Laurent for the *SeaOx* who signed a transfer of ownership. He then helped Laurent, still groggy, back to the boat; retied him to the v-berth, and injected him. Pelling returned to the chart table, looked over the transfer, and tore up the one-hundred-seventy-five-thousand-dollar cheque.

The following morning, June 1, Pelling cooked scrambled eggs, toast, and coffee in the galley of the *SeaOx*, and then brought Andre to the table in the salon. Andre ate in silence and drank his coffee, after which he began to regain his wits and asked, "What day is it? Where are we?"

"We're at the marina in Le Havre. I've ordered a rental car in your name to be delivered here shortly. We're going into Paris to see Pierre Turrin, your Merrill Lynch broker. But first, you'll phone him and instruct him to cash in your T-bills. Tell him we'll pick up the cheque for your account balance before noon."

Andre thought for a moment. *He has my boat and he'll have my money. Then what?* "So, after you have my money, you intend to let me go. Is that it?" he asked.

"I don't think you'll be much of a bother to me after I'm through with you," Pelling said.

Andre thought about that for some time as he slowly finished his breakfast. *That could mean when he's finished with me I'll be lying somewhere with my throat cut, my life gushing out of me. Damn, I'm as weak as a baby, but my only chance is to somehow alert Pierre of my situation.*

"You can make the call to your broker at the phone booth by the office," Pelling said. "Let's go, Laurent, and remember I have this blade at the ready. If you try anything stupid, I'll end your life in an instant."

Chapter 3
Marta and the Lake A-4

Marta Vander Riis banked her Lake Renegade amphibian onto the final leg of her descent into the Amsterdam Airport and spoke into her headset. "Schiphol tower, this is Lake Renegade *Baker Charlie Nova* 3639, on final for runway 26. Please confirm landing instructions and give me a time check, will you please?'

"Schiphol tower to Lake Renegade *Baker Charlie Nova*, we have you on final just crossing inner marker, one kilometre back, on active runway 26. You are clear to land. On touchdown, switch to 118 ground control. Time is 1142 hours local. Tower out."

"Roger tower. Lake Renegade *Baker Charlie Nova* out."

She landed without incident and switched her radio as instructed. "Lake Renegade *Baker Charlie Nova* reporting for taxi instructions, over."

"Baker Charlie Nova, proceed straight ahead and turn right at zero three, then straight ahead to tie down area in front of hangar 6."

"Roger that, ground control. *Baker Charlie Nova* out."

Marta had landed at Amsterdam's Schiphol Airport so many times since she'd purchased the plane she had lost count. She and Mathijs, her twin, had been given flying lessons on their eighteenth birthday by their mother. Mathijs, pronounced *Ma-tice*, stayed interested in flying until it was time to move from visual flight rules to the next level, instrument flight rules. He then decided not to continue with more instruction because he wanted to concentrate on getting a rock band together. Marta, on the other hand, was hooked on flying and kept taking more instruction after her IFR rating.

She now had a night rating and a float rating. She practiced continually until her twenty-first birthday when she and Tice, her twin's nickname, came into their trust funds of $5 million each.

Marta purchased her dream airplane for three-hundred-thousand US dollars—a new 1990 Lake Turbo Renegade four-seat amphibian, powered by a 270-horsepower Lycoming engine mounted on a pylon over the cabin in a reverse, or pusher, configuration. It had some remarkable features, such as the ability to take off from a dry strip in only eight hundred feet. On water, it needed twelve hundred feet of straightaway to get airborne, but only six hundred feet of arc, and it could accelerate through turns, which only the Lake series could do.

In boat mode, the Lake Renegade could reach one-hundred-five kilometres per hour, at which point it became a plane, like it or not. The price included checkout flight training, but Marta had only required twenty hours and used most of that time on touch-and-go practice on water. The Renegade could go from water to beach simply by lowering the landing gear, continuing forward from a floating position until the wheels touched bottom, then by adding power the pilot could taxi up onto the beach. Conversely, it was just as easy to go from land to water by simply proceeding into the water until the plane floated, when the pilot would bring the wheels up.

As well as teaching languages at the university in Utrecht, where Marta had become an assistant professor at twenty-six, she had a part-time job as an interpreter at the World Court in The Hague. She specialized in Dutch, German, French, and Spanish, with some expertise in Basque.

Marta flew to the coast when the World Court was in session, and whenever the mood struck her she flew into Paris. The farthest flight she had made was to Cannes for the film festival. She flew to Schiphol today to pick up her brother, due in at noon from New York on KLM flight 1200, and their special friend Lt. Robert Bizet of the Paris Sûreté. Tice had invited Robert to do some fly-fishing, when Robert had confided he was being forced to take some holiday time by his superiors but didn't know where to go. Tice didn't have to report to Merrill Lynch's Paris office for another two weeks. He also knew that Marta had a crush on Robert and that she was delighted he was coming.

Marta and Tice Vander Riis first met Robert Bizet when he was the investigating sergeant assigned to their case. They had witnessed the murder of the owner of the café where they were eating on a chilly Paris evening in October. There had been a student rally earlier that evening, which turned into a protest march and surged through the street where the café was located. Part of the mob leadership came into the café and demanded service. The owner could not accommodate the crush of the boisterous protesters and refused to serve them. At which time, one of the group drew a pistol and shot him. The mob dispersed quickly at the sound of gunfire. The twins went to assist the fallen owner, but he was already dead.

Later that evening, Marta and Tice identified the shooter and an accomplice while looking through the known-terrorist photo albums at Sûreté headquarters. Detective Sergeant Robert Bizet took their eyewitness accounts and thanked them for their help. That same weekend, both perpetrators were arrested and the Vander Riis twins picked them out of a police line-up. Detective Bizet informed the twins that the men they identified were members of the ETA, the terrorist arm of the Basque movement.

"Thank you both for stepping forward in this matter. However, it's my duty to advise you of the possible consequences of testifying against the ETA in open court," he'd said to them.

Marta and Mathijs put their heads together for a quick strategy session before Marta spoke, "Thank you for the warning, Detective, but we feel compelled to testify against this cold-blooded murderer and intend to see him punished."

The twins gave their accounts of the murder at the trial. The gunman was found guilty and sentenced to death. His accomplice received a jail sentence. During this time, Detective Bizet had on several occasions warned them, as well as their widowed mother, Elspeth, that they might be targets of the ETA and marked for retribution. He liked the twins, admired their tenacity at the trial, and took a personal interest in them. Whenever they or their mother were in Paris, they called him and invited him to lunch. For his part, the detective would discreetly arrange to have plainclothes police follow them to provide unobserved protection.

Tice informed his sister and mother of what he had learned on a lunch date with his new detective friend. Tice related how he had been teasing Robert about his frequent no-shows at their lunch get-togethers. He accused Robert of being a workaholic without a life outside his job. Robert told Tice that he hadn't always been so committed to his work. In fact, he did have a life in the recent past. He'd planned on getting married and settling down until his world was turned upside down. Robert admitted he had become obsessed with his work after the horrific tragedy he had witnessed when his car exploded with his fiancé inside, ETA retribution from his anti-terrorism police work. Knowing this, the Vander Riises agreed that a lesser man probably couldn't have continued in his line of work. However, Robert's resolve and strength of character allowed him to continue chronicling terrorist activity, with special emphasis on the ETA. This total dedication to his work earned him a promotion to the rank of lieutenant at the age of thirty.

Tice and Robert stayed in touch and became good friends. When Tice was hired by the Paris branch of Merrill Lynch and sent to New York to take his brokerage training at 1 Wall Street, they kept in touch by telephone at least once a week during his training. During their last telephone call, Robert advised Tice that his recent promotion to lieutenant gave him the authority to recruit, train, and assemble his own anti-terrorism squad. He told Tice his superiors insisted he take a holiday before beginning his new project.

"I told them I'd go somewhere just to get them off my back. Cripes, any travel I've done has always been work related. I haven't taken any time off in years. And to be honest, Tice, I don't know where the hell I'd go."

"Well, Lieutenant, I finished my broker training on Friday and don't have to report for work until the first of next month. We would love to have your company at the chateau. I'll arrive at Schiphol on Sunday, June 2 at noon. How about Marta and I meet you there, and the three of us can fly to Utrecht for some fun and relaxation? We could shoot some skeet, fly fish, or just hang out. What do you say?" Tice asked.

"That would solve the problem of where to go, and it does sound enticing. Okay, it's a deal. Just a minute, do you think your mother or Marta would mind? They may have other plans for this weekend," Robert said.

"Not a problem. Mother will be away. And as for Marta, even if she did have other plans she would cancel them as soon as she heard you'd be coming for a visit. I think she fancies you. What the hell she sees in you, though, I can't imagine. Besides, Marta is always looking for an excuse to fly *Baker Charlie Nova* somewhere."

* * *

Schiphol Airport, Amsterdam, Netherlands

Marta glanced up at the clock above the baggage area where KLM flight 1200 had unloaded. It read 12:06 p.m. She spotted her brother in close contact with a very attractive flight attendant. *Same old Tice,* she thought. *Just smile and they go gaga and fall all over you. Well, let's see if I can stir up your arrangements a little bit!*

Marta waved at her brother as she approached him, then threw herself at him, and gave him a big kiss hello. She glanced over his shoulder and saw the look on the face of the gal he had been talking with. The flight crew was holding the doors open for her as her wheeled luggage got caught in the doorway. It was evident they were enjoying the frustration of their crewmember.

"That was one of your better welcomes, Marta. You look fantastic as always, sis. And by the way, thanks a lot for scaring away my date. I'm supposed to pick her up at the Regent in an hour, but I'm not sure she'll even be there now. Did you come in the Lake?" Tice asked.

"Yes, and thanks for the compliment. Now I'm on the lookout for our favourite policeman. He arrives on Air France flight 1220, landing in a few minutes. We'll collect him, and then take a taxi over to the Regent Hotel to see if you still have a date. She's gorgeous, Tice!" said Marta.

"You're right, she is lovely, but you're just saying that because she resembles you. By the way, her name is Sylvie Bern."

"Really, you even know her last name! I'm impressed. I just hope she has a sense of humour. I get such a hoot out of trying to embarrass you when you arrive at airports."

He put his arm around her and she hip checked him, making him guffaw. "I really missed you, Marta. It's good to be home."

"Ditto, Tice!"

The luggage from the Air France flight had begun to spill onto the stainless steel luggage reptile as they approached. The twins stood off to the side talking quietly together, not noting the increasing crush of passengers pushing their way toward the metal conveyor in order to lunge for their bags before they passed them by.

"Hello there!" Robert smiled as he appeared beside the twins holding a single leather suitcase. He was wearing an orange leather sports jacket, cut more like a shirt, over a cream-colored mock turtleneck, and tan tailored slacks. He wore brown socks in tan loafers. He was casually dressed, but no maître d' enforcing the most rigid dress code would turn him away. Robert Bizet was six-feet tall and weighed a svelte two hundred pounds.

After he and Tice finished with their hellos, Marta stepped between them, looked up at the policeman, and said, "I'm so glad you came. You know, you haven't responded to our invitations in the past, Robert." And with that, she gave him a hug and a kiss of welcome.

Robert pulled himself together while Tice collected his luggage. Tice explained they were off to retrieve his date from the Regent Hotel nearby, after which they would have the taxi take them to the hangar where Marta had parked her airplane.

The Regent was a ten-minute taxi ride from the airport. Tice asked the driver to wait for them, hurried to the front desk, and asked to be connected to Sylvie Bern's room. The manager sent him to a house phone and connected him. After a short animated conversation, Tice returned and told his sister and Robert, "She will be down in five minutes. She's just changing and repacking her bag."

A short time later, Sylvie arrived in the foyer. "Hi Tice, hi everyone else, I'm Sylvie Bern." She smiled and gave him a devouring look. Tice introduced Robert and then his sister, Marta.

"The family resemblance is incredible. As a matter of fact, I bet my crewmate, Meg, that you were Tice's sister or cousin." Sylvie blushed, and said Meg had answered, "You had better hope she is after the welcome he got." Robert smiled but didn't get what they were laughing about.

"Welcome to Amsterdam, Sylvie. Tice is my twin, and ever since we were in grade school I've been trying to embarrass him upon arrivals. But as you can see, he's pretty cool about it."

After loading Sylvie's luggage into the taxi, Marta gave the driver directions to her plane. "Sylvie, we're going to fly to our home in Utrecht in Marta's plane. Not to worry, she's an accomplished pilot. Besides, we are in safe company with Lieutenant Robert Bizet of the Paris Sûreté with us," Tice said.

"Well then, I'll just relax and let events unfold as they will. This is beyond exciting," Sylvie said.

Twenty minutes later, Marta side slipped the Lake Renegade, descended from five thousand feet to level off at three thousand, and flew a circle around the perimeter of the city of Utrecht. Tice pointed out the bell tower for Robert and Sylvie, as well as the university where Marta taught. Marta added power and headed for the chateau minutes ahead. As they approached the estate grounds, it was evident that Sylvie and Robert were impressed at seeing it for the first time from the air. Marta flew around a second time at a thousand feet in slow attitude, affording them a marvellous view of the estate and its accompanying buildings.

"Okay, everyone, tighten your seat belts. We are going to set the plane down on the river," Marta said, then climbed to two thousand feet, levelled off, and began her descent to the river, which ran past the estate grounds and connected to a lake behind the chateau. Moments later, they came to a sliding skid along the water. Marta revved the engine, swung the plane around, and roared toward the opening to the lake beside a two-story structure on the shore. Marta lowered the wheels as she coasted toward the landing platform on the river bottom, which extended up onto the shore. The engine revved and they felt a little bump as the versatile little plane rolled out of the water and up onto the concrete pad. With a final rev of the engine, Marta swung the Lake one-hundred-eighty degrees to face the water. She then went quickly through her shutdown procedure.

"Okay, guys, we're here. How did you enjoy the ride?" Marta asked as she unlocked the cockpit doors and swung them open overhead.

"Wow! What a fabulous plane, super flight, Marta! Your place is awesome," gushed Sylvie, as she was the last one out of the rear seat, letting Tice help her from the ground.

"Very enjoyable flight, Marta," commented Robert. "The view from where I sat was exceptional." He looked into Marta's eyes for a response and got it as she winked at him.

Marta smiled and thought *I had to roll my skirt up pretty far to get comfy in order to operate the foot controls. At least, that's my story and I'm sticking to it.*

After tying the plane down, they loaded their luggage into a Land Rover parked near the landing area. Tice drove them to the chateau, a five-minute ride through a mini forest of beautiful trees. The roadway connected to a large circular driveway in front of the main entrance to the big house. Some of the staff was on the stone steps at the front entrance awaiting their arrival. As soon as Tice got out of the car, an elderly chap came forward to shake his hand and then bowed toward Marta, who rushed to hug him. Tice then introduced Henk Veldhoen to Sylvie and reminded Henk he had met Robert on a previous official visit. After Henk set the luggage on the front steps, he drove the Land Rover to the four-car garage, which looked like a two-story cottage. Tice and Marta introduced their guests to the staff and took them on a tour of the chateau.

Chapter 4
The Utrecht Chateau

First-time visitors to the Vander Riis chateau were always impressed with how modern the interior was compared to the exterior. Mathijs and Marta took turns explaining to Sylvie and Robert how their grandfather had the buildings constructed to appear as if they had been built in the eighteenth century when, in fact, they were built in 1930. The walls in all the hallways and against the horseshoe-shaped stairway leading to the second story were adorned with oil paintings of ancestors. The chateau did not contain an art collection; however, the paintings and tapestries hanging in various areas of the house could easily be classified as such.

The Vander Riises were wealthy, but not the least bit ostentatious. This chateau had been "home" to Elspeth and the twins for the past twenty-eight years. It had become their sanctuary since Elspeth took over the management of the estate after her husband, Karl, died of a stroke at age forty-three. The twins were just past their tenth birthday and Elspeth had just turned thirty a week before his death. It was a difficult time for the three of them, but they made the best of those years together.

At the time of her husband's death, they had a staff of six that looked after every aspect of their lives. Everything they could want was provided, so that the young widow could devote herself to her twins. Her first order of business as the new head of the household was to assure the staff that they would always be employed at the chateau as long as she was alive. Elspeth treated her staff more like family than servants, always addressing them by their first names and keeping keenly abreast of their families and welfare. She also kept a complete record of the staff's birthdays and all the important happenings in their lives. She grew to be admired and loved by them.

Henk Veldhoen and his wife raised two children who were now grown and living in Utrecht. Henk and his wife resided in sumptuous living quarters above the two-story garage. Henk had been in the employ of the Vander Riis family for almost forty years. The housekeeping at the chateau was a responsibility shared by the Voelker sisters, Alma, aged fifty-five, and Freda, fifty-seven. These remarkable ladies had never married and had been employed by the family for over thirty-five years. The eldest was a nurse and nutritionist, and her sister was a teacher who had training as a cook, interning for two years in a cloister of twenty-four nuns. They both had proven to be invaluable to Elspeth.

Elspeth also took a keen interest in the family business conglomerate, which included shipbuilding, insurance, metal fabrication, tool manufacturing, and extensive revenue property holdings.

* * *

After a quick tour of the chateau, Tice took Robert to a large guest room resembling a modern hotel suite, asked him to make himself at home, and to come down to the library for a cocktail after he freshened up. Robert had stayed in this room the last time he was a guest. It was a man's room, with dark wood from floor to ceiling and a wall of books. The adjoining wall contained a shelving unit complete with a stereo system, records, tapes, CDs, and videos. The furniture was burnt umber tufted leather, set against a screened off fireplace. The bath suite was all tile and mirrors with a step-down tub with Jacuzzi jets. The other half of the bathroom area was a walk-in closet, which contained many items of neatly stacked clothing, plus a compartment that held only boots and shoes. Robert hung his leather shirt jacket on the valet, washed his face with soap and water, and looked at his reflection in the mirror.

That was some plane ride. What a view! Marta is quite remarkable, he thought to himself. He was pretty sure they had connected when she noticed him ogling her from ankles to panties when she had her skirt hiked up. And when he looked into those incredible grey eyes of hers, she had smiled and winked at him. He definitely found her something to look at, yet he marvelled at how she was so natural and unassuming despite her beauty. *Methinks Ms Marta is on the hunt, and I seem to be her target. Hmm . . . and wouldn't that be special?*

Lieutenant Robert Bizet told his reflection in the mirror, "You must be on your best behaviour and just wait and see what develops."

Meanwhile, Marta had settled Sylvie in a similar suite decorated in a slightly more feminine theme. It had the same layout as Robert's, except the walls were a combination of fabric wallpaper in dark and light blue shades, and the furniture was covered in a multi-ribbon fabric of teal and purple. The main feature of the room was the huge canopied four-poster bed. The canopy of the bed was the same fabric as that of the furniture. The closet was full of every article of clothing imaginable, which Marta explained was her "overflow wardrobe."

Trying not to be too impressed, Sylvie smiled and asked, "Can I go shopping in your closet?"

Marta laughed and said, "Just help yourself to anything you like. Please, I insist. Wear whatever strikes your fancy. You are about an inch taller than I am, but I'll bet we are similar in size. Before I forget, I go for a run in the mornings. So, if you care to join me for all or part of my workout routine, you are welcome. Just put on one of my track outfits and come on down to the kitchen at seven. If you show, fine, if not, I'll know you've found something better to do and I'll just say, 'lucky lady' and go about my daily routine."

Hearing what Marta was implying, Sylvie wasn't sure what to say, so she just smiled, shook her head, and said,

"You and Tice are just too much . . . but thanks, Marta. We'll see how it goes, okay?"

"That's fine, Sylvie. Now freshen up and come on down to the library when you are ready and we'll have a cocktail. See you in a bit! I have to go get changed for my guy. And just between you and me, Robert Bizet has been here on other official occasions, but this time he is my guest and I'm planning a conquest. So, wish me luck, and I'll wish you the same."

"Deal!" Sylvie said and hugged Marta before she left.

Alone now, Sylvie took her bag into the closet, put the contents onto a vacant shelf, and set her shoes on the floor. She undressed as she went, grabbing a terry-cloth robe on the way to the glassed-in shower compartment. She reached in and turned on the water, adjusting the jet and temperature to her liking. She dropped her robe and underwear on the floor and stepped into the shower, letting the soothing warm water cover her as she began to wonder. *Who are these people? They're unreal! 'A place in the country' and then his sister flies us to this fabulous estate in her own plane. I'm trying to be cool, but I'm overwhelmed. You'd think anyone with all this would be sort of . . . snooty, but not these guys. And they're twins. Pinch yourself, girl!*

The truth was she was very impressed with the place, but she was even more impressed with Tice. From the moment she first laid eyes on him, she wanted to jump him. *What is with me anyway? I've seen lots of great looking guys on our flights and they haven't affected me like he has.*

What she loved was that he seemed so unaware of how devastating he truly was. She would have followed him anywhere. She remembered introducing herself and having him say the sweetest thing, "Sylvie would you like to come to my place and play?" *It was like we were in grade five or something, and it was his first day at school and everyone wanted to get to know him. Yet, out of all the others, he picked me to come over to his house to play!*

She hadn't been able to help herself; she'd burst out laughing. When she'd asked if he lived in Amsterdam, he said he lived in the country and his name was Tice. *Boy, talk about smooth!* He'd told her he knew she would be too busy to visit during the flight, but he'd insisted they have a chat before she left for her hotel so he could arrange to come by and pick her up. *So natural . . . and, God . . . I must have sounded like a dork when I blurted, 'Absolutely, you can count on it!' And what a doll his twin sister is. That cop hasn't got a chance. Never mind. I better get out of here, get dressed, and go find the library and my guy, Tice. Will you listen to yourself? Take it easy; just be cool!*

When Marta arrived in her own bedroom, she found Tice waiting for her. "Some catch that Sylvie gal—very nice person and a very attractive package, indeed! Of course, you hardly noticed did you, sweetie?"

Tice just smiled at his sister and agreed, "You're right, Marta. Sylvie seems like a very nice person, and you're right again, she is the type I'm attracted to. But never mind that. I'm a bit concerned about our friend, Robert. I know you, sister dearest. You wanted him here because you have designs on him. Just remember he is our special friend. Cripes! That sounded like a lecture or a sermon. Honest, I didn't mean it to be, even though I'm much older than you . . . six minutes, right? It isn't the same as me inviting someone like Sylvie for a weekend of fun and lust. Or . . . is it?" he asked.

Marta came close to her brother, laughed up at him, and kissed him on the cheek. "Listen up, you! I do have the hots for the lieutenant, and I mean to have my way with him this weekend. I don't know if it's just lust. I suspect it's more, and I think he's interested, but time will tell. You just busy yourself taking care of sexy Sylvie. My God, Tice, she lathers up at the mention of your name!"

That caused Tice to laugh and they both broke up. "What I want to know," Marta asked, showing a serious face, "is do you think we should offer the lieutenant some grass this evening, or should we just forget about it?"

"Well, Sylvie and I can have a toke wherever we end up, in her bedroom or mine." Tice said, not really answering his sister's question.

Marta thought a moment and said, "Let's just stay cool so it doesn't compromise him in any way. If he seems comfortable with my attempt to get him into my bed, I'll just ask him if he minds if we toke up, and then we play it by ear."

"Robert hasn't really opened up to me that much," Tice offered. "I've asked about the events of his fiancé's death and he told me about it, but it was like I was hearing a police report. As you know, I've spent a good deal of time with him, and I've got him on the list of candidates for brother-in-law, so this is as good a time as any to find out if he really is in-law timber, or just a cop on a vendetta pretending to be a good guy. Oh, by the way . . . how's Mother? I meant to ask you at the airport."

"You won't believe my suspicion. I think she has a fella. In these past three weeks she has been in a sort of a daze, smiles a lot but won't share. Now that's very unusual for her, right? And she's been like this ever since her trip to her Paris apartment in May. No kidding, Tice, she left for Paris this time and refused my offer to fly her to Schiphol. She just said, 'Not this time, sweetie.' When I asked her point blank if she met someone special, she looked at me like as if she wanted to tell me, thought about it, then said, 'I'll call you from Paris and let you know all about it. But not right now, it's really too soon. Please don't question me anymore, Marta. I'll call you two darlings from my apartment when I promise to tell all'. Then she had Henk drive her to Schiphol and took off two days ago. There was a message from her saying she would call again after you got here. So, she'll probably call later tonight. What do you make of it?"

"Awesome! I hope for her sake that she has met someone. She deserves to live a little. And your intuitions are usually bang on, so I'll keep my fingers crossed and hope like hell you're right . . . again." Tice shook his head in wonder and left the room, a hopeful look on his face, saying to himself, *All right, Mother!*

* * *

Marta, Tice, and Robert were having a Vander Riis Estate brandy when Sylvie joined them in the library. Henk was manning the bar dressed in a waiter's coat and bow tie. After pre-dinner drinks, Marta left to check with the kitchen, returned moments later, and summoned everyone to the dining room.

Marta and Tice sat opposite each other across the table; Sylvie sat alongside Tice, and Robert next to Marta. After a meal of roast beef, garden vegetables, sorbet, and tea, they retired to the game room.

A rousing game of eight ball took place, Marta and Sylvie against the guys. Marta suggested they play two out of three and each ante a hundred dollars to make it interesting. Sylvie turned out to be a very good pool player, and the girls easily won the first two games and the four-hundred-dollar pot.

"Wow, I'm going to buy my Granny Mandy a fabulous birthday present with this. Say partner, will you help me shop for her?" Sylvie asked.

"Sure, I'd be happy to help. How about we fly to Amsterdam tomorrow afternoon and see what we can find?" Marta answered.

"Oh, you're a pal! Thanks, but . . . I don't want to get in the way of your . . . ah . . . well . . . the lieutenant, I mean."

"Don't be silly, the night is still young. I'm taking Robert to the hunting shack in the morning to skeet shoot, and then I think he and Tice have plans to fish the lake in the afternoon. They won't even miss us."

Tice interrupted the girl talk, suggesting they all go into the spa area for a swim and hot tub. The inside swimming pool and spa area consisted of a complete workout facility with every possible machine you would find in the most upscale spa. There were three pools. One was moderate sized, four feet deep at one end, and eight feet at the other. Next to this was a lap pool that was five feet deep, five feet wide, and ten feet long. The entry was at either end via ladders. A lever at poolside set the water flow at slow, medium, or fast. A good workout could be had swimming against the flow, while remaining in one place. Ten minutes of swimming against the medium flow would tire the fittest of users. The third pool was half the size of the largest one, but had Jacuzzi jets coming from the bottom of the underwater bench seating, which ran from the entry steps at each corner around the inside perimeter. The change room along one side of the pool contained a sauna and shower, along with complete bath and vanity fixtures. There was a large cedar cupboard that contained various sizes of bathing trunks, towels, and dark brown terry-cloth robes.

Robert was the last to enter the hot pool. He sat by the entry steps nearest the cedar cupboards. When he was on the edge of the underwater bench between two jets of bubbles, he eased back against a jet, which burbled between his shoulder blades. As he slipped lower, the hot soothing water was up to his chin. He looked across the width of the pool and watched the twins passing a joint back and forth with Sylvie. Tice raised his frosty mug of beer and saluted in his direction.

Marta got up from the edge of the pool, caught Robert's attention, pointed at her stein, and then at Robert who nodded assent. Marta flowed over to the bar in the corner, went behind it, set her drink on the counter, opened the fridge, took out a frosted stein, and poured a beer into it. She reached under the bar for an ashtray containing wooden matches and a joint. She walked them over and set both beside Robert. Then, without a word, she walked slowly back to the bar to retrieve her drink.

Robert lifted his beer to his lips and watched the effortless grace of Marta's movements. They had a polarizing effect on him. It occurred to him that he had never seen a more perfect example of womanhood until this moment. Marta wore a bikini that was cut like the shortest of shorts and a halter-top, like a sports bra—silver in colour and very revealing, yet somehow modest. Robert glanced at Sylvie entering the pool, noticing she was wearing a white version of the same bikini. Robert sat up on the edge as Marta returned, seating herself close beside him to dangle her legs in the bubbling water.

"Thanks for this. It hits the spot," Robert said, lifting his beer in salute.

"My pleasure. I couldn't help noticing that you had me under surveillance as I brought the beer and the toke."

"I apologize for staring, but I do admire beauty, and you most certainly are one. I was captivated watching you walk. Was I leering?" he asked.

"Why, thank you for the compliment, Lieutenant. There may be hope for you yet. And, I don't mind if you were leering. Actually, I'm flattered." Marta smiled and scolded him. "But really, Robert, you shouldn't sit in this water much longer, or you'll melt."

Marta set her beer down on the deck, put the joint to her lips, and lit it. She took two deep drags and set it down on Robert's side of the ashtray. She looked across the pool at her brother and Sylvie who raised their beer mugs in her direction. She smiled at them, and with an undetected backward glance saw Robert lifting the joint to his lips. Marta slowly turned to smile at him with anticipation in her eyes.

After they finished their beer and the joint, Robert asked, "Just how far is it to my bedroom from here anyway?"

"Don't you worry, friend. I'll make sure you get there. If you've had enough of this hot tub, I suggest you dip into the large pool, then into the change room for a shower. Get into a robe and I'll show you up to your room."

"Yes, I'll do that. Otherwise, I might crash right here. I'm really quite wrecked."

Robert left the hot pool and walked into the regular pool, jarring his body with the shock of the cooler water. He swam to the opposite corner, exited, and noticed Marta and Tice having a chat with Sylvie at the bar. He observed once again how similar in body type the two women were. Sylvie was a bit taller and slightly slimmer, but their busts, waists, and hips were identical. As he walked past the threesome, he said he would have a quick shower and then hit the sack.

In the shower, Robert realized he hadn't felt like this since the last time he'd toked up with Marie-Claude. *How long ago was that? Five years . . . no, more like ten.* Marta Vander Riis was certainly a very exciting lady. He had gotten hard just watching her walk. *I better turn this water on colder, or I won't get out of here without embarrassing myself.* He didn't know why he was trying so hard to make a good impression. Was it because of Marta, Tice, or Elspeth? He definitely thought they were really all kinds of unique. *But those eyes of Marta's . . . incredible . . . I could fall into them. I better get out here. She's probably waiting.*

Whew . . . I'd forgotten how grass affects me. The sensation begins at opposite ends every time, in the back of my head and in my toes. The warm tingling spreads upward from my toes and down from my head to the ultimate destination, my genitals, which become the centre of my being. Like . . . right now.

While Robert towelled dry, thinking of Marta and the way she walked brought a documentary to his mind about a famous racehorse retired to stud, and how the handlers had paraded a mare around in front of him to get him in the mood to service her. Robert chuckled, thinking that ritual might be more easily accomplished by simply giving both animals a hoot.

Marta was waiting for him near the entrance smiling broadly at him, noticing his embarrassment and his attempt to conceal it.

Robert blushed, saying, "The cold shower didn't seem to work."

Marta giggled, circled her arm around his waist, and whispered into his ear, "I'd better get you to your room and out of sight."

They walked arm in arm to his room in a very friendly and sexy stroll. They kept shushing each other, while trying desperately not to giggle or laugh out loud. It was a bit of a struggle navigating the big staircase, but an expertly timed hip check by Marta got them back on course for his room. He felt her grip on him tighten when he stumbled. Realizing just how stoned he was, he told her so.

"And, is it any wonder? The brandy, the beer, and the hot tub, as well as the very best government marijuana should have knocked you out before now," Marta said.

Robert smiled at her as they arrived at his door and answered, "Indeed, all of those, plus a little jet lag and the most beautiful intoxicant of all, you Marta. You're a knockout, and before I forget my manners, I want to thank you and Tice for inviting me. I'm having a great time."

Marta looked up at him, grinned, and said, "You say the sweetest things. Let's get you to bed."

Chapter 5

The Twins' Guests and the Country Hustle

Robert awoke at 8:07 a.m. and lay there, searching the surroundings with his eyes. His foggy sleep-sated brain was beginning to send questions and answers. *Where am I? Oh yeah . . . at Tice's place, the Vander Riis castle. Not a castle . . . a chateau. That's right. What a night . . . didn't think I had that much to drink. Hmm . . . shared a big joint with Marta. Remember . . . she kissed you good night . . . those eyes of hers. That's why my head is a little fuzzy . . . let's see, this morning we are skeet shooting. I guess I could wear my jeans or . . .*

The answer came with a knock at his door. Marta entered holding a plastic suiter. "Good morning, Lieutenant. My father was about your size, and if these fit they'll be more comfy than your city clothes. Try on the jacket for me, please."

"Good morning yourself, and thanks, I thought I'd just wear jeans and a sweater. This is very thoughtful of you, Marta," Robert said, as she laid the outfit at the foot of the bed and unwrapped the plastic.

He got out of bed wearing only his boxer shorts. Slipping the sports jacket on over his bare skin, he walked to the full-length mirror at the closet. The expensive shiny lining sent cool shivers everywhere it touched his skin.

"You are absolutely right on. This suit coat feels like it was made for me." He pulled on the breeks she handed him, did up the zipper, and the waist flap. *Not bad at all,* he thought, *but what in hell do I do with the bloody pantaloons?*

Marta stood, smiling, watching him in the outfit, pleased with how it looked. She turned to leave and announced, "Breakfast in twenty minutes!"

Robert went through the rest of the things and found tan leg wrappings, long heavy socks, a tan chamois shirt, and a yellow leather and canvas shooting vest. He put the shirt and vest on, leaving it unbuttoned. Some things didn't need to be reflected in a mirror to verify that they fit. The feel confirms it.

He had a quick shower, dressed in the outfit, got the wrappings around the laced leggings, over which he pulled on the heavy socks. He tucked the chamois shirt into the breeks and wore the hunting vest unbuttoned over the shirt. He carried the sport coat and made his way down the big stairway in stocking feet. Halfway down, Tice spotted him, hailed him good morning, and hurried off in another direction.

Robert walked carefully into the small dining room, said good morning to Sylvie and Marta, and asked permission to join them before seating himself at their table. The housekeeper arrived with a large pot of coffee at the same time that Tice appeared with a rust colored pair of riding boots for Robert to try on.

"Like they were made for me, Tice," Robert said, walking away from the table, trying them out. "They feel very comfortable, beautiful leather. I'll take good care of them. Thanks."

While eating breakfast, the friendly back-and-forth banter centered on how Marta's leather biking outfit and their father's shooting clothes looked as if they had been tailored for Sylvie and Robert. Sylvie jokingly suggested, "It won't be necessary for me or the lieutenant to pack anything on our next visit."

After breakfast, they all walked to the front entrance. Robert liked the feel of the riding boots. They completed his outfit splendidly. He felt like a country squire. On their walk to the garage, Marta put her arm around his waist and hugged him to her. She grinned up at him like an imp and whispered in his ear, "So, tell me, did you have a pleasant dream last night?"

Robert, curious, looked into her grey eyes for more information, but only the sparkle answered. "When I get to know you better, I promise to tell you about the most incredible dream I think I had last night."

Marta seemed pleased and answered, "Sounds delicious. I can't wait."

Robert felt at ease, relaxed, and pleased with how this new friendship seemed to be developing into a real relationship. *A definitely exciting possibility*, he thought. Marta had selected a Volkswagen Thing from the four cars in the big garage. She drove along a well cared for road that wound around the estate's lake and through the mini forest. During the five-minute ride, they remained silent. Robert liked being squired about by Marta. He was mulling over what she asked him on their walk to the garage. Speeding out of the little forest, Marta continued along the shore and pulled up in front of the two-story hunting shack where her airplane sat tied to its pad alongside the building facing the river's edge.

Marta lifted the picnic basket from the back seat, handed it to Robert, retrieved an iron ring from her carryall bag, unlocked the massive oak door, and pushed it open. Inside, the huge room smelled faintly of furniture polish. Large tufted red leather chairs and sofas were clustered about rustic tables in four different settings, giving the room a clubhouse look. The floor-to-ceiling flagstone fireplace, extending from a corner, took up one third of the room. The other walls were floor-to-ceiling windows enclosed by double French doors at both the second story and main floor. An elegant wrought iron stairway to the right of the hearth curled up to the second level. A walkway wound all the way around that floor. Robert could see the bedroom doors and a French door, which led to the shooting tower. Pieces of animals adorned the walls and floor—a set of horns here, some trophy heads there, and a couple of complete skins on the hardwood floor.

They call this incredible lodge a hunting shack and their place in the country a chateau, which is a bloody castle! They understate everything they own, almost as if their wealth embarrasses them. And the way they treat their staff . . . like family. Always courteous, saying 'please to this', 'thank you' for that, and using first names, always first names. Seems to me it's natural: the way it ought to be. But I do wonder; what's next, Ms Marta?

Marta put the basket in a large stand-up fridge and opened a glassed-in mahogany wall cabinet containing guns of all description. She cocked her head, looked up at Robert and said, "I can offer you a preference in gauge and make." Robert shrugged, showing his indifference. "We should shoot for a small wager," Marta suggested. "If you're game, ten dollars a bird would make it more interesting."

Robert looked at Marta's face, studied her, then fell into her eyes and agreed, "Ten dollars a bird is just fine. It will give me a chance to recover the money I lost to you pool sharks." He walked to the gun case and admired the selection of handmade weapons. "A very impressive collection; which is your favourite, Marta?"

"Well, I have shot them all, but my favourite is the Beretta 687 because it's almost a pound lighter than the others. My father used to say it was the Ferrari of the Italian sporting guns." She removed the handsome handmade shotgun and handed it to Robert so he could examine the twenty-gauge over and under more closely. She asked again if he had a preference in the selection in front of him.

"I don't know a lot about shotguns, but this strange looking fella has caught my eye," he said, lifting the twenty gauge out of the case. He hefted both in each hand saying, "This Italian job is definitely lighter than this fellow."

"Actually, that funny looking fellow is a Lujic LM6 and was handmade for my father. The cast, the drop, and the comb were all cut to his body shape," Marta said, "Are you sure you don't know more about sporting guns than you are letting on, Lieutenant?"

Robert made a gesture of sincerity saying, "Guns interest me. In police work we come across them all the time, as you might imagine, so I've taken an interest in the handmade models. Here's one I've seen before. It's a Krieghoff, right? Mind if I use this one?" Robert returned the Lujic to the case and withdrew the double-barrelled, twenty-gauge gun.

"Yes, it is a Krieghoff and it just happens to be one of Tice's favourites," Marta said, "Now I'm sure I shouldn't be shooting against you for money." When they were all set to start Marta asked, "Would you care for a little drink before we begin?"

He thought, *what a hustler! Doesn't miss a trick, does she?* "Maybe after," he said, smiling and shaking his head.

Marta led Robert up the stairway through the French doors and onto the walkway to the shooting tower. She pointed out bedrooms as they walked, saying, "Dad designed this place. Mother says he thought it cool to be able to have drinks up here after a shoot. We use it a lot, actually."

They entered the tower and walked across the circular floor to a panel on the wall where there were a number of switches. Marta pressed a green button on the panel and one-third of the wall began moving upward, exposing the shooting range. She took Robert over to a cabinet containing boxes of shotgun shells. She handed him two boxes of twenty-gauge birdshot and took two for herself. During the setup, Marta explained how they loaded the automatic skeet throwers. She told him how the birds were programmed to fly every fifteen seconds up to ten birds, followed by a sixty-second pause, and then resuming for another ten birds until one hundred had flown. They flipped to see who would shoot first. Robert won.

He moved to the rail, lifted his gun to his shoulder, and wondered which side the bird would come from and how fast. A bird shot forth from the left side of the tower. He laughed as he poked the gun at the fleeing disc while trying to pull the trigger with the safety on. He released the safety, fired at the next bird, and missed. Marta watched with a trace of a grin on her face as he led the next bird with an easy swing of the gun, fired, and watched it explode. The fourth bird escaped as he tried in vain to shoot it with an empty gun. It took him too long to reload and swing it in the direction of yet another escaping disc. He paused, gun at the ready, aiming to the right, and killed the next two discs. He reloaded and made a long shot for a kill, and then dusted the next. He reloaded and disintegrated the tenth bird. He had six kills in eight shots at ten birds.

Marta, like a machine, swung the over and under—fire and kill, swing, fire, kill, reload and repeat until she had killed all ten birds. Robert got better as the contest continued, but the final tally was in Marta's favour, 48-41. He had lost seventy dollars to this beautiful hustler and didn't mind at all.

"How is a little country girl supposed to make any extra money if a mean old policeman spoils all her fun?" she said, pretending to pout. As he handed her the money she said, "You have a good eye. You are very dexterous. With a little practice you'd be tough to beat. C'mon," she said, "help me start a fire in the fireplace. You're a very good sport, Lieutenant."

She grabbed his hand and hip checked him for the third time in the past two days. A fire sounded good to Robert, as he needed to get some heat on his sore right shoulder. It was lit and roaring in short order. Robert pulled the screens in place then pulled the bearskin rugs closer to the edge of the hearth. He was content watching Marta in the kitchen, preoccupied with stirring cocoa and sugar into large mugs. She had removed her shooting vest, and the red turtleneck sweater she wore with the tailored khaki pants accentuated her figure. He thought her pleasing to the eye regardless of what she wore. But this red sweater . . . He was staring at her . . . uncool.

Marta noticed and asked, "Something the matter?"

"Just admiring the scenery."

"Come help, please?" Marta asked. "You carry the mugs and put them on the table by the hearth. I'll bring the kettle."

He did as he was told and sniffed a cup before putting it down. "Hmm, smells good. What are you making?" he asked as she hung the copper kettle on a swivelled iron arm, positioning it over the edge of the fire.

"My specialty: hot brandy toddies. Just as soon as the milk in the kettle heats, you're in for a treat. But while we wait, you and I are going to have a nice long talk," Marta said.

She squatted on the sofa opposite the one he sprawled on. She crossed her ankles and reached for and grabbed her toes. She looked at him and smiled as she began to slowly rock back and forth on her haunches. Robert wondered if she was sending a very subtle message. He could only hope.

"So, are you going to tell me about the dream you think you had last night?" Marta asked, still rocking slowly. Her grey eyes shone with mischief. "Why don't you come over and sit beside me?" She coaxed, patting the space next to her.

It was all the invitation Robert needed as he uncoiled from his sprawl and sat beside her. "I had too much fun last night and more than enough good cheer," he said, moving closer to her. "Thank you for helping me to my room." Robert looked into her eyes, as they got larger, drawing him in. They closed and she kissed him enthusiastically. He returned the kiss as she came into his arms with a telling urgency.

They both felt a release of tension in their embrace. They nuzzled, inhaling each other's fragrance, grooving on the unspoken anticipation building in them. Robert was enticed by the faint hint of her perfume, which was overridden by the cordite and wood smoke. Her voice was so pleasing; he just smiled whenever she spoke. Marta told him her plans for that evening which sent shivers up his spine.

"I'm going to tuck you in properly tonight, Lieutenant. But right now, I'm going to finish making our toddies," Marta said. "Tice and Sylvie ought to be along soon, so please come and give me a hand?" As she pulled him up off the couch by his hands, Marta couldn't help but notice the embarrassment in his trousers. She giggled, saying, "Maybe if you walk around a little it'll help."

Robert blushed, holding the mugs while she poured the hot milk into each, and then returned the kettle to the hook hanging over the fire. They smiled at each other as they stirred the contents of their mugs, adding sweet spice and brandy fumes to the room.

"When Tice invited me to come for a visit, his invitation became very intriguing when he said he knew for certain you would be pleased if I came," Robert said.

"As you know, Mathijs and I do have a very special bond," she said. "It's true, and we do like to please each other whenever we can. So, when he told me he persuaded you to come, I said, 'marvellous, Tice! I owe you one.' Then before he could make plans to whisk you away, I asked if I could be your chaperone during your stay."

Marta brushed a lock of her hair aside and looked at him to see his reaction. He reached to run his left hand through her hair. She responded to his touch, gently moving her head against his hand while closing her eyes. The spell was broken by the sound of approaching motorbikes. "That will be Tice and Sylvie," she said, looking down at him, "And you need another walk to loosen up again."

Tice and Sylvie came through the front doors in a rush of enthusiasm, saying they had a marvellous run all over the estate grounds.

"So, Marta, how much money did you win skeet shooting?" Tice asked.

"A paltry sum, seventy dollars," Marta said.

"Pay up, Sylvie. You owe me fifty bucks," Tice said.

"Okay, but my wallet is back at the chateau," Sylvie answered.

"What was the bet?" Robert asked.

Sylvie answered, "Tice bet me fifty dollars that Marta would win at least sixty from you, Robert. I took that bet because I just figured, as a policeman, you'd know your way around guns."

Tice and Marta told their guests that they had been playing this little scam on visitors since they were teenagers. After their toddies and lunch they made plans to fish the estate lake in the morning, and in the afternoon Marta would fly Sylvie into Amsterdam so they could shop. They locked up the hunting shack and headed back to the chateau.

Chapter 6
The Paris Broker and Attempted Escape

"Pierre Turrin here," a familiar voice on the other end of the line said. "How can I help you?"

"Pierre, this is Andre Laurent speaking. I want you to listen carefully at what I would like you to do. Cash in my T-bill account, and . . . and . . . take the fifteen-hundred-dollar commission we agreed upon and make up a cheque for the balance. I've been injured on my sailboat and decided to sell the *SeaOx* to an associate. We'll pick up the cheque before noon today." Andre's request was met with complete silence on the other end of the line. "Pierre, did you hear what I said?"

"Yes, Andre . . . the cheque will be ready when you arrive."

Andre began to panic, realizing that Turrin was completely without questions about his injury or sudden change in his lifestyle. So, in a desperate but feeble attempt, Andre said, "Pierre, my associate would be a great prospect for you . . . "

"I see . . . "said Turrin and hung up.

Andre hung up the phone when he felt the sharp bite of the knife that Pelling suddenly jabbed into his side.

The rental Jaguar Sovereign pulled up. The delivery guy, after walking around and confirming there wasn't any damage, obtained Andre's signature and his Visa gold card imprint.

Pelling drove with Andre Laurent buckled in the passenger seat. Laurent slumped over, completely defeated. The ninety-mile drive into Paris took almost two hours. They drove to the Merrill office at 11:00 a.m. and parked close by.

Pierre Turrin was at the counter with an envelope when Andre and Pelling walked through the main doors into the boardroom. "Your account balance as requested, Andre."

Turrin handed the envelope to Andre and moved along the counter to speak with Pelling. "And you must be Andre's associate. Glad to meet you, Mr Pelling. I have a new account form which needs to be completed in order to get your account set up quickly." He offered his hand to Pelling, who looked at it as if it were diseased.

Pelling said, "I won't be doing any business with you today. Give me your card and I'll drop in when I'm in Paris at the end of the month." Turrin produced his business card, which went quickly into a pocket of Pelling's coat, like a gum wrapper you would crumple and bury in your pocket for later discard.

"How far is it to the nearest bank?" Pelling asked.

"Turn to your left when you leave the front door; the Royal Bank is in the middle of the block."

Pelling helped Laurent walk to the bank. When they reached the teller, Andre put his portfolio case on the counter, withdrew the cheque from the envelope, and looked at the itemized statement on the stub. The redemption amount was $154,901.20, less the commission, for a net amount of $153,401.20.

"Can I help you, sir?" the teller asked.

"Yes, good morning. I'd like to cash this US cheque," Andre said. "Here is my passport and international driver's license. Can I have 1500 one-hundreds, 60 fifties, 20 twenties, and the rest in change? Thank you."

"I'll be back in about ten minutes with your cash, Mr Laurent. I have to go downstairs to the vault." The cashier took Andre's signed cheque and left for the vault. She was back within minutes with a tray containing packets of hundred-dollar bills and bundles of fifties and twenties. They verified the amounts and the total and placed the bills into Andre's carry portfolio.

Andre thought, *it's now or never, I'll make a break for it. It's my best chance for help. The two bank guards will come to my assistance. I'll occupy Pelling's hands by giving him the case of money, then get quickly to the bank guard and tell him I'm a hostage. He should be able to get his gun quickly on Pelling. It is my best chance to escape so far.*

As Andre approached the guard, he swung the money case backward hitting Pelling in the stomach, who clutched it to his body to keep it from falling. Andre started toward the guard, stumbled, and fell. The guard took no notice. Pelling went quickly to help Andre to his feet, and with a steadying grip walked him roughly out onto the street. While leaving the bank, they looked to passers-by like a friend helping someone under the influence as they walked up to the corner and into a large hotel, stopping at the payphones in the lobby.

Pelling drew Andre close to him and said, "Your last chore, Laurent. Call your widow friend and say you will be at her apartment in about a half an hour. Go ahead and make the call. I'll be right beside you. Just say you will be along shortly, nothing else. Then hang up."

* * *

12:30 p.m., Paris apartment of Elspeth Vander Riis

When her telephone finally rang Elspeth thought, *It has to be Andre.* As she lifted the receiver, she said, "Thank heavens," into the phone. She was so thrilled to hear from him that she ignored Andre's clipped voice. She heard only what she longed to hear, that he would be at her door in thirty minutes.

After scurrying about with redundant last minute tidying, the buzzer sounded Andre's arrival and his voice crackled over the intercom, "Hi, it's me, Andre." Elspeth buzzed him in. She hugged herself to get control of her excitement as she looked at her reflection in the hall mirror. She fussed with her hair and waited until she heard the elevator chime faintly at her floor.

There was a rap on her apartment door. As soon as she turned the doorknob, someone pushed it in on her and stepped into the foyer. Elspeth was pinned against the wall and momentarily stunned. The man pulled the door away from her, kicked it closed with his heel, then gripped her by the throat with his left hand in a choke hold that kept her pinned to the wall.

Elspeth's terrified eyes tried vainly to focus on the typewritten sheet of paper he held directly in front of her face with his right hand. She couldn't read the note in her frightened and confused state.

"I'll release you now and follow you to your bedroom so that you can sit and read these instructions. If you scream you will die instantly. Move!"

Elspeth fought to regain her breath as she stumbled toward her bedroom, her attacker right behind, hurrying her along. He forced her to sit on the side of the bed and handed her the page of text once more. He stood in her space on purpose, looking down at her as she read. Elspeth took a few deep breaths, glanced up at the smug intruder, and began to read:

My Dear Elspeth:

I have sent my partner in my place. His purpose in life is twofold: he likes accumulating large sums of money and satisfying his deviant sexual appetite. I have told him of your abilities under the covers, and while he is most anxious to sample you, he will restrain himself if you will follow instructions and arrange to give us the sum of one million guilders in US dollars. At the present rate of exchange, the equivalent should be about $435,000. We suggest you call your home and tell either your son or daughter you have been taken hostage by the Basque ETA and that they mean to kill you if their ransom is not paid. You will tell them that your *personal cheque for one million guilders will arrive by courier tomorrow morning and you will call with further instructions. Either your son or daughter is to be driven to the bank by your driver in your Rolls Royce, but they are not to leave for the bank until you give them final instructions on where to deliver the money. Impress upon them that if they contact the authorities you will be executed, and the ETA will see to it that both of them follow you to the grave.*

Andre

The chill began at her lower back and rose up her spine, causing her to shake. She wouldn't let the scream come out of her mouth and all her attacker heard was "no, oh . . . no!" after which Elspeth became silent.

"Get yourself together. You have a telephone call to make," the man ordered.

Elspeth picked up the receiver and dialled her chateau in Utrecht. She took a number of deep breaths and noticed the difficulty she had in swallowing. She asked to speak to her son and waited until she heard Tice's greeting on the line. She spoke clearly and demanded his complete attention. After she described her situation, Elspeth asked that he comply with her instructions to the letter, so as not to endanger their lives. He was to stay at the chateau to receive her cheque, which would arrive in the morning by courier. She would call in a couple of days to tell him when to pick up the money from the bank and where to deliver it.

Elspeth hung up the phone and looked up at the intruder who was still standing very close to her—too close. His smirk had given way to a more speculative look, which alarmed her, but she managed to keep the fear from showing. She would not challenge him and curbed her bravery by remaining silent.

I'd like to slap that snide look from his face, she thought. *Easy now, just answer him when he speaks to you. Do not, for God's sake, get sarcastic or give him any reason to attack. He really is full of himself. Probably terrifies women into having sex with him. I'll just bet that's what's going on in his perverted mind . . . so damn sure of himself . . . probably expects me to accommodate him just because he's terrified me.*

The man kept looking at her, all over, then finally reached into his suit jacket pocket, withdrew a business card, and handed it to her saying, "Call this courier and have them come here to pick up an envelope to be delivered to your chateau in Utrecht."

Elspeth did as she was instructed, and after ending the call to the courier, she reached into her purse for her chequebook. She wrote a cheque to her son, Mathijs, for one million guilders. Remembering where the ransom money was going, she began to shiver again, saying to herself, *Damn you, Andre! Stupid me, how could I have been so completely wrong about you?* Her hopes suddenly shattered, and she wondered if she'd been so emotionally starved that she'd let him turn her inside out, and for such a meagre amount of money! *So utterly cruel, didn't you know I would have shared everything I have with you, if only you were who you said you were? Damn you! Damn your eyes to hell!*

Elspeth addressed an envelope to her chateau in Utrecht and enclosed the cheque. She looked up to find her captor still watching her. *He is a brute of a man, much younger than I first thought, eyeing me like a wolf would his prey.*

She stood, and with as much composure as she could muster said, "I've done exactly as you have instructed. I do not wish to bring harm to my children or myself. I'm now going to call my bank in Amsterdam and speak with the manager, Dirk Visser." The man nodded but said nothing.

After speaking with the bank manager and arranging for the various denominations making up the ransom, he assured her the money would be available when her son presented her cheque. Within the hour, the UPS deliveryman buzzed her apartment. When he arrived, Elspeth opened the door and handed him the envelope. She asked the cost and paid in cash.

She turned toward her captor, looked him over and thought, *okay, mister, I've done what you've asked, what now?* The man didn't speak, but they kept eye contact until, suddenly, she noted the look in his eyes change, as if he had just made a decision. "We're going for a little car ride now," he said. "I suggest you wear a wrap or a sweater."

Elspeth selected a sweater from her bedroom closet, put it on, and brushed by her captor leaning against the bedroom doorway. Elspeth felt certain she knew what he was silently inferring. The bastard is waiting for some cue from me. God, does he really think I might be interested in him sexually?

The man walked her around the block to where he'd parked the rented Jaguar. After settling her in the front passenger seat and buckling her in, he quickly rounded the back of the car and got into the driver's seat. As they headed toward Le Havre, Elspeth was unaware that she wasn't the only captive in the car.

The man did not converse with her and she gradually fell asleep with her head up against the side window. She awoke, noted the car was stopped, felt a sting at her hip, and made a sweeping grab at the pain, but he caught and held her wrist until he emptied the syringe. Elspeth mumbled something incoherent and passed out.

When they arrived at the marina in Le Havre it was nearly five o'clock. Elspeth was barely mobile. Pelling held her tight and walked her, unnoticed, down the jetty and aboard the *SeaOx*. He stripped her clothes off down to her bra and panties, and then secured her in the berth in the main salon. He left her there, bound at the wrists to the headboard, and bound by her ankles to the bottom legs of the berth. He stood and admired her for a moment, all spread-eagled—nice and ready. However, Pelling was only hungry for food just then. He made himself a sandwich, opened a can of Beck's beer, sat down at the table, and went over his day.

Pelling thought, *Laurent can stay in the trunk of the Jag until it gets dark enough that I won't be noticed bringing him aboard. The injection I gave him was a full shot and should keep him very still until tomorrow sometime.*

He'd been concerned when that little prick Turrin had almost screwed the whole deal by pressuring him to open an account and called him by name. *Don't think Laurent even noticed though.* He was surprised how much Laurent managed to straighten up at the bank to get the cheque cashed. He was pretty sure that he'd tried to escape when he swung the money case at him and made a move toward the bank guard, but he could barely stand, let alone run, and fell on his face. *I got him out of the bank in a hurry without incident. But when I forced him to call the widow, he knew I wasn't about to let him go free.* He had considered it, though. He knew his brain had absorbed enough of the special Valium mix that it was likely to be irreparably damaged. He envisioned Laurent at a police station trying to convey what had happened to him and then getting taken immediately to a psyche ward.

Chapter 7
Widow Kidnapped

The Chateau

"Robert, I must ask a favour of you." Tice studied his friend closely. "What I'm about to tell you cannot leave this room. It must be held in strict confidence. Can I have your word as a friend?"

"Yes, of course," Robert replied. "You have my word. What's the matter?"

"That was Mother who just called. Basque ETA terrorists have kidnapped her. She just gave me some of the instructions about the ransom. She said she was calling from her Paris apartment and would call me again with the ransom delivery instructions. She asked that we do not leave the chateau until we receive the cheque for one million guilders payable to me, which she is sending by courier."

"My God!" Robert said.

"Mother said she would be released after the ransom is delivered. She said they would kill Marta and me, as well as her, if we contact the authorities or fail to comply with their demands."

"Did I hear you correctly that the ransom demand is for one million guilders?" asked Robert.

"Yes, that's correct. Not a lot of money is it? about four hundred and thirty thousand US dollars. The cheque is supposed to arrive tomorrow morning, but I'm to wait for her instructions before cashing it at our bank in Amsterdam. She said she would make arrangements with Dirk Visser, the bank manager, to have the denominations ready in US currency. She said I was to have Henk drive me to the bank in the Rolls, but to wait to hear from her with exact instructions on how to deliver the ransom."

"How did Mother sound?" Marta asked her twin brother, adding, "Good Lord, some of the things those ETA terrorists have done to their captives in the past! She must be terrified."

"That's what seems so strange. She didn't sound the least bit concerned about her safety. Instead, she sounded pissed off. You know how she gets when she's angry? Well, she sounded just like that, yet, very much in charge."

Sylvie suggested, "Maybe your mom knows the kidnapper."

Robert and the twins both looked at Sylvie, and then at one another. It was Marta who said, "Of course she knows him! She was going to meet a man in Paris, but she wouldn't tell me anything about him. Remember what I told you, Tice? Mother said, 'It's too soon, but I promise to tell all very soon. I'll call you from my apartment after Tice gets home.' What if her meeting turned out very badly and she is, indeed, pissed off at him and at herself for trusting him."

Robert frowned. "Does she know I'm here at the chateau?"

Marta and Tice looked at each other and Marta answered, "Yes, of course. When I offered to fly her to the Amsterdam airport, she said no, she would have Henk drive her. I said I was going to pick you and Tice up. Mother gave me a wink and a hug and said, 'we are all very fond of Lt. Robert Bizet, dear. I always hoped you and he would become special friends.' And with that, she left for the airport."

Sylvie asked, "Could you tell if anyone else was there with her while she spoke with you, Tice?"

"There may have been, or she wouldn't have been so . . . severe . . . and . . . instructive. Mother didn't ask about my flight or anything personal. There *must* have been someone there."

Robert went over to the bar, poured himself a brandy, swallowed some, and felt the burn begin when the liquid was halfway to his stomach. He put the drink down on the bar counter and turned toward the others. "We must do exactly as Elspeth requests," he advised. "When the cheque arrives we must be out of sight. We'll have one of the staff answer the door, just in case the delivery person is an ETA member casing the chateau. If this is an ETA kidnapping scheme, then it could be an elaborate setup to kidnap either Tice or Marta, or both." The twins looked puzzled.

"Let me explain," Robert said. "You may, or may not, know that my work with the Sûreté has to do with trying to keep up with all terrorist activities, and especially the tactics of the ETA, the terrorist faction of the Basques. They are known to take a member of a wealthy family and ask for a small amount for the safe return of the hostage. They then capture the family member delivering the money and demand a very large ransom for both."

"Let me ask you, Tice," continued Robert. "Did your mother say to bring the money back here to the chateau?"

"No, she said she would call and give me instructions on where to deliver it," Tice replied.

"I may be completely off base about my suspicions, but better to err on the side of caution. If Marta is correct and Elspeth has been taken in by this anonymous new suitor, it would certainly explain why she won't accept that she is in any danger and thinks she will be released as soon as the money is handed over. I do hope for her sake she's right, but it could still be a plot to extract a little at the outset and then a much larger amount as the plan unfolds."

Robert continued, "I'll say it again. The best way we can help Elspeth is to comply with her instructions, but we can help the situation by setting up a command centre here to record all telephone calls from now on. They may well come in handy at a later date. Could we use the library for this purpose?"

The twins nodded their consent. "I'll rig up a tape recorder to the telephone," Tice said. "I don't think we should alert the staff just yet. Let the household go about their regular routine. The main phone line can be tape recorded from the library and will pick up any extension in the chateau. I suggest the four of us get our heads together after every incoming call."

* * *

Late night, Bassin de La Manche Marina, June 3
Andre Laurent's world was filled with the faint smell of gasoline and rubber. Everything was black until he suddenly experienced a rush of fresh air. He was standing upright and being helped to walk, as the smells changed to those of the sea. The blackness overhead also changed and was now sprinkled with diamonds winking at him. He was being helped along a narrow walkway made of jelly suspended just above the water, when a doorway suddenly opened as he stepped into a moving house. Andre's brief attempt at consciousness ended the instant his face struck the deck inside the pilothouse of the *SeaOx*.

Pelling lifted Andre up, carried him down the stairway through the salon area, and dropped him on the v-berth. He removed Andre's raincoat, then stripped off his clothes down to his underwear. He hung the clothes in the hanging locker. Looking down at the sailor, Pelling made a decision. He rolled him over on his back and bound his wrists with sail ties. He wrapped a stronger cord around the wrists, pulled Andre's secured hands over his head, tied them to a headboard post, and then tied each of his ankles to the nearest bed leg. Pelling said aloud, "You won't be going anywhere tied like this, even if we run into rough seas."

Pelling checked on his other hostage in the main berth. Elspeth was still out cold, exactly as he had left her. He went ashore and methodically cleaned the rental car trunk, then went over the front seat where Elspeth had sat. He checked under the seat, in the door pockets, and even the crease of the seat. He found nothing. After leaving the keys under the floor mat on the driver's side and that door unlocked, he walked to the telephone booth near the marina office and telephoned the car rental agency. He advised them the location of the car and the keys and asked them to come pick it up.

As Pelling piloted the *SeaOx* away from the dock, he saw a truck from the rental agency drive up beside the Jaguar. It was 10:00 p.m. He had four-hundred-eighteen kilometres to sail and calculated his arrival at The Hague before noon on Thursday the sixth. He'd have Elspeth call her son at that time and give him the ransom delivery instructions. Once he had the ransom in his possession, he'd drive Elspeth somewhere and release her.

With Laurent's money and this four-hundred-thirty-thousand dollars plus for the return of Elspeth Vander Riis, he would be half a million over his goal of three million dollars. But as soon as the ETA had confirmed Agent Pelling was missing, his control, Raoul de Vascos, would send others to sanction him. Pelling was aware of this and planned to have his face restructured in Switzerland, downsize his body considerably, let his hair grow in, and grow a beard. He had spoken to Raoul in the past two weeks; so, for the present, everything was cool. This little escapade was for extra cash and a sailboat, which Raoul knew nothing about. If Pelling and his friend Ruth could obtain the estate they wanted to purchase in Bordeaux, they could settle into a lifestyle where the ETA wouldn't find them.

Pelling weighed the pros and cons of what to do with Andre Laurent. His inclination was to kill him and not leave any loose ends. He knew that the boat sale and transfer of ownership wouldn't hold up under scrutiny. It would be chancy to just let him go, because his first step would be to get his boat back. If the Valium mix did what Raoul promised, another dose should make Laurent just short of a babbling idiot. Raoul had said the bad effects were cumulative, but Pelling wasn't so sure. He'd already been amazed at how docile Laurent was at the brokerage office, but still managed to straighten up at the bank while cashing the cheque. And then there was his feeble getaway attempt when he fell in the bank, but he'd returned to putty when he was taken out of the trunk and brought aboard. Pelling figured he'd awaken with a massive headache, judging from how he crashed face first into the deck.

If I kill him, I shouldn't have any problem keeping the SeaOx, Pelling decided. *I could have it repainted and renamed. Hell, I could keep the boat a secret from everybody, Ruth included, but especially Raoul.* He figured there was no sense wasting any more of the drug on Laurent if he was just going to kill him and dump him in the sea. *But what if he really does have another T-bill account that could be had as easily as the Merrill Lynch account? Ah, don't get ahead of yourself, Teddy—first things first.* He decided Laurent should be able to stand another small dose to keep him quiet while he collected the ransom and turned Elspeth loose. He could deal with sailor boy then.

* * *

At nine in the morning on the sixth, Pelling could see the Scheveningen Marina at The Hague looming ahead. He would be at the dock alongside the harbourmaster's office shortly. Pelling had looked in on both his captives earlier in the morning. Laurent was sleeping soundly, but the widow was beginning to stir.

Pelling finished with the customs entry process and arranged for a slip out of the way of the other marina traffic. He advised the marina manager he would be staying three or four days and planned to catch up on his sleep. After securing the *SeaOx* to his assigned slip, he connected water, electricity, and the telephone. He could now have Elspeth call her son from the security of the boat. He went to the master stateroom and untied her.

"Why did you feel it necessary to remove my clothes?" Elspeth glared at her captor.

"You might have soiled your outfit if I hadn't. Doing laundry isn't one of my favourite things. Besides, you are very entertaining when you sleep, especially after I untied one of your wrists. You are a very randy lady." He smirked.

"Where are my clothes?" Elspeth asked in an angry tone, which turned his smirk to an icy stare.

"Your clothes are hanging in that locker. Get dressed. It's time to make a phone call to your son and read the typed instructions I've prepared."

Elspeth opened the locker and put on her clothes with such deliberate indifference he might just as well not have been watching her. When she was dressed, she looked at him and asked, "Where is the telephone?"

"Sit at the chart table and read through these instructions before you place the call." Elspeth did as she was told, nodding to her captor when she finished reading. She reached for the receiver and dialled the number at the chateau.

The housekeeper answered the phone and went immediately to summon Master Mathijs. "This is Tice speaking. Who is calling please?"

"Tice, did you receive the cheque I had delivered to you?"

"Yes, it arrived by courier Tuesday morning about nine thirty. Are you all right? We have been expecting your call," Tice said, trying to remain calm.

"Yes, dear, I'm okay. Now, you must listen carefully as I read you these instructions. Please do not interrupt me until I have finished. Do you understand?" Elspeth asked.

"Yes, go ahead. I'm listening."

"You are to leave for the bank in Amsterdam at three o'clock this afternoon. Henk is to drive you in the Rolls. Go straight to the manager's office. Mr Visser will cash the cheque. The money will be waiting for you. Return to the car, drive to Schiphol Airport, and park in the visitor's parking area. People will meet you and tell you where to pick me up in exchange for the ransom. Now, Tice, no heroics please, and do not involve the police. Just follow these instructions to the letter and I'll see you this evening." Tice repeated the instructions to his mother and said he would do as she asked.

Pelling reached over, took the receiver from her, and placed it on the cradle. "Elspeth, we'll have some hot chocolate and toast before we leave. We won't get much chance to stop until I release you later today."

"Humph," responded Elspeth, who wondered what had caused his sudden interest in her well-being. Her answer came shortly after she finished drinking her cocoa, when everything she looked at began to melt and then quickly dissolve into a batter. Realizing what he had done to her caused her to scream at him, but it came out in a pitiful gargling moan. She slumped forward on the dinette table.

Pelling secured her in the main berth once again, tied spread-eagled and fully clothed. He took a look in the forward v-berth to see Laurent still out cold.

He arranged for a cab at the marina office and was driven to the nearest Hertz rental agency. Pelling looked at his watch, 10:30 a.m., still plenty of time. He drove the maroon rental van out into traffic and quickly consulted one of the two pages torn from the payphone directory. One page listed highway patrol stations, and the other listed lumber companies. He headed for the lumber company closest to the marina that he had highlighted. It took him less than thirty minutes to complete and store his purchase in the back of the van.

He arrived at the Dutch Highway Police station and parked in an inconspicuous spot with a good view of the coming and goings of police officers on their big BMW motorcycles. As three officers came out to their bikes, Pelling made his choice and followed one who appeared to be headed in the direction of the airport. Pelling trailed him at a respectable distance until he saw him pull over beside another motorcycle policeman. Pelling drove by and noticed the second motorcycle take off with a wave. His shift was probably over for the day, Pelling assumed.

Three kilometres down the highway Pelling turned off onto a side road and drove along it for a short distance. He turned around, re-entered the highway, and drove back past where the motorcycle policeman was watching for speeders. Pelling did a U-turn and headed toward the policeman. When he roared past the motorcycle, he was doing one-hundred-twenty-five kilometres per hour. Pelling looked into his rear-view mirror and saw the patrolman join the chase. There was no mistaking the siren was meant for him as the policeman came alongside, waved him over, and pulled in behind the van. Pelling signalled as he approached the exit ramp, then drove up the access road he had previously scouted, slowing as he went. The policeman was growing impatient as he revved his engine and blipped his siren, demanding that the van stop.

Pelling pulled over, rolled down his window, and watched as the policeman got off his bike and approached. When he was even with the door, Pelling stuck his revolver fitted with a silencer out the window and shot the officer in the forehead. Pelling stepped out of the van, opened the back door, pulled out a plank, and wheeled the motorcycle up it and into the van. *No traffic so far*, he thought, but he took no chances and lugged the dead cop into the back of the van as well. He undressed him, careful not to get blood on the uniform. He stripped himself down to his ultra light tailored overalls, which were designed to be worn under other clothing and could be discarded when a quick change was needed.

Pelling, now dressed in the policeman's uniform, checked his watch and decided he had lots of time to get to the turnoff on the A-9 for traffic going to Schiphol Airport. He dumped the policeman's body in the ditch and covered it as best he could. It didn't appear to be visible from the roadway as he drove back to the A-9 heading toward the airport.

* * *

Henk pulled the Rolls Royce to the curb and let Mathijs off at the entrance to the Bank of Amsterdam. Overhead, Marta was at the controls in her Renegade. In the passenger seat, Robert observed the Rolls pull up and then move slowly away from the curb. They saw Tice carrying the leather grip up the steps and into the bank. Marta was flying a grid at two thousand feet so the lieutenant could keep the white Rolls in sight at all times. The chauffeur began his slow rounding of the block by driving three blocks past the bank, then three blocks to the right, and six long blocks to the right again, three blocks again to the right, and then finally turning right and driving until he pulled over outside the bank.

Tice entered the back seat, set the grip down, and spoke to Henk. "Please drive directly to Schiphol Airport and just keep it at the speed limit."

Overhead, Marta had lengthened her flyover passes, widening the grid so as not to appear to be buzzing the Rolls, which was now entering the A-9 and proceeding toward the airport. It was on the third long north and south leg that Robert noticed the Rolls stopped on the side of the highway by a motorcycle policeman. As they flew by overhead, they witnessed the patrolman take off with a leather grip between his handlebars. They watched the motorcycle turn off A-9, drive down a side road, and park beside a maroon van. On their next pass overhead, they observed the patrolman wheeling the motorcycle up a plank and into the back of the van.

"That patrolman made the ransom pickup," Robert said. "That briefcase was the one Tice took to collect the money."

"I'm going up to five thousand feet to fly a little wider grid so we don't lose that van. It looks like he's heading for the coast. If so, he'll be at The Hague in about twenty minutes. I'm going to call Scheveningen harbour and ask permission to land at the marina, just in case he parks somewhere close by."

Robert kept the powerful field glasses fixed on the van, dropping them occasionally to rest his arms. "Very clever fellow, our kidnapper. He appears to be working alone, —so far anyway. No one would have expected him to pick up the ransom dressed as a highway patrolman. See, he's turning off onto the A-10, which, according to this map, will take him right into The Hague."

He watched as Marta levelled off at five thousand feet and witnessed the van pull into a marina parking lot. A man exited the van, but he wasn't dressed as a policeman. He wore overalls now, but was carrying the same leather grip, as he made his way down the jetty and jumped on board a big green-hulled Pilot House sailboat.

Marta circled lower and landed on a clear stretch of sea by the marina and taxied up to the slip she regularly used by the gas dock. She was always a welcome visitor to the crew, who were on hand to grab a wing and pull her gently to the dock so that she and her passenger could step out of the sporty little amphibian.

Marta smiled. "Hi, fellas, would you fill my tanks and charge it to my account. We'll be back in a little while."

Once inside the marina office, Robert took the manager aside and introduced himself. "How many boats have docked here in the past two days?"

The manager looked carefully at the badge of the lieutenant from the Paris Sûreté before he answered. "Four in all, Lieutenant, three yesterday and one at just past ten this morning. Why do you ask?"

"Could I please see the entries for those boats?"

"Of course, Lieutenant."

The manager stepped behind the counter and swung the registration journal around and pointed to the last entries. Robert and Marta both leaned forward to read the latest entry. The *SeaOx* arrived from Le Havre at 10:10 a.m. skippered by a Ted Pelling, with no passengers listed. The slip was paid for three more days. The sailboat was a Hans Christian 44-foot Pilot House cutter tied up at slip D-22.

"The *SeaOx* and her owner Andre Laurent have been reported missing," Robert said. "Would you describe the skipper, Ted Pelling, for us?"

"Actually, he walked past the office with his arm around a lady a few minutes after you came into the office. The lady looked like she had a little too much to drink," the manager said, then described the lady and Pelling.

"Robert, he's got Mother!" Marta said.

As the threesome made their way to the *SeaOx*, Robert explained to the manager that Pelling was a terrorist suspected of murder and involved in a kidnapping. It was necessary that they board the boat and investigate. The manager opened the door to the pilothouse of the *SeaOx*. They made their way down into the dinette area. Robert looked into the master stateroom and then into the galley, noting the two cups and two plates left in the sink. When he pulled the louvered doors open in the forward v-berth, he let out an exclamation that sounded like, "Mon Dieu!" Then, in a louder voice, he said, "Bring me a sharp knife from the galley. And hurry, please!"

Chapter 8

Basque Assassin in Control

The marina manager dialled the local harbour police and handed the cell phone to Robert, who began his routine used to identify himself to police who didn't know him. "Harbour police, Staff Sergeant Ryker speaking. How may I help you?"

"Lieutenant Bizet of the Paris Sûreté speaking. Do you have a computer in front of you, Staff Sergeant?"

"Affirmative, sir."

"Good! Please type the Sûreté access code 129ps3344. The screen will ask for your user ID which is 'stop it' in uppercase. That should bring up my picture, Staff Sergeant."

"How may I be of assistance to the Sûreté, Lieutenant Bizet?" he asked.

"You see on the screen that I have special duties concerning anti-terrorism, Sergeant. I would like your help by providing two of your uniformed policemen to stand guard duty on the *SeaOx*, a sailboat presently tied up at slip D-22 at the Scheveningen Marina. The *SeaOx* is a Hans Christian 44-foot Pilot House cutter with a dark green hull and white upper body. A Basque terrorist is suspected of hijacking the boat. I'll need two men to guard it for the next seventy-two hours. Would you please send the first shift to the marina immediately, Sergeant? I'll fax the proper paperwork to you before their shift is over."

"Certainly, Lieutenant. Officers Volker and Franson will be at the marina in one half hour. I'll watch for your fax."

The sergeant gave his fax number to Robert, who recorded it in his notepad. He then turned to the marina manager, Karl Schenk, and said, "It would be in the best interest of the marina that you forget what we witnessed. It is a matter of life or death for the woman being held by Teddy Pelling. The tipsy woman seen leaving with Pelling was probably his captive. I'd suggest that you just go about your business as if nothing happened and let the police arrest Pelling if he returns to the *SeaOx*."

Robert made a thorough search of the sailboat, turning up Andre Laurent's passport and the transfer papers showing the ownership change of the *SeaOx* from Laurent to Pelling. The surprising find was the leather grip in the hanging locker amidships. It contained a large brown envelope on top of stacks of US currency. *This is likely the ransom, so Pelling will be coming back for this money,* Robert thought.

He took a good long look at the passport then attempted, once again, to question Laurent, who had a nasty bruise on his forehead and continually asked for water. He was incoherent, mumbling something about T-bills he could cash if they took him to Bordeaux. Neither Robert nor Marta could understand what the man was trying to tell them. Robert didn't know yet how Laurent figured into the kidnapping of Elspeth, but thinking he was also a victim of Pelling's, he would keep him close until he got to the bottom of his identity. When the two harbour police arrived, Robert introduced himself and one of the policemen asked to see his ID. Robert then briefed the two about their guard duty, telling them they were to arrest anyone that came aboard, or anyone that seemed too curious about the boat.

Robert shook hands with Schenk and thanked him for his co-operation. All three then escorted a very unsteady Andre Laurent to the fuel dock where Marta's amphibian was tied up. After nearly losing him off the fuel dock, Robert and Schenk finally got him secured into the rear seat of Marta's plane. Marta set the leather grip containing the ransom beside him.

Prior to getting in her plane, Marta used Schenk's cell phone to call Tice at the chateau. Sylvie answered and said

Tice hadn't returned. "How are you doing there all by yourself, Sylvie?" Marta asked.

"Oh, I'm fine, but I've heard nothing from Tice."

"I'm sure he's okay. When we flew overhead, he was pulled over on the side of the highway . . . looked like they had a flat tire. He was heading in the direction of the airport. Please ask the housekeeper to call our family doctor and have him come to the chateau. We're bringing a guest that is very much under the weather. I'll explain when we get there. We'll see you soon—in about forty minutes."

As soon as Sylvie put the receiver down, the phone rang again, startling her. The caller simply said, "Elspeth Vander Riis is free and waiting to be picked up. She is in a booth at the Schiphol Airport arrivals lounge cafeteria." Before she could ask who was calling, the person hung up.

Sylvie didn't know whom to call with this wonderful news. While telling the housekeeper about Marta's call asking to have the family doctor come to the chateau, the phone rang again. The housekeeper answered and said, "The call is for you, Miss Sylvie."

"Sylvie Bern speaking."

"Hi, Slim. It's Tice. How are you doing?"

"Oh Tice, thank God it's you. A call just came in and the caller said that your mom is free and in a booth at the arrivals lounge cafeteria at Schiphol Airport! Are you all right? Marta also called from The Hague and said they would be home in forty minutes. She also asked that the housekeeper call the family doctor because they have a passenger who is quite sick. She said she would explain when they arrived."

"We had some car trouble, which I'll tell you about later. We are at the Schiphol now. I'll pick up Mother and call you when I have her with me. Talk with you soon."

Sylvie was back on the phone with Tice twenty minutes later. "Hi, Slim, we have Mother with us. She's very likely been drugged and is quite woozy. Please ask the doctor to stay until he has a chance to examine her. We should be there in forty-five minutes. Hang in there, Slim."

The doctor arrived at about the same time Marta was landing at the hunting lodge on the edge of the estate. While the doctor attended to Andre Laurent, Robert advised Marta and Sylvie of who he was. "Our Paris office has had several calls from an Ava Haas from Hamburg stating that the *SeaOx* owned by Andre Laurent was sold to a Ted Pelling. Haas is adamant that Laurent would not have sold the boat to anyone but her. She demanded the boat be boarded and Andre Laurent be rescued as she was positive of foul play. I initially thought Ms Haas was some hysterical ex-lover stalking Laurent, but she played a tape she received from him that confirmed he could very well be in trouble."

When Robert looked through the suitcase, it contained the ransom money, as well as a large envelope containing cash and a brokerage cheque stub. The amount of money in the case totalled four-hundred-thirty-thousand dollars, the amount of the ransom less five thousand. The cheque stub in the envelope was for $153,401.20. The cash in the large envelope matched that. The purchase and sales slip from the Merrill Lynch office in Paris was for Andre Laurent's T-bill account.

Robert fished out another envelope and some typewritten notes stuffed amongst the ransom money. Robert said, "This is a legal transfer of ownership of the *SeaOx* from Andre Laurent to Theodore Pelling for one-hundred-seventy-five-thousand dollars. It states on this document that Pelling's cheque accompanies this transfer."

Marta said, "So, that explains who Andre Laurent is. He was the owner of the *SeaOx* before he sold it to Pelling. So, why did we find him tied up and drugged on the boat?"

"Seems Laurent had a brokerage account in Paris with Merrill Lynch containing one-hundred-fifty-four-thousand dollars in T-bills, and he sold his boat for another one-hundred-seventy-five thousand dollars. So why wouldn't he put that money into more T-bills?" Robert asked. "Instead, he cashes out his present account and that money ends up in Pelling's possession, along with Elspeth's ransom."

Sylvie, quiet until now, said, "What if Andre Laurent is also a victim, along with your mother?"

Once again, Robert and Marta looked questioningly at Sylvie. Robert scanned the two typewritten notes and said, "This is a note to Elspeth from Andre introducing his partner, who is to collect the one million guilder ransom or else suffer some deviant sexual assault. He warns against involving the police, or the Basque ETA will kill Elspeth and her son and daughter. Rather damning admission of who they are and what they're after, wouldn't you agree?"

"It explains who Andre Laurent is, doesn't it? Obvious to me, he is the man Mother was to meet in Paris. He just wasn't who she thought he was. Seems he's a bloody confidence man and an ETA terrorist to boot," Marta said.

"Doesn't explain why he was drugged and bound on his former boat if he was, in fact, a partner of Pelling, or where the cheque is for one-hundred-seventy-five-thousand dollars that Pelling gave him for the sale of the *SeaOx*? And why did he cash in his T-bill account?" Robert asked. "We need to interview Laurent and Elspeth. They might be able to answer these questions."

The doctor reported that he had bandaged Laurent's head wound, gave him a strong sedative, asked Marta to have plenty of water by his bedside, and allow their patient to sleep off the sedative. The doctor would have the blood and urine samples he took analysed, and fax the results to the chateau. He was just making himself comfortable in the study when Tice and Henk arrived with a woozy Elspeth.

The doctor and Tice helped her up to her bedroom suite. After he gave her a complete check-up, the doctor took blood and urine samples before administering the same sedative he'd given Laurent. He told Robert that her test results would be included, along with Laurent's, in his fax.

They walked the doctor to the door, and as he was about to leave he asked, "I don't suppose you care to tell me any more than you already have about how Elspeth and Andre Laurent came to be in their present condition."

It was Robert who answered. "We've told you what we know for certain, but I'll make sure to let you know further details after my investigation is complete. I'll look forward to the results of the fluid tests you took."

Tice added, "We are grateful to you for your quick response and attention to Mother and Mr Laurent. Thank you again for your confidentiality. We will see you in the morning."

The following morning, June 7, Andre Laurent made his way carefully down the stairway, taking note of the portraits on the wall. His muddled mind didn't wonder who they were. He walked toward the sound of voices. Looking in, he saw Elspeth and four young adults sitting around a coffee table engaged in conversation.

"Elspeth, thank God you're safe. You have no idea how worried I was for you. I'm to blame for this awful predicament. Could I please have some water? And then I'd like to try to explain what happened," Andre said.

Marta left the study and returned momentarily with a pitcher of ice water and a glass. Robert produced a tape recorder. Elspeth introduced Andre to the others. Robert turned on the machine and spoke into it.

"June 7, 8:45 a.m., the study in the Vander Riis chateau at Utrecht, interview with Andre Laurent. Mr Laurent, please tell us everything you remember since you last saw Elspeth Vander Riis in Paris one month ago," Robert asked.

"I provisioned my sailboat, the *SeaOx*, at my slip at Baie Des Ange in Nice, where I had it berthed for a short time. I sailed from there on May 17, headed for Le Havre to have my radar equipment checked out. I had an appointment with the dealer there to bring my boat up to his dock the morning of June 1. He's located right by the marina office. I intended to fly to Paris after I'd tied up at Le Havre, in order to keep my date with Elspeth later that same day. By the way, I did file a float plan at Baie Des Ange in Nice and stated that if the weather and sailing time permitted, I would stop at Brest to top up the water and fuel. What a mistake that was!

"Well, the weather was favourable. I made very good time and stopped at Brest. I arrived at the Radi Abri Marina at eleven in the morning on May 29. I took the boat's papers to the marina office, emptied the garbage, and topped up the fuel and water. I motored the *SeaOx* to the slip assigned to me and tied up. I was only staying that afternoon. I took an envelope containing an audiotape I'd made of my solo voyage. I mailed it to Ava Haas in Hamburg, Germany. She sold me the *SeaOx* and taught me about the boat in a shakedown cruise from Hamburg to Oostend, over to London, and back to Le Havre. I picked up the provisions needed for the rest of my trip into Le Havre. A delivery kid helped me back to the SeaOx with these parcels. We put the bags of groceries on the deck by the boat, and I remember giving him a tip. I began loading the bags down into the galley. On my way down the stairs to the galley with the last two bags, my head exploded and . . . and . . . everything went black."

"Please continue . . . what do you remember after that?" Robert asked.

"I woke trussed up, naked, and was confronted by . . . this is embarrassing . . . He was a heavily muscled character who looked to be thirty- to thirty-five years old. He did not respond to my questions. I asked him if I could have my jeans and some water. He thought about it, then left for the deck and operated the winch, which dropped me to the floorboards. He came back with my jeans, untied me, and watched me struggle into them. I was woozy but the pain in the back of my head kept me awake. The guy said he had given me a shot to relax me. He needed my boat . . . that was the extent of his information. I asked to look at his navigation. His shrug suggested his total disinterest. My nautical chart was open on the chart table. While I was focused on his navigation, he handed me a cup of soup, which I devoured. I checked his position lines and waypoints, and measured a four-hundred-fifty-kilometre track into Le Havre. His last fix indicated we had covered three-hundred-five kilometres, and we were presently sailing off the Cap de la Hague. This guy definitely knew how to sail. I figured it would be another fourteen hours to make Le Havre if the winds held.

"The bulkhead clock chimed 1:00 p.m. We would arrive at 3:00 a.m. I wondered if he knew about my appointment with the Furano dealer at the Basin de La Manche. When I asked if I could take a look at the sail trim from the pilothouse, he nodded and let me walk partway up the stairs so that I could see the sails. He had the jenny up, and it and the main were drawing nicely. I was convinced he knew what he was doing and I said so, my second big mistake.

"He obviously didn't like the tone of my voice because he knocked me to the floorboards with a vicious backhand that I didn't see coming, then told me what was in store for me. He intended to keep me alive until he accompanied me to the Merrill Lynch office in Paris to pick up a cheque for the proceeds of my US Treasury bill account, which we would cash. After that, he planned to take my place at Elspeth's apartment. At that point, he said I would become expendable. So my worst fears were happening, and I couldn't think of any way to get out of a mess that was my fault.

"He found the notes I had made from what Pierre Turrin told me about you and your family, Elspeth, as well as what you told me yourself. I'm such a damn fool. You must despise me, and I don't blame you, but I can't for the life of me figure out why this happened, or who would have reason or motive to hijack my sailboat. Elspeth, I really owe you an apology. It's my fault that you are involved, because as he was rummaging through my personal papers he came across those Polaroid pictures we took of each other. He undoubtedly read the details of our meeting on June 1 at your Paris apartment. If that information hadn't fallen into his hands, you would have been spared this terrifying ordeal. I don't know how I'll ever make it up to you. I've been just sick about it.

"The guy planned to take ownership of the *SeaOx* by a legal transfer when we docked at Le Havre. I thought I'd be safe at least until he made me call Pierre to instruct him to cash my T-bill account. How bloody naive of me to think Turrin might help me. During my telephone call to him, I couldn't think of anything that would alert him to my predicament. I had a tough time composing my thoughts. I couldn't stay on track very long before I'd drift off into a stupor. My head has since cleared, but I still drift off at times. I figured I was being drugged, and whenever I awoke I'd have this awful thirst. I need to have another drink. I can't seem to quench this thirst."

"You describe your captor as thirty- to thirty-five years old, six-feet tall and about two-hundred-twenty-five pounds, with a muscular build. Is that correct?" Robert asked.

"Yes, that's right. He has short blond hair, a military cut, and grey-blue eyes that reveal nothing. I didn't see any marks or tattoos or disfigurements that might identify him. He is built like a body builder, but moves like an athlete. He moved around the boat like a cat. He's very sure of himself. When he did speak, it was just to tell me what I was going to do. He's one cold and calculating character.

"I awoke to hear the *SeaOx* settle against the dock when we arrived at the Basin De La Manche in Le Havre. He walked me to the marina office to record our arrival. I was unsteady on my feet, and judging from the pain coming from the swollen right side of my face, I figured his blow had broken something. The clerk in the office asked me what I had done. My captor answered that I was hit by the boom in an accidental jibe and asked the clerk where we might go to have a legal transfer of boat ownership drawn up. We were directed to a law office close by. The clerk requested a copy of the transfer. I paid for a week's stay with my gold card. After that, we went directly to the Avis rental agency close by and arranged to rent a Jaguar Sovereign. It was to be delivered to the *SeaOx* the next morning. I paid for the rental with my card."

"Was your captor armed? How did he keep you under control?" Robert wanted to know.

"He had shown me a nasty looking switchblade he kept in his jacket pocket and stayed right beside me at all times, holding my arm and helping me to walk. He had no problem righting me whenever my knees buckled—very strong dude. I was woozy from the drug he must have put in my drink. I wasn't up mentally or physically for a fight or flight. But, I knew it would come to that.

"At the notary's law office we had drawn a title transfer to Theo Pelling. That was the first time I knew his name. He gave me a cheque for one-hundred-seventy-five-thousand US dollars for the *SeaOx* to complete the deal, and I paid one-hundred-fifty dollars with my card for the fees. We went back to the marina office and gave a copy of the legal transfer to the clerk to put with the boat's papers. Lieutenant, I'm going to ask for your help in unwinding that bogus sale and transfer. Is the *SeaOx* still in custody at that marina?"

"Yes it is. Fingerprint experts from the Amsterdam police have examined it. You won't have any trouble recovering your boat as soon as we're through with it. By the way, Andre, do you still have that cheque Pelling gave you?"

"No, I don't. Just as soon as we left the law office he took it from me. We walked back to the *SeaOx* and he tied me up in the v-berth again. I had a drink of water before that and went quickly to sleep. It was probably drugged.

"The following morning Pelling cooked breakfast for us. As soon as we finished, he walked me over to the phone booth outside the marina office where I called the Merrill Lynch office in Paris and asked to speak with Pierre Turrin. I asked him to please cash the T-bills in my account and have a cheque for the balance ready as I'd stop in with an associate to pick it up in a couple of hours. There was no response from Turrin. That's when I had this glimmer of an idea and told him to take the fifteen-thousand-dollar commission we agreed upon from the T-bill proceeds. Turrin remained silent." Elspeth harrumphed at this and shook her head.

"I then blurted into the phone how I'd had an accident on the sailboat, was through with sailing, and sold the boat to my associate. That's when I said; 'He would make a good prospect for you.' Turrin finally said, "I see," and Pelling brandished the blade, motioning me to end the call."

It was Tice who spoke up, "You don't take commission off a T-bill redemption. There isn't any commission charged. Turrin must have known something was up or wrong."

"Just a minute now, back up a bit," said Robert. "Now really, Laurent, did you expect that Pierre Turrin would have the police there at the brokerage office awaiting your arrival?"

"No, of course not, but I gave him an opportunity to ask if anything was wrong and he ignored it. Perhaps he couldn't get past the fact that I was closing my account. When we arrived at Paris and walked into the Merrill Lynch office, Turrin came bounding to the counter and handed me the envelope with the cheque in it, without any conversation about my future plans. Turrin went right to Pelling and pushed a new account form toward him trying to get him to make a deposit. Pelling gave him a cold stare and in a threatening voice told Turrin to just give him a card and he'd be in touch when he returned in July. Turrin handed him the card and offered his hand to shake, but Pelling just looked at it.

"We left the brokerage office and walked up the street to the Royal Bank of Canada to cash the cheque. I noticed two bank guards on duty in the area. It was my first real chance to escape. My plan might have worked, but my knees buckled from the effects of the drugs, and Pelling helped me to the counter. At the cashier's window I straightened up, presented my passport and international driver's license, then opened the envelope and studied the cheque before endorsing it. I looked at the purchase and sales slip that accompanied the cheque; the net amount was $153,401.20."

Robert turned the tape recorder off for a break while Andre went to the washroom. Marta and Mathijs were having a quiet conversation. Elspeth and Robert had their heads together. When Andre returned and took a drink of water, Robert turned the tape back on and asked, "What happened next?"

"When the proceeds of the cashed cheque were stored in the case, I turned and shoved the case at Pelling's midsection, which kept his hands occupied while I dashed, or rather attempted to dash, for the nearest bank guard. I planned to get behind him and tell him Pelling was a terrorist and had a knife he was threatening to kill me with. But the guard was looking the other way; my knees buckled halfway to him, and I stumbled and fell. Seconds later, Pelling helped me to my feet and led me out of the bank. He walked me down the block into a hotel lobby and over to a bank of telephones. That's when I made the call to you, Elspeth, saying I'd be along in half an hour.

"I was shoved into the trunk of the rental car when we stopped in a park. That time I felt a sting in my rear before the lid closed. I don't remember much after that. The boat was moving. I would wake and couldn't make out why I was tied to the berth. I remember being helped into an airplane at a marina, I think, then climbing a big staircase . . . a doctor asking me questions. That's it . . . that's all I can remember right now."

Elspeth said to all of them, "It's clear to me that Andre was the victim of pure circumstance. For your information, if none of this had happened I would have brought him home with me and introduced him to all of you. And there is something else you should know. I had a detailed inquiry made about Andre through Pierre Turrin, which I will let you read. I'm convinced Andre Laurent is who he says he is. I believe him." She looked at Andre and smiled. "I had the report all ready to show you at the apartment, Andre, when that Pelling character burst in on me."

Elspeth continued, "Andre and I were to be introduced to one another at Pierre Turrin's annual customer party back in May. Andre told me he had been out to dinner with Pierre who invited him back to his apartment for drinks where he saw a picture of me taken at last year's party. Andre said he questioned Pierre about me, learning I was in Paris at the time to see the new lines at the courtiers. Back at his apartment, Andre told me he made notes of what he'd learned about me. He said he dreamt about me that night. The following morning he decided he wouldn't wait to meet me at the party and set out to intercept me, if he could. He found me at one of the courtiers. That's how we met.

"I thought his actions very charming, to tell you the truth. It was chemistry at our first meeting. We hit it off right away and spent that week together. We even spoke on the phone with Pierre and told him we would not be attending his party. He didn't seem at all concerned and asked what our plans were. I was unsure, so I didn't offer much information."

Elspeth stopped to take a drink of water and went on. "To hold Andre responsible for what happened is pure nonsense. We are both victims of this Pelling person, who Andre described so well. He's definitely the same brute who burst into my apartment and nearly choked the life out of me, then forced me to read that letter that was supposedly from you, Andre. And it had the desired effect on me. I became so furious at being duped by Andre that I just did as I was ordered, while I fumed inside."

Andre looked surprised and spoke up, "What letter are you talking about, Elspeth?"

Robert chimed in, "I found that letter along with another typewritten note giving Tice instructions on how to deliver the ransom."

Elspeth said, "Show it to Andre so he knows what we are talking about, please. It is a typewritten note addressed to me and purportedly signed by you. It introduced the brute forcing me to read it as your partner. It said you had told him all about our . . . get together . . . at my Paris apartment, and how his partner would like to have me as well. But, because he liked money as well as sex, he would restrain himself if I would pay them a ransom of one million guilders for my safe return. Pelling said when I spoke to my family about the ransom I was to say agents of the ETA—the Basque terrorist arm—were holding me, and if their demands were not met they would kill my children and me as well. This letter so completely unnerved me that I began to seethe with anger at being so easily duped. I managed to hold myself together and followed instructions to contact either Tice or Marta and make arrangements to cash a cheque for the ransom amount.

"But, since I've had time to think this through, I think Pelling just used that letter to crush my spirit in order to control me. He never contacted any associate or was contacted by anyone while I was in his custody. I'm convinced he was acting alone. Whether or not he is an ETA agent, I can't say, but I did believe his threat to kill the twins and me if I didn't pay him off. As Pelling reminded me, it was a good deal for me—a mere million guilders for my life. I'm obviously conflicted right now. I'm thrilled and thankful that I'm home safe, and that Andre has been rescued. I believe we are both innocent victims. But I'm terrified for us that Robert and Marta recovered the ransom money. I can't help but feel like I've reneged on a contract that gave me back my life."

Nobody said anything for a few minutes. Then Andre spoke, "Pelling is clever and a truly evil creep to have implicated me with that letter. I did not write it, nor was I aware of it."

"Well, thank God for the way everything worked out," Robert said. "But, don't for one minute think you owe this Pelling anything for turning you loose. If he is an ETA agent, you will hear from him again, mark my words."

Chapter 9

Suspects

Robert thought to himself, *Elspeth may be convinced of Andre Laurent's innocence in this matter, but I'm not so sure. It certainly could have happened exactly the way Laurent said it did, but the only way we will know for sure is if we obtain a confession from the real villain, Theo Pelling, but that doesn't seem likely.*

Robert kept at his police procedure of clearing everyone involved in the events of the past couple of weeks: Elspeth Vander Riis, Ava Haas, Theo Pelling, and the broker, Pierre Turrin. *Elspeth passes critical scrutiny: she made inquiries of Andre Laurent. That's due diligence on her part. Still, something in the back of my mind keeps flitting about.*

Robert reverted to the basics of his police training. "Elspeth, that inquiry you made of Andre was directed to Pierre Turrin, was it not?"

"Yes, that's right. I thought about making a formal inquiry through our family lawyer, but I remembered something my husband used to say about lawyers, which made me change my mind. Paul used to say lawyers were all members of the same club and liked to practice one-upmanship with the confidential information they were privy to. I pictured my innocent letter, —my attempt at some form of inquiry about Andre Laurent—arriving at the law firm, opened, read, and recorded, then passed on to our dear friend for his personal attention. He would read it and probably hand it off to some junior person to handle. I then imagined our lawyer friend with this information and, if my late husband Paul was correct, how easily it might get into the social stream. Very cynical, I know, but that's when it occurred to me to ask Pierre to tell me what he knew about Andre. I know for a fact that brokerage account information is very extensive. This is the very complete report Pierre sent about Andre's net worth, along with information about his sailboat and where it was located."

Robert read it and asked, "What was your reaction to this report?"

"Well, I was thrilled and relieved because he was single, and his net worth indicated he was self-sufficient. Please forgive me, Robert, I know how that must sound. But, I don't really have any parameters I use in eliminating new friends who might be fortune hunters. In retrospect, when I read the report it confirmed he was who he said he was. As I said, I was relieved, thrilled, and anxious to see him again. The sailboat seemed to add another dimension that I thought was rather exciting."

"Thank you. One more question, and it will be my last. What has the doctor concluded about your health, and did he make any recommendations?"

"Thank you for your concern. The doctor told me this morning that I appear to be all right. He said when he knows what I have been given, he can advise what after effects there might be, if any. He is a true family friend and assured me his visit here would be kept a secret between us. Now, I know you are Marta's guest and are not here on official business. Can I have your word that you will stay uninvolved officially, at least until we resolve this situation with this Pelling person?"

"Yes, I'll do as you ask for now, but I must warn you and the others of what we're dealing with here. This whole misadventure is about money. Pelling hijacked Andre's boat for resale and came across his brokerage account, a bonus. Then he found out about you. Jackpot! But for the life of me, I can't imagine why he left both the money and Andre unguarded as he did. The only thing that makes any sense is his arrogance at not getting caught. And he would have gotten away with the boat and the money if we hadn't been able to trail him from the air to the marina.

"If he planned to keep the *SeaOx* after setting you free, he most certainly planned to murder Andre, and he had all avenues covered. If, and when, you gained your composure, Pelling knew you would turn your anger toward Andre, thinking him to be the mastermind in your kidnapping, but you would then have been looking for a dead man. The second concern I have is that Pelling never returned to the *SeaOx* for the ransom—very strange. Then again, he could have returned to the marina, spotted the police on guard, and figured the money and Andre were gone. In which case, he had no choice but to disappear. It will surprise me if we find any of Pelling's fingerprints on the *SeaOx*."

Andre excused himself and left the study for the washroom. Robert spoke to Elspeth and the others saying, "Pelling's actions so far suggest to me he is a professional, if you disregard his careless and cavalier actions yesterday. I'd bet money we haven't heard the last of him. But there is another possibility you all must have considered. This could be a confidence game of grand proportions. What if Andre and Pelling really are partners? The only sure-fire way to gain your confidence would be to have events unfold exactly as they have so far. So, their next step would be to do something violent to get your attention in order to extract a much larger ransom. We must all be vigilant. You and the twins are his targets. Please, everyone, take extra precautions, and be on your guard. Thank you for your candour. You've cleared up a few things for me and have been very cooperative."

"Robert, I'm so glad you're here to advise in this dreadful business. But, as for your conjecture that Andre had anything at all to do with this whole matter, I hope and pray you are wrong. Nevertheless, I do respect your expertise, and I promise I will consider your intuition and shake the stars from my eyes where Andre is concerned."

"Very well then," Robert replied.

Andre returned to the group as they were leaving the study. Robert remained and telephoned his office at the Sûreté in Paris and spoke with Sergeant Moline.

* * *

After releasing the very groggy widow at the Schiphol Airport, Pelling drove back to the marina. He noted the time on his wristwatch was 5:00 p.m. He parked the rental van on the upper deck of the parkade across from the marina. He had a good view of the boatyard and located the *SeaOx* through his powerful little telescope. Pelling thought to himself, *I had a feeling everything was going along too smoothly. Two uniforms appear to be standing guard at the boat. What's that about?* He was pretty sure Elspeth wasn't in any shape to have called the cops. Even if she were, she wouldn't know where to send them. *Christ! Laurent must have gotten loose, but how? I gagged him and made sure he was tied securely before I left with the widow. Maybe he made a ruckus and someone came aboard and rescued him. Shit, shit, shit! Why in the hell didn't I take the money with me? A little bit overconfident, old son?*

He kept looking to see if perhaps the cops were there for some other reason. Nope, one of the cops stepped onto the boat and into the pilothouse and disappeared down the stairs, probably to use the head. *So, Laurent got free somehow and called the cops, which means he has tried to contact the widow by now. Let's see . . . I left at 1100 hours. If he got free in the first hour I was gone, he could be at her chateau by now.* He didn't think Elspeth could have been picked up and taken home yet. Judging from her condition when he'd left her, he knew she wouldn't be much help to the authorities, if in fact the family even reported her kidnapping. *Christ, Laurent's head ought to be full of wool and utter confusion from all the special Valium mix I shot into him. Serves me right, I should have killed him as soon as I had his money. Greedy! Greedy! Greedy!*

Pelling figured Laurent would be back for the SeaOx soon enough, but not before the police lab would swarm all over it looking for his prints, as if that would help. He decided he had no other choice. He had to get to the widow's chateau.

But first he needed to stop at his bank in The Hague to clean out the two-hundred-fifty-thousand dollars in his safety deposit box. *It wouldn't do to get caught short again. Then, after I'm finished here with the widow, I'll go home to the farm and ask Ruth to join me.*

He thanked God that he'd given most of his earnings to Ruth to invest for them, but not all of it, mind you. He'd kept a little stashed here and there. There was the quarter million at The Hague, about the same amount in Marseille, and two boxes in Paris with a little over a half million. *Damn it all to hell! I figured with this score from the sailor and the widow I could retire. Well, widow lady, the stakes have just gone up.*

She'd learn that he was serious about his threat, just in case she thought he didn't have the power of his convictions. He decided he'd execute her daughter and promise her that her son was next. *Hell, she'll probably bring me the money herself. Yes siree, I've always been able to read the ladies. And I do believe the yummy widow would be willing to satisfy me in just about any way I choose, just to seal our bargain.* He figured she was the type who definitely kept her word. So, right now it was time to get her attention.

I'm starting to feel better already. When I demand a higher amount from her now for my trouble, it will cast even more doubt on Laurent. Yeah, it will appear we set her up for the big score by returning the smaller amount, which is undoubtedly what he has done.

* * *

Back at the chateau, Robert's little exercise of "what if" turned his attention to the broker, Pierre Turrin. He thought Turrin's actions were more suspicious than aloof. First, there was the phone call that Laurent made, requesting he redeem the T-bills and take a healthy commission. No response. Then, when he was told Andre sold his boat, obviously his home since he'd been in Europe, Turrin appeared uninterested and didn't comment. Being the aggressive sales type Andre said he was, why didn't he go after the proceeds of the boat sale? And when they arrived at his office, Turrin just handed Andre his cheque and turned his attention to Pelling. Turrin's actions seemed more than rude or callous. Something seemed wrong. Why no conversation, and why no mention of his best client, Elspeth Vander Riis? Was his very unusual behaviour aloof and uncaring? Maybe, but Robert thought otherwise. Pierre Turrin failed scrutiny on all counts.

Robert went over all the notes he'd taken while talking with Sergeant Moline. *What if Turrin had set this whole thing up?* He knew the location of the *SeaOx* and could have easily obtained the float plan from the marina. He could have told the hijacker how easy it would be to get at Andre Laurent's T-bill money. Turrin could have also set the possible kidnapping of his wealthiest client in motion as well. Wasn't he about to lose her account to her son very soon anyway? Turrin could make a chunk of easy cash for his part in the abduction—more than enough of a motive. *Yes, Pierre Turrin, you are definitely a person of interest. Maybe the reason you snubbed Andre Laurent was that you believed he would be dead soon.*

Robert had instructed Moline to check with the Baie Des Anges Marina office in Nice to check on the float plan filed by the *SeaOx* and to put round-the-clock surveillance on Pierre Turrin. Nevertheless, it still didn't leave Andre Laurent completely in the clear.

* * *

Up in his room at the chateau, Andre went over the events that had happened down in the study. He had told them everything, at least all he remembered. Still, he did not have a good feeling about whether or not they believed him and that bombshell of a letter Elspeth mentioned. The accusing looks on their faces were like blows to his delicate psyche—shock and awe. They were shocked and he was awestruck. *How the hell is anyone supposed to deal with that?*

Andre thought that his denial at writing that letter seemed kind of lame. Even after Elspeth had stood by him saying she believed he was an innocent victim, Andre felt a curtain of suspicion, like a mist, hanging between his innocence and her endorsement. He couldn't stop thinking that unless Pelling was apprehended and made a complete confession, he was still a suspect. *I'll ask the lieutenant to arrange for me to take a lie detector test to help prove I'm innocent,* he decided. *I'll ask to go along with Marta and the lieutenant when they fly to The Hague. I'll need his help to regain possession of my boat.*

Andre felt better having formulated a plan of action. First, he would unwind the title transfer of the *SeaOx*. Then he'd have it hauled and completely scanned for anything electronic that Pelling might have installed. He would check the clever hiding place Ava had shown him where he stored his pistol and its permit, which Pelling obviously never found. *If only I had put all those papers and pictures and my financial statements in there as well, Pelling wouldn't have found them.* After that, he'd hitch a ride with Marta and the lieutenant into Paris, get the lie detector test done at the Sûreté office, and then pay a visit to Pierre Turrin.

Andre looked at his watch, 6:00 p.m. *What a day, but I'm very much alive!* He still couldn't believe his luck at being rescued. He definitely had to thank Ava for her bugging the lieutenant to look for him. He knew right away what the *SeaOx* looked like, and when he followed Pelling's movements with the ransom from Marta's plane, he made the connection as soon as Pelling stepped aboard the boat at the marina.

Even though I've been treated kindly by the lieutenant, Marta, Tice, and his friend Sylvie, I still detect some coolness from Elspeth, and I don't think it is embarrassment or shyness. So here I am, shaken but alive . . . and I'm getting more pissed off by the minute at having been put into this situation. Cripes, I had no idea that Pelling forced Elspeth back to the SeaOx after taking my place at her apartment.

I had no idea we were both captives aboard. Hell, I was drugged most of the time and bound to the berth in the forward cabin. My carefree lifestyle will have to be put on hold until I get to the bottom of this bloody fiasco.

Andre Laurent wasn't going to be satisfied until he was completely exonerated and had his good name back.

Chapter 10

Revenge of the Basque Assassin

Upon leaving the marina parking lot, Pelling drove the van containing the stolen BMW police motorcycle to a deserted cement plant located thirty kilometres north of the Scheveningen Marina. There, he covered the chrome trim on the bike with masking tape and spray painted the silver BMW a flat black with quick-drying paint. He stripped off the masking tape and, voilà, had a brand new motorcycle. He siphoned gas from the van to fill the bike's tank. Next, he offloaded the motorcycle and drove the van into a large storage bin, swung the cement flow pipe above it, and started the stream. The van was completely covered by the time he walked to the motorcycle.

Pelling had no trouble finding the Vander Riis estate after checking at a gas station on the outskirts of Utrecht. The grounds of the estate were vast, and he had to travel back roads in order to enter near a mini-forested area, which was close to the chateau and a two-story structure with an airplane tied down beside it. Pelling hid the motorcycle under branches he cut from bushes nearby. When he was satisfied the bike couldn't be spotted by anyone out for a drive around the estate grounds, he went to work. His first stop was the two-story building. He did a quick walk around the amphibian airplane tied down on a landing pad. He admired the sporty little plane and thought he just might like to get one for himself in the future.

Pelling broke the glass on the rear kitchen door of the building with his elbow, which was protected by the heavy olive green military greatcoat he wore. Once inside, he checked all the rooms to make sure he was alone. He opened the custom-made case he brought and took out four pieces—the barrel, scope, body, and silencer—and assembled his handmade rifle. It had been designed to look like a competition model. Pelling put three .22 calibre hornet shells into the breach and jacked one into the chamber. He cleaned up the broken glass, pulling the remaining jagged pieces from the door, and threw them into the fireplace ashes. The fridge yielded cold cuts, bread, cheese, and milk. He made himself two sandwiches and drank half the milk from the container. The sandwiches went into the side pocket of the greatcoat.

A very useful map of the estate grounds hung on the wall beside the gun cabinet. On it, he located the spot where he hid the motorcycle and estimated the distance to the rear of the chateau where the pool and tennis courts were situated. He would make his kill shot from a place halfway between the hidden bike and the tennis courts. Four hundred yards was an easy enough shot if the widow's twins decided to swim or play tennis. It was now 9:35 p.m. and there wasn't likely to be any evening activity on the courts; however, the pool might yield an opportunity.

Pelling found a large tarp at the lodge that he could conceal himself under at his shooting position, which he'd occupy as soon as it got darker. If he found it too uncomfortable waiting in the field, he'd retreat to the woods and make himself a shelter out of branches. He thought briefly about the beds inside, but dismissed it as an imprudent choice, even though it was probably safe enough.

Watching the chateau through his telescope, Pelling saw figures inside, their shadows passing windows, but nobody ventured out. Prepared to wait in this optimum place until someone came to the pool or the courts, Pelling realized it didn't matter who he shot and killed because the widow would feel responsible and realize he meant what he said about killing her and her family.

Pelling verified the distance of approximately four hundred yards by pacing it from the pool and courts to his vantage point early that morning while the occupants of the chateau slept. He made a practice run, carrying the rifle with the tarp fluttering about his shoulders, to where he'd hidden the motorcycle. Back at the shooting position, he set his watch and slept until the wristwatch alarm wakened him at 6:00 a.m. His rifle lay loaded under the edge of the tarp. Pelling saw one elderly woman come out of the rear of the chateau to retrieve a tray of glassware. He assumed she was a kitchen worker judging from the apron she wore. At 7:05 a.m., morning at the chateau suddenly began in earnest as two young people came out of the rear entrance dressed in white tennis garb. They made their way to the courts laughing and enjoying some good-natured pregame taunting.

Pelling brought the high-powered riflescope to bear on the young couple. He settled in and watched them play two sets, biding his time, until the match was over and they were standing still beside each other. *That's the son and his sister all right, out for a bit of exercise—same guy who handed me the suitcase from the back seat of the Rolls. There is a family resemblance. The girl does take after the widow. Ah, that's it . . . a handshake at the net . . . hold it right there . . . I could kill them both . . . but only the daughter this time. Aim just below her left shoulder and squeeze . . .*

Phhiitttt the muffled sound of the rifle exclaimed. Pelling kept the scope on the target and saw her pitch forward and the back of her left shoulder blossom red. Kill shot! Her brother caught her in his arms and stumbled to the rear entrance of the chateau.

Quickly now, move! Pelling ordered himself.

Robert, watching from windows in the study, saw Tice and Sylvie about to finish their match and thought about how they had not been able to spend much time together—about as much as he and Marta—thanks to the events of the last couple of days. His thoughts were interrupted when he saw Sylvie pitch forward as if pushed, and Tice's quick reaction, catching her before she fell. The sudden red blossoming on her back sent an alert to his brain. *She's been shot!* He looked away from them, toward the direction he thought the bullet came from. He caught a glimpse of what seemed like a huge dark green manta ray flapping toward a wooded area.

Instinctively, Robert lifted the receiver of the study telephone, intending to call the Utrecht police, but paused and replaced the receiver as he remembered his promise to Elspeth. He went to the hubbub of servants surrounding Tice carrying Sylvie.

"I saw the shooter, Tice. He scurried toward the woods at the edge of the field out back," Robert said.

Elspeth hurried away to call the family doctor as Tice lay Sylvie down carefully on the leather couch in the study. Marta stayed beside her and ordered the staff to bring towels and hot water.

"My shoulder went numb, but now it's really starting to hurt. What happened?" Sylvie asked, as she looked up into the concerned faces of Tice and Marta.

"You've been shot. It looks like the bullet creased your shoulder and left a groove. There's been a lot of bleeding. Marta will fix a bandage to stop it. Mother has called the doctor. Here, drink this shot of brandy. It may help calm you. Just try and relax, Slim. God, I never dreamt we were in any danger out here, or I wouldn't have asked you to go outside. Damn it! Robert was right; we're dealing with a cold-blooded killer," Tice said and stepped back out of the way to let Marta tend to the wound.

Elspeth arrived, and in an excited voice announced, "The doctor is on his way, Sylvie. He'll be here in twenty minutes." Elspeth took a few deep breaths, calmed herself, and announced to Robert, Tice, and Marta in a quiet but determined voice, "I will pay the ransom Pelling demands just to get him out of our lives. I feel I'm responsible for what happened here, Tice. I just shudder when I think of what might have happened to her."

Robert said, "The shooter was obviously Pelling, and I'm sure we'll hear from him soon for further demands. In the meantime, it would be wise to stay inside the safety of the chateau."

Elspeth turned to the housekeeper and asked her to gather the rest of the staff in the kitchen for a meeting. Elspeth informed them that their guest, Sylvie Bern, had been shot but that she was not in any danger and would be treated shortly by the family doctor. Elspeth suggested they all go about their regular duties, promising them a further update after Lieutenant Bizet completed his confidential investigation and the doctor attended to Sylvie.

* * *

That shot should kill her instantly, Pelling reasoned as he rapidly crab-walked in a half crouch toward the cover of the trees. When he arrived at the hidden motorcycle, he broke down the rifle and placed the components in the carrying case, secured it in the saddlebag, then left the grounds the same way he had entered. The BMW motorcycle was now wearing a new coat of military khaki paint that he had applied overnight. Pelling roared away, heading to the nearest main road into Amsterdam. Forty-five minutes at the speed limit and he'd be there.

Amsterdam swallowed the khaki motorcycle and rider until they turned into an underground parking area at a hotel with a secure area. Pelling bundled up his belongings from the bike and checked in as Rolf Erik Studer. Later, at a department store near the hotel, Pelling purchased a leather suitcase and a matching over-the-shoulder carryall. He also bought a pair of loafers, two pairs of socks, a pair of tan corduroy trousers, a belt, two lightweight pullover turtleneck sweaters, and, finally, a yellow leather jacket.

* * *

It took Robert about an hour to search the chateau's grounds. Upon his return, he asked Marta to accompany him while he checked out the hunting lodge.

* * *

After Sylvie had been attended to, Tice helped her to her feet and walked her up to her guest bedroom. Tice eased her onto the bed and under the covers. She reached up with a grimace and pulled his head down to her face to kiss him, saying, "Honey, would it be all right if I stayed here for a while longer? I'm supposed to report back for work tomorrow, but I could book off for a week or so and take some of my holiday time."

"Slim, you can stay here as long as you wish. I would be delighted if you'd stay. Go ahead, book off, and rest up. We wouldn't think of sending you off in this condition."

Sylvie smiled, surrendered to the sedative, and fell fast asleep before Tice could finish his sentence.

When the doctor was leaving he said to Elspeth, "I read the lab findings on your tests. Both you and Andre Laurent where given a Valium mix that can be very dangerous, but in your case both samples indicated the drug was a very low dose. It would knock you for a loop, make you a little cuckoo, cause you to sleep, and muddle your mind for a few days, but there aren't any long-term side effects. So, just take it easy, and I'm sure in a day or so you will both be back to normal.

"Elspeth, we've been friends for many years, and while you choose not to tell me the details of how you and Mr Laurent came to be in this condition, I want you to know that I've seen enough gunshot wounds in my day to recognize one. Miss Bern is very lucky that the bullet didn't hit an inch lower, or you would be dealing with a coroner instead of me. Please don't worry about this call compromising me. I did not extract a bullet; therefore, I won't have to report a gunshot wound. Satisfied?" the doctor said, smiling.

"Thank you so much, Arnold. Sometime in the near future we will have a quiet evening together. We will have much to talk about—I promise," Elspeth said.

* * *

At the noon meal, Robert informed everybody of what he found when he'd investigated the grounds after the shooting. He told them the shot was fired at Sylvie from a point halfway between the tennis courts and the wooded area at the edge of the field north of the tennis courts. He told them he'd witnessed the shooter scurrying toward the woods. He said he had requested a team from the Utrecht police to collect fingerprints from the hunting lodge, which had been broken into, and also to take plaster casts of the tire tracks left by the gunman's motorcycle. Robert did not mention that he suspected the motorcycle was the same one ridden by the highway patrolman that had stopped the Rolls and hijacked the ransom. He had learned from the duty sergeant at The Hague police department that a missing motorcycle patrolman had been found shot dead in a ditch about ten kilometres from his patrol area on the A-9.

* * *

Pelling showered at his hotel room then got dressed in his new cords, sweater, and jacket. He put the rest of his clothes in the new suitcase, along with the two-hundred-twenty-five-thousand dollars in cash. He took the bike boots and his old clothes and dropped them down the garbage chute on the way to the elevator. He left the suitcase and a hundred dollar tip with the concierge and ordered a taxi to take him to the train station. Upon arrival, he entered a telephone booth and placed a call to the Vander Riis chateau in Utrecht. When he looked for the number in the hotel room telephone book, he found two Vander Riis listings, one for an apartment in Utrecht and another for the chateau. That surprised him. They certainly didn't appear sheltered like most wealthy families. A servant answered and called Elspeth to the telephone.

"Yes, this is Elspeth Vander Riis, who is this please?"

"Your safety and that of your son will now cost you one million US dollars. Is your daughter dead, or did I just wound her?" Pelling asked.

"She is badly wounded. And, yes, I'll pay you the money to be rid of you forever."

"You realize I intended to kill her to show you I will carry out my threat. I meant what I said. I will kill you and your family if you don't pay. The police are likely already involved but that won't stop me. Do you understand?" Pelling asked in a tone that terrified her.

"Yes, I understand!"

"I will let you know tomorrow morning the details of how I want the money delivered."

"Andre Laurent was never involved in my kidnapping, was he?" asked Elspeth.

"Just arrange for the money to be at your chateau and I'll tell you how to deliver it." Pelling hung up the receiver.

Robert played back the taped telephone conversation for the third time. "There is no doubt in your mind this voice is that of the man who abducted you from your Paris apartment?"

"Yes, absolutely, Robert. I will never forget that voice. It's the same man."

"And you are going to pay him the million dollars he demanded?" he asked.

"Yes, I've already arranged for an additional five-hundred-seventy-thousand dollars in hundreds, fifties, and twenties. Andre and I counted what was left of the previous ransom amount. It came to four-hundred-thirty-thousand dollars. Pelling must have taken the missing five-thousand dollars. I remember what you suggested to me about keeping an open mind, as well as what Pelling's next move might be. And even though it has happened just the way you predicted, I still cannot for the life of me imagine Andre having anything to do with this shooting and extortion," Elspeth said in exasperation, hoping to counter the sceptical look on Robert's face.

"Professional scepticism, Elspeth, nothing more I assure you," he replied, smiling this time. "I do agree paying him this ransom is the right thing for you to do for your own peace of mind. Besides, there's always the chance we'll pick Pelling up and recover the money later."

Robert stroked his chin, looked Elspeth in the eye, and suggested, "I'd like to deliver the money to him when he gives you the delivery instructions, and for good reasons. I don't think any member of the Vander Riis family should be involved in handing over this money. You are all worth many times more than what he is asking this time. He could be planning to grab the family member who brings the money and demand a much larger sum for their safe return."

"I don't think so, Robert. Pelling had his chance to extract a huge amount from us when he kidnapped me. It must have been a spur of the moment idea, which came about after he took Andre's sailboat. He knew I was rich after reading Andre's notes. I think he probably thought another half a million was a tidy sum in addition to Andre's money and sailboat."

Robert countered, "On the other hand, if he is only interested in the money, he won't give a damn who brings it."

Elspeth shook her head and said, "Except for the fact that you are a policeman, and that would be a betrayal in his mind, whether we paid him or not. I know you mean well, but I insist on doing everything he asks so that he has no cause to come after us again. Besides, we don't know yet how he plans on taking delivery, and until we do I don't want any interference. I know as a friend you understand, so please, we must be patient and await his instructions."

Chapter 11
New Ransom Demand

Pelling left his hotel and took a taxi to the nearest UPS office. He ordered an envelope, inserted his instructions to Elspeth, sealed it, and addressed it to her at the chateau. The instructions directed Elspeth to give the UPS delivery person the suitcase containing the ransom, which was to be brought back to this office. Simple enough, but because it was a delivery and a pickup, he was told it would be done by a subcontractor, rather than a regular route van. Pelling asked the details of the delivery vehicle and the route so he could advise the chateau who to expect. The delivery/pickup was scheduled for 11:00 a.m. the following day. He paid for the service in cash.

* * *

Andre and Elspeth hadn't been alone together since Marta had flown him to the chateau after his rescue. Elspeth placed her hand on his arm and smiled, saying, "You could be the greatest swindler in history, Andre, but I don't think so! I believe what you told us, and I sympathize with your predicament."

"I'm exactly who I said I am. I'm no swindler, Elspeth," Andre replied. "As for my predicament, the only way that'll be resolved is when Pelling is caught and we find out who actually is behind the hijacking of my boat and our kidnapping."

"I know, Andre. It's a terrible blow to your dignity and self-esteem, but I'm very confident that when I pay Pelling his ransom demand he will not bother any of us ever again."

"I wish I was as certain as you are. But he's such a cold-blooded bastard, shooting Sylvie like he did. I'm sure he thought he was shooting Marta, since they look so much alike. And when you told us about that letter, I . . . I was dumbfounded. Good Lord! The insidious SOB just kicked you in the stomach with that little gem. I'm telling you, he's nobody to bargain with. He's a stone-cold killer, and I'm really not sure if he has others involved with him or not. He has already shot and killed two people and wounded Sylvie. As God is my witness, I'd never laid eyes on him before he grabbed my boat.

"Talk about a complete reversal in my life. There I was, literally on top of the world when I sailed into the marina at Brest. As I said before, I'd made an audiotape for Ava and mailed it to her in Hamburg from the marina in Brest. I only stopped long enough to offload the garbage and top up the fuel and water. I decided to get a few provisions, just in case I was able to convince you to come for a sail with me; in which case, I'd be ready to leave. I figured I'd be two more days getting to Le Havre where I'd leave the *SeaOx* with the Furano people at the marina, and I'd fly into Paris to meet you at your apartment, just like we planned.

"I was excited about seeing you again. I was smiling and whistling as I carried the last bags of groceries down the stairs when, *boom*, everything went black. When I awoke, I was strung up naked, hurting like hell, trying to recall what happened. I . . . I could tell we were underway and I was in a bad situation. Well, you know the rest . . . "Andre trailed off, turning his head away in embarrassment.

"Andre, before you called I was fussing around the apartment, excited with anticipation, but when you called, I sensed from your voice that you weren't happy. I began to worry about our meeting. You had a month to think about us. Were you having second thoughts? Then you called up on the intercom and I realized I must have imagined problems. Then that frightening character forced the door in on me and almost choked the life out of me. I was terrified and had difficulty breathing. He shoved that typewritten note from you in my face, which I couldn't read. So, he walked me back to the bedroom, sat me on the edge of the bed, and let me read it while he stood over me, so close his belt buckle was at my nose. Your note told me to do exactly as I was told, or your partner would enjoy raping me before he murdered me. I nearly became sick to my stomach when I read that you told him intimate things about us. The only thing holding me back from throwing up was the anger welling up inside me. I was so steamed at your treachery, but twice as angry at myself for acting like a silly romantic school girl." Elspeth attempted to smile at him while she dried her tears and continued.

"The twins and Robert getting involved with the ransom delivery was very risky on their part, but because they did you've been rescued and are safe. For that piece of luck, I'm very thankful."

Andre leaned forward from his chair and kissed the tears from her face, "I was certain I was going to die, but I kept thinking about your safety. I was terrified and concerned about what could happen to you because of my carelessness. I'm beyond relieved that he didn't harm you."

Elspeth kissed him gently on the lips and whispered, "Come with me." She led the way down the hall to her bedroom suite. When she closed the door behind them, she smiled, saying, "Oh Andre, I need you to hold me close."

The chateau, June 8, 10:30 a.m.

Pelling telephoned Elspeth and told her to expect a UPS courier who would deliver a letter to her within the hour. He instructed her to give the suitcase containing the ransom to the courier. The late model red Nissan UPS pickup truck arrived at the chateau three minutes before eleven. The female UPS driver, holding a clipboard and the letter, rang the doorbell and awaited an answer. A servant opened the door, asked the UPS driver in, and went to fetch Mrs Vander Riis. Elspeth appeared with a suitcase, signed the driver's clipboard for her letter, and signed it again for the pickup and delivery of the suitcase. The driver left at 11:09 a.m.

It took the UPS driver another six minutes to get to the turnoff to the main highway to Amsterdam. She pulled up behind a blue NSX-300 sports car, its parking lights blinking. The well-built young man in the sunglasses came back, leaned close to the rolled down window, and put a gun with a silencer in the driver's face.

"Hand me the suitcase you just picked up at the chateau," Pelling said. She did as she was told. The last thing she heard was the burp of the gun that ended her life.

Pelling had an exhilarating drive back to Amsterdam, putting the NSX through its paces, accelerating up to 180 kph then cutting back to the speed limit. Reaching over, he snapped open the suitcase lying on the passenger seat. He fondled the stacked cash and noticed a folded note on top of the bundles. He picked it off and snapped it open with his right hand. He seemed pensive after reading the note and stuffing it into his shirt pocket, saying aloud, "Yes indeed, Elspeth, you do have spunk!"

Concerned the suitcase may be bugged, he pulled into a rest stop, and put the bundles of cash into the Gucci bag he brought for this purpose. As he picked up each bundle of cash, he gave it a top-to-bottom flip to ensure a minute bug hadn't been implanted in one of them, but found nothing. He placed the stacks in the Gucci bag in order of denomination—hundreds and fifties on the bottom and twenties on top. He'd count it carefully later. He examined the empty suitcase but found nothing. He tossed it into a trashcan, pulled back onto the highway, and drove to the rental agency to return the sports car.

* * *

Elspeth brought the UPS envelope she received into the study, opened it in front of Robert, Andre, Marta, and Mathijs, and read what was inside aloud.

Elspeth,

This letter is to assure you I will never contact you or your family again. I think you and Laurent both realize how fortunate you are to be alive. This money will allow me immediate retirement. You have nothing more to fear from me.

T. Pelling

"Well, as Robert has previously stated, putting any trust in this criminal is a fool's game, but I feel I must. As you have all heard from my telephone conversation with him yesterday, I asked him if Andre had anything to do with my kidnapping and he wouldn't answer me. But I feel he has now done so in this letter. It clearly indicates he intended to kill us both. I don't think we will hear from him again, and I intend to put this nasty business behind me and get on with my life." The twins went to their mother's side and gave her a group hug.

Robert was not pleased with Elspeth's insistence that there be no interference from anyone during the delivery of the ransom money. *The lady does have her moments*, Robert mused. He wondered just how rich or how important a client had to be to arrange for the delivery of almost six-hundred-thousand dollars in cash to their home, in exchange for her personal cheque at the door. Her bank did aim to please, though, as the bank manager had delivered the money that morning in a limo. *What a lady. I marvel at her resolve after all she has gone through these past weeks.*

Robert also picked up on a very special connection, albeit restrained, between Elspeth and Andre Laurent. He intended to do as she asked and not interfere in any way until this business with Pelling was over. Robert felt Elspeth had made a bargain with the devil and was adamant about keeping it because Pelling had kept his word to her and let her live after payment of the first ransom. She had told everyone that she felt she owed the money to the kidnapper for sparing her life and releasing her unharmed, but when that ransom money was returned to her, she just knew in her heart that something terrible was going to happen to them. She felt responsible for Sylvie getting shot.

Elspeth summed up her actions, saying, "I could have been attending the funeral of either Sylvie or Tice, or both of them. I've paid the money he demanded and expect him to keep his promise that our family will now be left alone."

Robert wasn't going to waste his time trying to convince Elspeth or the twins that expecting this criminal to keep his bargain was foolish. He had to hand it to her, though. She had written a note to Pelling that summed up her resolve:

> *Here is the one million dollars I give you for your promise to never bother my family or me again. We have a bargain. I expect you to keep it. However, if you are apprehended you can rest assured that neither my twins nor I had anything to do with it. If you or your associates ever contact us again, or bring harm to us in any way, you have my solemn promise that I will put a bounty of considerable millions on your head, dead or alive. I will have a description and police artist sketch of you running continually in newspapers, billboards, and magazines all over the world.*
>
> *EVR*

When the suitcase was picked up that morning, Lt. Robert Bizet did not intercede, nor did he have the UPS truck followed.

* * *

Sylvie awoke with a numbing pain in her left shoulder area and quickly remembered why. The room was darkened as she tried to focus on her wristwatch, which read 5:25.

There were no hints at all in her surroundings of whether that time was morning or afternoon. She recalled it was just before nine in the morning when Tice helped her into this bed.

She finally decided it must be afternoon. *Poor Tice, and poor me, too! We were playing the tennis match for us,* she recalled. *Whoever won would pay for a candlelight dinner in Utrecht tonight.* It went unspoken, but Sylvie knew what they were planning for dessert later. *Poor us!* Tice had won the match but Sylvie had put up a good fight. She remembered them meeting at the net when the match was over and feeling as if someone had hit her in the back with a crowbar. She'd staggered forward and would have fallen on her face if Tice hadn't been there to catch her.

Now that I think about it, it's very scary stuff. If he had been standing a bit more to my left the bullet could have killed him. I wonder if they've caught the guy yet? She decided to go peek out the window to see what time of day it was, but found herself rather woozy as she unsteadily made her way over. She looked outside to confirm her deduction. *It's definitely afternoon, by the look of the sun, a lovely day, and a lovely day indeed.*

Sylvie just made it back to the edge of the big bed and collapsed face first into the softness. The sudden shock of pain from her left shoulder brought her immediately awake. She turned away from the pain onto her back, but was unable to lift either arm to wipe the perspiration off her face. She closed her eyes, felt the cooling effect of the gathering moisture, and fell into a deep sleep.

Chapter 12

UPS Driver Killed, Ransom Missing

"Hello, Mrs Elspeth Vander Riis?" the voice asked.

"Yes, speaking."

"This is the manager of the United Parcel Service at the Amsterdam office. I'm checking on a delivery made to your address this morning."

"Yes, how can I help you?" Elspeth asked.

"Did our driver arrive at eleven o'clock this morning to deliver a letter addressed to you and pick up a suitcase?"

"Yes, that is correct. I signed for a letter and gave your driver a suitcase to be dropped off at your office. Is there a problem?"

"We think so. It's nearly 2:00 p.m., and we have been unable to raise the driver on her radio. We are backtracking to see if she had truck or radio problems. Thank you, ma'am, we will send a driver out from Utrecht and trace her from your address."

"Very well, then."

Elspeth hung up the receiver and went directly to the study to tell Robert about the phone call. He had already reversed the tape on the recorded call and turned up the volume. Marta and Tice came into the study after every incoming phone call to hear the playback of the tape recorder. Robert kept all of them in the picture, even though they were all aware of his promise to Elspeth not to interfere with the ransom delivery. Nevertheless, they knew him to be a very conscientious detective. Tice looked at his watch, two fifteen, and noted three hours had gone by since the UPS driver had delivered the letter and left with the suitcase.

Robert looked up the UPS telephone number for the downtown office in Amsterdam. When he called and asked to speak with the manager, he switched on the speaker and put his finger to his lips asking for silence. They all heard him confirm he was indeed speaking with the gentleman who had just called Mrs Elspeth Vander Riis, inquiring about his delivery person. The manager advised that moments before he had been informed that the UPS delivery driver had been found shot dead in her truck. A helpful motorist had pulled up behind her red truck. He didn't see anyone at the wheel, yet the motor was running. The motorist discovered the lady driver slumped over onto the passenger seat. His first thought was that she had a heart attack or a stroke until he saw the blood seeping from her left temple. Hearing a crackle of noise coming from the radio on her belt, he spoke to the caller, explaining what he found. An ambulance was requested and the Utrecht police were notified. Robert asked the UPS manager if the attending officers had completed their investigation of the crime scene and was informed that they found the driver's clipboard with her delivery schedule in the front seat.

The schedule showed her first delivery was a letter delivered to, and signed for, by Elspeth Vander Riis at the chateau, as well as a pickup at the same address to be taken back to the UPS office in Amsterdam. The police officer confirmed that the suitcase was missing. The manager told Robert the delivery pickup truck was being towed back to the police lab at Utrecht, and if anything more was learned by the forensic team he would get the information to him. Robert hung up the receiver and looked at the inquiring faces.

"It appears our kidnapper was proactive on the ransom delivery, just in case we had some sort of reception waiting for him at the UPS office. We'll have to wait and see what the forensic team turns up, if anything. I'm willing to bet Pelling killed the UPS driver and is working alone. If the Basque ETA were involved, they would have had a team of agents take over this chateau and demand a much larger amount of money. My growing suspicion is that while Pelling may be an ETA agent, he is just moonlighting, picking up a little extracurricular work for himself, or a person unknown, by hijacking Andre's *SeaOx* and kidnapping Elspeth.

Elspeth issued a quiet sigh at Robert's summary saying, "Well then, until we hear differently, we can assume Pelling murdered the driver and has the ransom money. He has definitely shown his true colours, emphasizing just what he's capable of."

Andre had come down the stairway from his bedroom suite and stood just inside the study. Elspeth spotted him and went to his side, scolding him, "Andre, you look so pale! Are you sure you're well enough to be up?"

"I'm okay, just a bit unsteady. I'll be fine. I heard the lieutenant's conversation with the UPS manager. I'm beginning to wonder if this really is the last we hear of Pelling."

"I know, I know. Robert doesn't think for one minute Pelling will keep his word," Elspeth said. "But we have no other choice. We'll just have to wait and see."

Tice, Marta, and Robert came over to join in the conversation at the doorway. Andre assured them he was fit enough to be up and asked Marta if he could catch a ride with her and Robert to The Hague. He wanted to get to the *SeaOx* and recover it from police custody.

"Of course you can. Robert and I will leave early tomorrow for Amsterdam. We'll drop you off at the Scheveningen Marina."

Andre then inquired about Sylvie and was told Tice spent the night as her nurse, who said she slept peacefully and was still in bed when he checked on her right after lunch.

Although Robert had agreed not to interfere in the delivery of the ransom, he felt he had to do something. He had called Sergeant Moline in Paris and told him to circulate a description of Pelling throughout the Netherlands. Robert dictated the contents, which stated that Pelling was considered to be involved in ETA terrorist activities and should be classified as armed and extremely dangerous. He was wanted in connection with two or more murders in the Netherlands.

Robert explained this to Elspeth, assuring her that nothing was mentioned about Pelling's recent activities. It was, at best, a minimal attempt to capture Pelling. He further explained that advertising Pelling's name would invalidate that particular passport, and may even cause him some grief from the ETA if he had broken ranks with them. It was a long shot, he told them, but it was his duty and the very least he could do while Pelling's trail was still warm.

* * *

Pelling had not spoken with his control in the ETA, Raoul de Vascos, for two weeks. When he finally did check in, he was surprised to be given a new assignment. "Corporal, the information you requested has been left for you at site ten," the voice said.

"Very well, Sergeant. I'll pick it up later today," Pelling said and hung up.

Site ten was the main post office in Brussels, Belgium, and "the information you requested," meant he had a priority assignment. Pelling drove from Amsterdam in a new Volkswagen van he had purchased immediately after checking out of his hotel. He made the deal for cash and had the registration made out using his present passport, Rolf Erik Studer. From there, he drove to a motorcycle dealer and purchased a complete set of tools. After a quick stop at a lumberyard, he loaded an eight-foot plank into the van. He pulled alongside the BMW motorcycle and rolled it up the plank and into the van. He worked for a couple hours, taking the bike apart and storing it in four boxes. The wheels he strapped together and laid flat. He could have just ditched the bike somewhere, but he liked it and thought it might come in handy. He would put it back together at the farm workshop. Later, he crossed into Belgium without incident and registered at a hotel complex on the southern outskirts of Antwerp. While he didn't really have to check in with his control, he did so as matter of habit every two weeks. After telling Raoul he would be at site ten later in the day, he decided to head directly into Brussels, just thirty-eight kilometres directly south of Antwerp. On the off chance his control planned to intercept him at the post office later in the day, he decided to go there now to pick up his next contract.

Just a bit of caution on my part. He recalled that two of his contracts in the past two years had been for ETA agents. His instructions had been very specific, "he will be coming out of the Bank du Nationals at 2:00 p.m.," or "he will arrive at the restaurant at 3:00 p.m." If, in fact, Raoul had issued instructions such as, "the corporal will be at site ten later this afternoon," by then, he would have come and gone.

Pelling drove by the post office building and didn't see anything that looked suspicious. Nevertheless, he parked in a parkade three blocks away, walked back past the front entry, turned the corner, and walked down the alley. There were no parked cars with people inside, so he entered the rear of the building and went to the general delivery wicket, where he showed his driver's license and asked and signed for mail addressed to T. Pelling. Raoul did not know of his identity transition to Rolf Erik Studer, so he would have to remain Theo Pelling until this new contract was finished. Moreover, Pelling knew that his status as the ETA's most effective agent could be over if the Basque ruling council learned he had gone rogue. So, he walked a tightrope between the ETA and the hijacking and kidnappings he had just pulled off.

His plan to retire, disappear, change his looks, and move to an estate immediately after taking Laurent's sailboat and money was put on hold by Raoul's latest contract. *Has he found out somehow?* This latest caper would top up his stash nicely. Pelling figured he must have lost about one-hundred-fifty-thousand dollars, which he would have easily gotten for the sale of the *SeaOx*, but he had turned a million guilders in ransom into a million US dollars, so he was still ahead.

I better pull over and take a look at what's in this envelope from Raoul. Pelling pulled into a roadside inn, went inside, settled into a booth, and ordered a meal. He noted the time was 11:35 a.m. Satisfied he wouldn't be bothered until his meal came, he pulled the envelope from under his shirt, opened it, spread out the pictures, and read the instructions:

Corporal:

You will be paid the sum of $150,000 US cash for the immediate sanction of this person. The ETA council wants him eliminated. Proceed immediately to Paris and carry out this assignment. Details below. Call control, announce yourself, and say "Corporal has agreed," and we will know you have accepted this contract. If for any reason you can't proceed, call, announce yourself, and stay on the line for further instructions.

Sergeant

Pelling turned over the black-and-white glossy of Pierre Turrin. *Now whom have we got here? Why it's that pompous little fuckwit broker Ruth hooked me up with.* She'd insisted he was an old friend who needed someone to hijack a sailboat and easily extort the money from the owner's brokerage account. The deal was that Pelling was supposed to open an account with Turrin, putting twenty-five-thousand dollars into a margin account and give him discretionary trading privileges. *Yeah right! I was also supposed to send him his half of Laurent's money, leaving me with about fifty grand for all my trouble on the SeaOx, which I could keep or sell.*

Pelling decided to change the plan when he brought Laurent into the Merrill Lynch office to collect the cheque, and Turrin was such a little dickhead, calling him by name and trying to get him to open an account. On the way to the bank he decided that Pierre Turrin could go fuck himself. He'd get nothing. He didn't know anything about his plan to kidnap the Vander Riis widow. *Hell, that was an opportunity that just appeared out of the blue. Turrin can't do a thing. Who is he going to complain to, Ruth maybe?*

Pelling went through the envelope and found the usual expense money for a hit, seventy-five-thousand US cash. He couldn't believe his luck. Here he was trying to retire and suddenly getting swamped with new wet work. *What did you do, you little peacock, to get yourself on the ETA elimination list?* Pelling wondered. Pelling quickly scanned the address and pertinent location info, shuffled the photos back in the big yellow envelope, and put it under his shirt. He'd wait until later to call Raoul and agree.

* * *

The evening Sylvie was shot turned into an evening of passion and discovery for Robert and Marta. She had brought a tray to his suite shortly after he said good night to the others. On the tray was a bottle of the chateau's brandy, two snifters, and a fat marijuana cigarette. Marta knocked softly on Robert's door, then turned the handle and let herself in. She heard the shower, so she set the tray down on the bedside table, opened the drawer, withdrew a lighter and ashtray, and set them on the tray. She then stripped out of her clothes, went to the bathroom, and standing in front of the glass shower panel asked in a voice that could be heard above the sound of the shower, "Can I join you?"

Robert, momentarily startled, drew the glass panel open to see the beautiful, naked Marta who stepped into the shower and into his arms. They kissed and she turned so her back was to him. She brought his hands up to her breasts and reached back for him. Later, after towelling off, they sat on the side of the bed sipping the brandy and sharing the joint. They then crawled under the covers and began learning each other's body. While their fingers, lips, and tongues gathered information, their brains signalled the inevitable next step and they joined in the intense embrace of lovers.

The combination of euphoric drugs and lovemaking sated them, and they fell asleep in the spoon position.

Chapter 13

Chateau Love, Lust, and Other Arrangements

Sylvie made it down to the evening meal, but it was evident to all that she was hurting. She managed to eat a couple of mouthfuls and asked to be excused. Tice helped her back up to her bedroom and kept her company.

"Come closer, honey. I really want to kiss you," Sylvie said when they reached the room. He kissed her very gently, careful not to hurt her, but Sylvie crushed her lips to his, holding his head in her hands while saying, "You have no idea how much I want to be with you. Please promise you'll stay with me after the doctor leaves?"

"I promise, Slim, as soon as I see the doctor leave, I'll be back in here and help you undress for bed. Okay?"

"Kiss me again and touch me," Sylvie whispered.

Tice kissed her passionately and felt her nipples through her bra. The knock at the door separated them, and Elspeth entered with the doctor. Tice remained sitting, hoping his embarrassment would subside. Finally, he stood, turning away from his mother and the doctor and said over his shoulder, "I'll come say good night in a little while."

Tice went across the hall to his room, leaving the door ajar so he could see across the hallway to Sylvie's suite. He wanted to be with her as much as she wanted to be with him.

Twenty minutes later, Tice saw his mother and the doctor leaving Sylvie's suite. After saying good night to the doctor, Elspeth came across the hall to her son's suite and said, "Tice, the doctor changed Sylvie's bandage and gave her another shot for the pain. She wants you to say good night before she drifts off."

Elspeth smiled at her son as he passed her and gave her a wink. She said a prayer to herself. *Thank you, God, for sparing them both.* As soon as she saw Tice enter Sylvie's suite and close the door behind him, she went straight to Andre's bedroom.

"Oh, sweetie. That stuff the doctor gave me is starting to make me tingle all over. You have no idea how excited I am. I'm not usually like this, honest, but if you don't come over here and help me out I'll have to do it myself."

Tice sat on the side of the bed, helped her sit and then stand in front of him. He slipped her nightgown off, letting it drop to the floor. She smiled down at him as he carefully unhooked her bra. Sylvie shrugged out of it, exposing her breasts and her jutting nipples. He snuggled his face into her flat stomach, his chin rubbing over the top of her dark curly pubic patch. He turned, threw the covers to the other side of the bed, fetched a pillow, and held it while he pulled the one Sylvie had used to the middle of the headboard.

"Stretch out in the middle of the bed and try to get comfy, okay?" Tice asked.

"Okay, but I've shown you mine, so take your clothes off so I can see all of you, handsome." Sylvie crawled to the centre of the bed and lay slightly on her right side, her legs apart, looking back at him while he undressed. "That's much better, lover. I've been dreaming about holding you and kissing you all over, but right now I really need you to hold me real close."

Tice slipped into bed and snuggled up to her back. Careful of her shoulder, he kissed her neck, nuzzling the hair at the nape. His left hand moved up her side and found her breast. Sylvie murmured and stretched her head to the left to be kissed. His hand left her breast and travelled down her left side, found her curly patch, and his fingers slipped easily into her wetness. Sylvie's orgasm happened quickly as she clamped his hand inside her and moaned her release into his chest.

"Oh, I'm just buzzing. I want you so bad."

"I want you now, Slim. Can you back into me and lift your leg up over mine?" He was able to enter her in this position and began to thrust. Sylvie forgot her shoulder injury as the pleasure of her second orgasm overtook her senses. Tice groaned with his release, which seemed to continue for a long time.

Sylvie was as spent as Tice and she started mentally drifting as the drug began its magic. "Kiss me good night, lover. I'm going to sleep fast so I can kiss you awake first thing in the morning."

"Good night, Sylvie Bern. I can't imagine a nicer wake-up call." Afraid he might roll into her during the night, Tice left her bed as soon as she fell asleep.

Just before he got into his own bed, Tice set his watch alarm for six, so he could return to Sylvie's bed so he didn't miss his promised wake-up. He went over every lovely inch of her in his mind and fell asleep thinking how special she was. The contented look on his face bespoke wonder, not conquest.

The bedroom scene involving Elspeth and Andre that same night did not go as well. Elspeth had joined Andre in bed, but he seemed standoffish, not really caring to engage in any kind of lovemaking at all. She was in an amorous and giving mood, but her advances were not met with much enthusiasm. He persisted in talking about making his *SeaOx* safer, and how he planned to have it hauled away in order to have the hull inspected for any surprises Pelling may have left for him. Elspeth soon grew tired of this and said good night. She kissed him on the forehead, went to her own suite, and began examining her feelings for him. She wondered if anything more would come of their brief relationship. Was she now too bothered by her recent misadventure to continue their relationship? Was Andre? Or could it be just an aftereffect of the drugs they'd both been given by Pelling and her family doctor? Elspeth didn't know, and she didn't like not knowing.

Andre touched the spot on his forehead where Elspeth had kissed him good night and wondered about it. It was strange that he wasn't really feeling anything at all. Maybe it was just seeing her here in her real environment, in charge, the mistress of the castle. *Something isn't quite right. I don't care how much she says she believes in my innocence and me. I still detect coolness, and she must realize it too.*

The heat has gone out of them, and Andre couldn't explain it. They couldn't get enough of each other before the shit went down. *Now, well that little bang we had the other night was more of an "I'm so relieved you're alive" thing, devoid of passion. Christ, I could hardly get it up.* Something had changed. Even if that psycho, Pelling, was caught today and admitted everything, he wasn't sure they could get back to where they were. And boy, if ever a guy got a 'kiss off', that good night peck on the forehead just now said it all. It was as if she were saying, "Andre, my dear fellow, we had an ecstatic sexual fling that turned into a horrifying event, which we both somehow survived. So let's just leave it at that, no regrets. Get some sleep now, and then . . . get lost!"

Andre didn't blame Elspeth if that was what she felt. He finally fell asleep after he decided on a plan of action. The first order of business, before he took possession of the *SeaOx*, was to get in touch with Ava and thank her for her persistence in getting the police to look for him. When he couldn't think of anything to help save himself during his capture, he held on to the slim chance that Ava might go looking for him. It was the remotest of possibilities, but it was the only thing he found to cling to once he realized Pelling was going to kill him. By the sound of Ava's voice on her calls, he figured she must have started looking for him as soon as she heard that tape he'd sent. Then when she learned about his uncharacteristic behaviour, such as not keeping the appointment with the Furano people when he was docked within spitting distance of their shop, she must have just known something was very wrong.

He found out later that's when she went into action. She contacted the local police in Brest and insisted that a coastal search be made for him and the *SeaOx*. Robert told him that he was aware of the missing boat because Ava, not satisfied with "the nothing to report" she got from the local police, had contacted the Paris Sûreté and was turned over to a Sergeant Moline. She played him his tape and told him what she suspected. The sergeant turned it over to his boss, Robert, who personally advised her he'd sent a circular to Interpol and would get back to her if anything turned up. Robert told Andre he recognized the missing *SeaOx* from Ava's description when they flew over the marina and watched Pelling step aboard. *Thank God for that! And thank God for Ava's persistence. I'll call her just as soon as I get to The Hague.*

What with the events of the past week, Andre had been out of circulation, so to speak. Prior to this week he used an answering service whenever he was in port. He checked in with his service from the chateau and was told he had eight messages since he'd docked the *SeaOx* at Brest. The most recent message was left two days ago. He had messages from Ava, Giles Ruel, Ava, Cecil Audette, and four more from Ava. Hearing these messages again, Andre was touched by the concern in Ava's calls. In the first message, she sounded perplexed that he had not returned her call. In subsequent calls she got more and more worried. Then she left him a threatening message, saying that if she didn't hear from him immediately she would contact the authorities and report him missing. Her latest call told him she had informed the Paris Sûreté about his strange behaviour prior to his disappearance.

While listening to Ava's concerned voice, he detected something else, something vaguely ominous. Andre dismissed it as a verbal foot-stamping tantrum because he wouldn't return her calls. He wondered what Ava had read into that innocent informative audiotape about his solo sail aboard the *SeaOx*. Her dogged search for him and his boat went way beyond the possible disappearance of a friend. It started to seem to him that her concern was more for the *SeaOx* than for him.

The calls from Cecil Audette and Giles Ruel in Montreal, Andre figured, were to advise him of their decision to purchase the Bordeaux estate from Anatole Hubert. Andre tried twice to speak with them, but was unable to reach them. He busied himself getting ready for the evening meal at the chateau and a party in the study later.

* * *

Elspeth had meetings every day with Marta and Mathijs, one in the morning, and one after the evening meal. They all felt it necessary to keep up with the events and needs of their guests. They all agreed that the Vander Riis family would underwrite Sylvie Bern's medical requirements from here on. They also decided to compensate her for the injury she sustained while at their chateau. They didn't think of it as hush money. Nevertheless, a guest of lesser character might have begun an action for a considerable settlement, which would have caused sensational headlines and an unwanted swarm of paparazzi following and bothering the family everywhere they went. Any such sensationalism in the press might provoke Pelling into changing his mind to never bother them again. Elspeth, Tice, and Marta agreed that not doing the right thing for Sylvie, Andre, and Robert, all of whom were a part of this extraordinary past week, would be less than honourable. Elspeth made out three cheques and they all signed them.

* * *

Pelling hadn't called in to his control's telephone number to agree to or refuse his new assignment, thus telling Raoul de Vascos he was no longer steadfast and would be slated for elimination by the ETA, but before Raoul actually had his most effective agent sanctioned, he planned to relieve him of the money he had stashed. Raoul already had a handle on the millions Pelling had amassed with Ruth Meikle. Raoul knew Ruth to be a practical person. Hadn't she offered Teddy Pelling's share of their money to him the moment he told her that he and the Basque council had pulled Pelling from active duty and scheduled him to be sanctioned? Pelling, however, knew nothing of his latest status with the ETA. Ruth also learned that it didn't matter to the council if he successfully carried out this last contract on the Paris stockbroker or not; the corporal's days were numbered.

* * *

Pelling arrived in Paris at 6:00 p.m. Hoping to find the broker home on a Saturday night, he telephoned Turrin's apartment and got the answering machine, advising callers he would be out of the city all day Sunday, but back at his office first thing Monday morning. Pelling calculated the time it would take him to drive through downtown Paris and arrive at the broker's apartment building. Pelling looked forward to offing the officious little snit and hoped he hadn't left yet.

If he was lucky enough to catch the broker at his apartment, he could finish his assignment and drive back to the farm in Bordeaux tonight. First though, he must call Ruth and ask her to meet him at the farm tomorrow afternoon. Pelling calculated after his wet work was done in Paris that he could drive back to the farm at the speed limit and arrive just after 8:00 p.m., call Ruth, have a quick nap, then go to work on the VW van, and maybe get the BMW bike back together as well.

I have way too much cash on me, Pelling thought. He wanted to get most of it stashed before Ruth arrived. The little bundle was his mad money, and he didn't want anyone to know about it. It totalled almost 1.1 million US dollars. He had another seven-hundred-fifty-thousand dollars between Marseilles and the two banks in Paris. *I'm flush, just with this total. I'll get an update from Ruth on how she's coming along with the purchase of that vineyard in Bordeaux.*

* * *

Ruth Meikle-Werner had a client in her elaborate apartment atop a Paris high-rise. She had fellated him near to orgasm when her telephone rang. Shrugging and smiling while squeezing him as hard as she dared without causing pain, she put him in a holding pattern. "Hello, who is speaking please?" Ruth asked.

"It's Teddy. Are you busy right now?" Pelling asked.

"Hi, lover! Yes, actually, I am. Are you in Paris?"

"I was, but I'm on my way to the farm and will be there in three or four hours, depending how long I stop on the way. Will you be able to get away?" Pelling asked.

"Sure. I can leave first thing in the morning and be there by noon."

"I'll see you when you get there then. Bye."

Ruth walked toward the couch, dropping the robe she wore onto the carpet. Her guest was slowly reviving himself as she straddled him and rubbed her crotch onto him. "Was it the corporal?" her guest inquired.

"Yes, it was," She sighed into his ear. "Now take it real slow, baby, while I get you off." He did as he was told for a few strokes and then began rapid thrusting as lust took him over. She waited until he was on the brink, and then began to squeeze him with her velvet tightness, causing him to come as she shuddered with her own release.

* * *

Pelling hung up the receiver after his brief conversation with Ruth. He was sitting comfortably in the living room at the farmhouse in Bordeaux at 10:30 p.m. He had always trusted her implicitly, but after what he had heard Pierre Turrin say about Ruth to Andre Laurent just before he shot him nagged at him. So, Pelling thought it was prudent to get quickly to the money he had given her or it may no longer be there. He purposely misled her about his whereabouts and the time he would be at the farm. It took four hours to drive from Paris at the speed limit if the traffic was moderate. He had made it back in less than that. If she planned anything in the way of a special reception, it would happen this evening or early in the morning. Pelling had only three hours to make the changes in the van that would hold his weapons box, extra clothing, as well as his cash and passports. He left for the big barn across the farmyard, entered the elaborate shop he had set up there, and began removing the metal floor panel of the VW with the cutting torch.

* * *

Later the same evening, Ruth and her guest, Raoul de Vascos, left her apartment to drive to the farm in Bordeaux. While driving through Paris, Raoul had checked with his people and related what he learned to Ruth, who was driving. "Pierre Turrin was shot dead, twice in the face. The Sûreté are holding a Canadian, Andre Laurent, who was found unconscious at the scene, a gun fitted with a silencer in his hand. The apartment building doorman told the Sûreté he had seen the Canadian once before when he had come for a visit. One of our agents is a brother-in-law of this particular doorman who sells us info. Anyway, it's nothing to worry about. However, Pelling may suspect you, depending on what he learned from Turrin before he died. I would guess it's the reason he wants you at the farm."

"You may be right. If he does want his money, he'll want me close until he gets his share, which at this time is a little over five million. Our portfolio is almost twelve mil."

"The corporal knew Turrin from the Laurent hijacking, which he was obliged as a loyal ETA agent to tell me about, but chose not to. When you mentioned that Turrin had you arrange for Pelling to snatch the Canadian and his sailboat to extort his brokerage money, that's when I set a little test for Pelling. I gave him this contract on Turrin. If the corporal were still steadfast he would have called as soon as he saw pictures of his target and told me he couldn't do the job since the broker knew who he was. But because he didn't comply and report to me, he automatically asked for his own elimination. Before we take him out, though, we'll recover what we can of his stashed money. You say you think he has over a million cash in bank boxes, right?"

"I'm not really sure how much, but I know he deals with five or six different banks and has safety deposit boxes in all of them," Ruth said, smiling at him.

* * *

Teddy Pelling finished installing the wide metal storage area under the floor panel on the van and hinged the top back in place. He replaced the floor covering and made one last conversion to the flap cover of the gas tank. With the conversion complete, he put two changes of clothing into the new compartment, all of his cash, as well as his other passports. His stash of cash in the compartment totalled $1.13 million US. He had almost five-thousand dollars in cash in the glove compartment. He drove the VW to the edge of the farm, stashing it in a wooded area off of a side road. The walk back to the farm took him ten minutes.

It was now two and a half hours since he had spoken with Ruth. He had accomplished what he needed to do to get mobile. No one who knew him, or anyone who might want to cause him harm, knew about his new van. Pelling needed to spend some time with Ruth and planned to keep her close while she unwound their investments. Her last statement of their account showed his total deposits made over the years at $2.5 million. Hers totalled five-hundred-thousand dollars, and she had turned the total into $12 million. It was time to turn the portfolio into cash. Ruth's share was to be half of the cashed-out amount. She was responsible for the growth of his money. She acted on sure things, which she gathered from pillow talk with some of her wealthier clients, one of who was Pierre Turrin. Pelling trusted her with his money and wasn't interested in her methods or how she managed it. Now, it was time to settle up. It had occurred to him that Ruth might have him killed so she could keep all the money that they supposedly had accumulated. Phony statements were easy to arrange. She, in fact, may have spent all the money by now. It was going to be interesting to see her reaction when he asked her for his share. *Whenever we're together, my impression is that she is totally satisfied and very enthusiastic when we get it on. Then again, she wouldn't have the clients she has if she wasn't a great actress.*

Pelling smiled and wondered what the true cash-out value would turn up. If Ruth hasn't arranged an elimination party for him tonight or tomorrow morning and does show up alone, he'd know he was just being paranoid. He could have waited by her apartment and brought her here after her client left, but what if he stayed all night. *What if? What if?* His thoughts took him back to Pierre Turrin's apartment.

The noise and steam coming from the broker's bathroom allowed him to enter, shoot the little prick twice in the face, and club Andre Laurent with the silencer on his pistol. He thought maybe he should have killed Laurent as well, but it was such a natural setup to frame him for Turrin's murder, he couldn't resist. He'd wiped the pistol clean, put it in Laurent's hand, and left. Laurent looked in good shape and had been in the middle of interrogating Turrin. *Christ, he had wired Turrin's hands behind him with a coat hanger, and by the look of the little shit, Laurent was using scalding water to get info out of him. Damn, I'll have to remember that little trick.*

Pelling snapped himself out of his memory. He had to get prepared. With this kind of money at stake, Ruth could have someone fly out here. *If nothing happens until she arrives at noon tomorrow, I'll confirm to Raoul that Turrin has been sanctioned and I'll arrange to collect the balance of the contract.*

When Pelling returned to the farmyard after hiding his van, all was quiet. He made his way to the converted old barn, which contained living quarters as well as his workshop. The powerful motion lights he had installed would light up the whole yard, exposing any unwelcome visitors. He took up vigil at a shooting position on the second floor. He planned to remain there until sunrise in order to welcome any visitors, just in case Ruth had arranged to kill him. He reasoned the value of their joint investments was motive enough. Watching and waiting for a target was what he usually got paid to do, but this was different. He was the target. Would there just be one assassin or many? His survival mechanism told him to lie in wait, just in case.

Chapter 14
Ruth and Her Basque Clients

Ruth let Raoul de Vascos out of her car a kilometre before the turn into the farmyard, warned him again of the motion lights, and suggested he enter the barn via the back entrance. He made it to the farm in good time without encountering any traffic, from either direction, and managed to get to the rear of the barn without being detected by the motion lights. Once inside the barn, he began eliminating the places Ruth indicated Pelling could be lying in wait. When Raoul came upon his agent's stand on the second floor, he watched from cover, thirty yards away. Pelling, kept nodding off, but Raoul kept still, remembering his stealth training. Finally, Pelling's head settled against his chest. Raoul made his move.

* * *

Ruth continued along the country road, past the farm, for two more kilometres before parking in a treed area out of sight. Raoul's instructions were for her to spend the night and morning in her car and arrive at the farm just before noon. After a couple of hours and much soul searching, there was no way Ruth could sleep. *Why didn't Raoul want me with him when I dropped him off near the farm? I'm supposed to remain here in my car overnight and for the morning just because I told Teddy I'd be here before noon. If Teddy happens to have his money stashed at the farm, Raoul would have time to get to it then kill Teddy before I arrive. Of course, then he wouldn't have to share. Bastard!*

She decided she wasn't waiting until tomorrow to show up, but knew she'd have to be real careful. Raoul needed to make Teddy tell him where he hid the money he didn't give to her. Raoul had said the ETA paid Pelling three million US for wet work to date. She knew Pelling didn't live a rich lifestyle, and that's why Raoul figured he had a stash of at least half a million bucks. *That's what I get for playing both ends, thinking I'd make out big time. Greedy bitch me!*

She thought she was being clever having Raoul as a client after that Basque banker introduced him to her. Raoul had told her on their first get together that he was Pelling's control, and if she wanted to keep getting the large deposits of cash he turned over to her, Pelling wasn't to know about their relationship. No problem. Pelling never asked about her clients. Raoul tipped her off when Pelling had an assignment; that way she knew when to expect he would bring more money.

Damn it! Teddy has been such a darling all these years, by far my best customer. So how come I'm running around the bloody country trying to cajole his petty cash—if you can call half a mil petty cash. Hell, she knew Pelling would probably give it to her if she asked him for it. She'd gotten greedy, but Raoul convinced her that all his agents eventually were terminated, and Pelling was next immediately after they located his money.

How things change. On the way here, Raoul, the lying bastard, tells me he has to give five million to the ETA, like I'm little Miss Gullible. Those murdering Basques would take the money and shoot us on sight. Well . . . me anyway. She knew Raoul was the nephew of the boss of the Basque council and probably had immunity. No, she decided a more likely probability was that Raoul would keep all the money, once he had his hands on it, and kill both Pelling and her. Hanging with Raoul wasn't going to guarantee her any money or safety. On the other hand, Teddy Pelling had trusted her all these years with no strings attached. He understands that information is what she deals in, and that she sleeps with rich and influential clients in order to obtain it. *That's how I have been able to turn our money into over twelve million. Jesus!*

What have I done? I've got to get to Teddy and hope the hell he's still alive. If he's in trouble, I'll have to find a way to rescue him.

At two that morning Pelling awoke as the barrel of the silencer touched his temple. Pelling's cornered eyes showed his embarrassment at being so easily taken.

"Easy now. Take it nice and easy, Corporal. By the look of your stand here, you're prepared for 'unfriendlies'. On your feet, stand still, back up to the pillar, and reach around and clasp your hands together." Raoul secured the hands together with curtain cord and said, "You won't be going anywhere until we've had a little chat."

Pelling said nothing. "I'm sure you know why I'm here, so let's get on with it." Raoul said, continuing, "I warned you when I hired you, and many times since, what happens to agents who didn't report right after their missions are completed to make arrangements to meet with me to receive the balance of their fee. We have done business many times so it should be routine procedure, Corporal. Imagine my disappointment when you didn't check in. Don't look so confused. You also neglected to tell me that you knew the target in this last sanction. You should have called me as soon as you took a look at Pierre Turrin's picture, told me you knew each other, and refused the contract. But, you didn't."

"Let me explain, Sergeant." Pelling said, "I planned on completing the hijacking of the Canadian's boat and extorting his brokerage money. When I had the loot in my hands, I planned to contact you to tell you what I did, and ask you the best way to dispose of the sailboat. It was to be a pretty good score after I kidnapped the widow. I just had to wait until the ransom was paid and I had it in my hand to call you. That's how it was, Sergeant." Pelling said.

Raoul replied, "I learned from your friend Ruth that she had you do this hijacking of the Canadian's boat, but I knew nothing about the kidnapping of the widow. I decided to send you the assignment to sanction Pierre Turrin to see if you would refuse the hit, but, of course, you didn't because you wanted the proceeds of this outside work for yourself."

"So, what is it you want from me, Sarge? I earned the money you paid me. And as for not reporting in, I did plan to call this morning and tell you I'd met the broker before," Pelling said.

"Don't be coy, Corporal. You know the rules. You advise control before the hit, not after. Case closed! What's done is done. The decision on how I handle your fate is mine. If we recover enough of your money, I'll let you buy your way out of the ETA—your life for your stash. Of course, we'll keep the money you invested with our mutual friend, Ruth. I think in light of the usual death penalty for breaking our rules, this isn't such a bad deal."

"So, if I don't lead you to my money, you'll kill me and try to find it on your own," Pelling said.

"Not the preferred choice for either of us, is it Corporal?"

"I figured we would someday come to a mano-a-mano situation, Sarge, where I wouldn't have to hold back and let you win," Pelling said, sizing up his control. Raoul's eyes narrowed when verbally challenged by Pelling, who sensed incoming and changed his tone abruptly, saying in a friendly manner, "Man, you really freaked me out when you woke me. But you're right, Sarge. I did suspect Ruth might have gotten greedy and set some amateurs on me. That's my excuse for being careless. I wasn't expecting a professional. And the moment I doze off, *wham*! You're in my face and I'm in a very bad place. Honest to God, Sarge, you are the last person I expected to see."

"You admit you were holding back in those vicious tussles we had while in the Legion, in order to let me impress the French officers whenever they set you on me? I suspected as much. Well Corporal, you just remember this, I was keeping a little in reserve myself. I just scrapped you enough to convince the Frenchies that I was in control of my men," offered Raoul.

"Okay, Sarge, I'll admit I was getting set to retire from the ETA. So, rather than take a bullet in the head, I'll take you to my money. Plus, I'll turn over the money I took from Andre Laurent, and the money you sent me for the hit on Turrin. I assume you will be Ruth's protector from now on?"

"You always struck me as a practical fella, Corporal. You've made a very sensible decision. Yes, Ruth decided to devote her time between both of us until we have converted all of your joint holdings to cash. She is in the midst of liquidating the portfolio now. She'll know the final amount in US dollars this week. I thought after I have all the money in my hands, I'd turn Ruth over to you as a bonus for your cooperation," Raoul said and went on. "You ought to get by on the money you have left after you pay the ETA. Hell, I'll even give you a little wet work from time to time as long as you abide by our strict routine."

Pelling smiled saying, "I'll look forward to semi-retirement on your terms, Sergeant, but I'd prefer to get paid for eliminating Ruth for you."

"Indeed, I'll bet you would," Raoul said shaking his head. "Corporal, you are a piece of work."

"How long are you going to keep me tied up like this, Sarge?"

"I'm going to have a look around, and then I'm going to crash for some much-needed sack time. I'll see you sometime before noon when Ruth gets here. We'll all go hunt up your money after that," Raoul said, leaving Pelling sitting on the floor with his back to the beam and his arms stretched backward around it with his hands tied.

Down on the main floor, Raoul made note of the time, 3:00 a.m., then looked around the workshop. *Pelling has been busy working on this motorcycle by the look of things. Must have been welding and cutting metal as well; the torch nozzle is still warm.* After completing his search of the barn, Raoul turned off the motion-detecting lights and went to the farmhouse. Completing a thorough search of the house, he set his wristwatch alarm for 9:00 a.m., settled on the big couch in the living room, and pulled a comforter over himself. He was fast asleep in minutes.

Chapter 15

Basque Money and Capture

The Bordeaux Farm 3:45 a.m.

Her mind made up, Ruth drove to another sheltered area near the farm, left her car hidden, and walked back to the farm. When she arrived at the back of the converted old barn, she circled the two-story building and the yard and peered into the front window of the familiar farmhouse. Was that Raoul or Teddy asleep on the couch? *What if Teddy managed to capture Raoul? He could have extracted info from him that would put me in danger. No, not to worry, I'm safe as long as I have control of the money. I'll look in the barn. If that is Raoul asleep on the couch, he's got Teddy restrained. He needs him to take us to his money.*

Back at the barn, Ruth entered the back door, stopped, and listened to the quiet. She heard only the sound of her heart thumping. Teddy was nowhere to be found on the first floor. Ruth climbed the circular staircase to the second floor in her stocking feet. When she reached it, she thought she heard a noise. Was it just her heart thumping madly? Nope, louder, there it was again. She moved toward the sound. It seemed to be coming from the large windowed end of the floor. As she neared the moonlit part of the room, she caught sight of feet moving back and forth. They belonged to someone who sat with his arms tied behind him and around a vertical beam. The man's head was swinging side to side as he sat there. The noise she'd heard was the shuffling of his feet as he tried to stand up. He wasn't going anywhere and posed no threat to her. Emboldened, Ruth moved closer. He was gagged. It was Teddy Pelling.

Ruth knelt beside him and kissed his sweaty face. The kiss startled him, as his head jerked away. Recognition spread across his face as she pulled the gag from his mouth. "I'm sorry, honey, but I couldn't warn you that Raoul was with me when you called."

"Where is he?" Pelling whispered.

"About five minutes ago, I looked through the front window of the farmhouse and saw someone asleep on the couch. It has to be him."

"Can you untie my hands?" It took Ruth some time to work the knots loose and free his hands. She helped him to his feet. "Where are your shoes?" he asked.

"Bottom of the staircase. Let's get the hell away from here, Teddy!"

"We will. Get your shoes on and go out the back way. Go straight south across the field. I'm going to take a quick look and see if sleeping beauty is still crashed on the couch. I'll catch up to you. Go on now!"

Moments later, Pelling looked in through the front window of the house and saw Raoul still asleep on the couch. He thought that it might be him under that quilt, or it could just be a rolled up blanket or pillow. *I go in to cut his throat and he shoots me from cover. Not worth the risk. Besides, I have a more interesting fate planned for you, Sarge. Rest up, comrade, you're going to need it.*

Five minutes later, Pelling caught up to Ruth halfway across the field and they continued to the wooded area without incident. Arriving at the van, Pelling screwed the gas cap off, lifted the inside of the cap away, and exposed an ignition key. They drove to where Ruth left her car and she followed him into Bordeaux, where they parked in a hotel parkade. She took her suitcase to the front desk, registered with her real credit card, R. Anna Werner, went up to the room, and left the suitcase there. She was scheduled to meet Teddy in half an hour downstairs in the lounge.

Teddy parked the VW in the same parkade away from Ruth's car. He took a change of clothing and all his cash from the hiding place under the floor rug. Two hundred and fifty thousand dollars went into one of the Gucci bags. Then he stuffed clothes on top of the money. The remaining one million plus fit into the other Gucci bag. He locked the van, carried both bags up to the lounge, set them down beside Ruth, and joined her table, saying, "Whew, I'm starting to hum! I'm in need of a shower. Let's go up to the room."

After Pelling had a quick shower, he sat in his towel, called the Bordeaux police, gave them directions to the farm, and told them they could arrest Raoul de Vascos, the notorious ETA terrorist.

The desk sergeant answering the phone at the Bordeaux police department asked far too many questions. Pelling insisted the clerk advise his superiors of the whereabouts of this wanted terrorist and send a helicopter swat team to apprehend him. Pelling added he would see that the Sûreté had enough information on this key ETA insider to convict him and send him to the gallows. Pelling noticed the change in the duty cop's interest when Pelling said he would provide them proof of Raoul's involvement in the bombing of Sûreté Lieutenant Robert Bizet's car, which killed his fiancé instead. This choice bit of info spurred the desk sergeant into action, who rousted his superior from his sleep, who, in turn, contacted Lieutenant Bizet in Paris. The lieutenant quickly arranged for two helicopters with special squads aboard to be sent from their Bordeaux station to the farmhouse.

After the call to the police, Ruth told Pelling all she knew about Raoul, holding nothing back this time, feeling safe again. She told him Raoul's plan to capture him, relieve him of his money, and kill him. She told him how Raoul had ordered her to turn the portfolio into cash immediately, which she had done.

"All our money is in an account in my real name, Ruth Anna Werner, at the Royal Bank of Canada in Paris. Raoul thinks it's in the name of Ruth Meikle in another bank easily accessible at his command. He thought his grip on me was so complete that I would follow his orders to the letter.

Raoul told me you were marked for elimination and that none of his agents ever got to retire from the ETA. He had them all killed. So, what could I do? I went along with him.

"After we relieved you of your money, he said we would split it down the middle. While driving here from Paris, he mentioned a new split. He would have to give half of all the money to the Basque ruling council, but we would still have the balance to split. I wondered if Raoul had just helped himself to another five mil? I felt I was in jeopardy of losing everything because I could no longer trust him."

Pelling listened quietly during her story, but he grunted at her last remark and said, "I wonder if I'd still be here now if Raoul had kept to his original promise to share all the money evenly?"

Ruth smiled at him and said, "Teddy dear, what would you have done if you were in my place? Raoul convinced me you would soon be dead."

"Ruthie, you will learn that I'm not that easy to kill. Tell me, how did you meet Raoul in the first place?"

"He was recommended to me by George Yaro, a Basque money man and a regular of mine. In the past five years, I've seen Raoul maybe four or five times a year—until this year, that is. He's been asking a lot of questions about you in the past couple of months, and I've only seen you once during that time, lover. I intended showing you a picture I'd taken of him just to confirm with you that he really was your boss. He set me up for sure."

"When did you meet Pierre Turrin?" Pelling asked.

"I've known Pierre for almost as long as I've known you. When I first went into this business, Pierre was very helpful in introducing me to wealthy people. All my clients, including Raoul, know me as Ruth Meikle, but all the business you and I have done I have conducted in my real name. I didn't do any brokerage business with Pierre, simply because I wouldn't take a chance on him being discreet. All of my transactions have been done through four different banks. I haven't had a chance until now to tell you what our final total is—it's $12,210,000 US," she said, grinning with satisfaction.

"You certainly know how to make things grow." Shifting the topic, he said, "Let's hope the Sûreté acts quickly. If they get there before Raoul awakens, they can pick him up without too much trouble. It's now almost six thirty and Raoul doesn't have any transportation. I also cut the telephone wires from the barn and the farmhouse. So, when he wakes he'll find I'm gone and head to where he thinks you are waiting in your car. He'll be on foot and it's ten kilometres to the nearest neighbour."

"We have to be extra careful from here on out," Pelling said. "Raoul will put a contract out on us as soon as he is able to speak with his lawyers. When he finds out he has no chance of getting out of jail, he'll give us up for some leverage. What is the easiest way to transfer our money to a safe place?"

"I have an offshore bank account set up in the Cayman Islands. I can transfer it immediately; I just have to do it in person at any Royal Bank branch. The transfer takes a few minutes."

"All right then, check in the telephone book and find out where the bank is located," Pelling ordered.

"I know where it is. I asked the front desk when I registered. It's within walking distance—four blocks straight east of the front entrance."

"I'd like you to transfer all of it except two million dollars. Buy eight US cashier's cheques of one quarter million each, okay? Purchase the cheques first, and then transfer the balance to your Cayman account. I'll be with you, but in disguise, as I'm sure the surveillance cameras will be rolling. If they get on to you and check back, they won't find anyone resembling the description they have of me."

"Why, you in a disguise? This I have to see!" Ruth was amused.

"When Raoul realizes how hopeless his situation is, he'll tell the Sûreté everything he knows about us. Does he know where our money is? Does he know you transferred all of it to the Royal Bank?" Pelling asked. He was becoming agitated because he didn't know for sure that Raoul was in custody.

"No, dear. Raoul only knows about the two other bank accounts in the name of Ruth Meikle. He thinks I've put the liquidated assets into those accounts. And you, my dear partner, are the only one who knows where our money really is, the Royal Bank of Canada, soon to be wire transferred to their Georgetown branch on Grand Cayman Island."

"Hmmm, maybe a long peaceful cruise to the Cayman Islands would be just the ticket for us, but first I have to get information to the Sûreté in Paris so that they understand who Raoul really is, and keep the back-stabbing bastard locked up tight until they execute him. I believe he'll give them my description and tell them about all my passports, after he talks with the ETA lawyers. Then he'll issue an order to have me shot on sight. He will also have plans for you, Ruthie; you can count on it. That's why, from now on, I'll be in disguise."

Teddy Pelling scanned the news channels on the television in their hotel room, still no word of Raoul's capture. They would visit the Royal Bank when it opened at ten o'clock.

Chapter 16
Andre, the Broker, and the Basque Assassin

Elspeth Vander Riis watched the midday television news, featuring the Sûreté capture of the ETA terrorist, Raoul de Vascos, while Marta was speaking on the telephone with Robert. "Excuse me, did you say the anonymous tipster that informed the Bordeaux police about this ETA terrorist was Pelling? How can you be so sure?" Marta asked.

Overhearing that question, Elspeth turned the volume on the TV down so she could hear their conversation. "One second, Robert, while I put you on speaker phone. Mother's here with me and will want to hear this."

"Hello, Elspeth," Robert's voice came across the speaker. "Well, we know it was Pelling because his voiceprint matches the calls he made to the chateau. The Bordeaux police played the call over the phone and I recorded it. Elspeth, please don't worry about this! Only Sergeant Moline and I know about the matching voices. There won't be any publicity. I had a hunch it was Pelling when I heard the replay of his call informing us of Raoul's whereabouts. There isn't any doubt the calls to you at the chateau and this call to the Bordeaux police were made by the same person.

"He also said he would send evidence implicating Raoul in the bombing of my car, which killed my fiancé. The Bordeaux desk sergeant familiar with that case had his superior contact me in Paris. As near as we can figure, Pelling is a triggerman for the ETA and took an assignment set up by Pierre Turrin to hijack Andre Laurent's sailboat to coerce the money he had in his brokerage account. Turrin admitted this to Andre who forced a confession from the broker. Andre took a tremendous gamble once he targeted Turrin as the only possible instigator in his abduction. He went after the little broker with a frightening vengeance. Turrin had no choice but to tell him everything or risk being scalded to death in his shower. Andre had the foresight to conceal a tape recorder in his pocket, which he produced after regaining consciousness.

"When we arrived on the scene, we found Pierre dead in the shower, shot in the face, and Andre unconscious on the floor, a gun with a silencer in his hand. At first, it looked like Andre had shot Turrin after his bizarre questioning technique. But when we listened to the taped conversation, we heard the sound of the two muffled shots and the blow that knocked Andre unconscious. The recorder then picked up a Willie Nelson tune he was singing, "On the Road Again", while he was rearranging the murder scene. It was Pelling's voice pattern again. I told Andre that if Pelling had searched him and taken the recorder, we would have had no choice but to book him for Turrin's murder."

Elspeth looked concerned. "Robert, are you sure the details of my kidnapping will be kept quiet?"

"Nobody knows anything about your kidnapping, Elspeth," Robert said. "It was I who made the tests of the voice patterns. Those tapes are in my custody; the technician doesn't know whose voices I was comparing. The tape recording of the confession Andre got from Turrin is in my possession as well. It's all about the plan to hijack his boat and obtain the proceeds of Andre's brokerage account. You are referred to as the widow and not mentioned by name. We will just have to wait to see what further evidence Pelling delivers. My reports to date don't mention anything at all about the unfortunate events that happened to you and your family. You have my word, Elspeth."

"Thank you. You know, I've been suspicious of Pierre Turrin myself, especially after he stopped calling me for business when Andre came on the scene. I won't shed any tears on his behalf. Now, Robert, please tell me, how is Andre? Did he say what his plans are now?"

"We released him after we cleared him of Turrin's murder. Turrin's confession answered all of the lingering questions we had of his involvement in your kidnapping. I reminded him how fortunate he was to have come out of this misadventure with his life. He agreed with me, but told me he couldn't imagine anything worse than the limbo he found himself in. The risk he took interrogating Turrin had been necessary to get the truth. He was beyond relief to have been able to provide proof of his innocence. He had the *SeaOx* hauled and scanned for anything electronic Pelling might have installed. Nothing was found. The boat is in fine shape.

"As far as his plans, he told me he was meeting a friend at Orly, and then he was going back to the Scheveningen Marina to get the *SeaOx* ready to sail. He did say he would be in touch with me. And, oh yes, he asked me to tell you that he gave me the cheque you gave him. I know . . . I know . . . I said I wouldn't accept your money, Elspeth. I couldn't, but Andre convinced me to accept the money to further my work. He said my work was extremely worthwhile and deserved funding. As you know, I've been reluctant to accept your generous gift for two reasons—my superiors at the Sûreté probably wouldn't allow me to accept it, and my motivation for my work is narrowly focused, as I've felt compelled to find the terrorists who murdered my fiancé. However, Andre reminded me how terrorism strikes at the heart of many innocent people. For example, he said, 'Look no further than what happened to me and Elspeth.' He was very convincing and positive that my work in anti-terrorism will save lives. So, I've changed my mind. I have decided to accept Andre's cheque and the one you gave me, if you can convince the Sûreté to authorize an account where I can deposit these funds and other donations that I can draw on for use in my work."

"A wise decision, Robert. Our lawyers and accounting department will handle the details, but should your superiors, for any reason, not want your special group to have this type of private funding, then they will have no alternative and will have to provide it themselves. Either way, your group will be adequately funded from now on. Please don't worry about this; we will see to it the money is at your disposal."

"Well, ladies, I thank you both with all my heart. I promise to keep you up on events as they unfold. One more thing, Elspeth, do you recall meeting a Ruth somebody at any of those annual client parties given by Pierre Turrin?"

"No, I can't recall meeting a Ruth. Why do you ask?"

"Turrin's confession said he had Ruth arrange for Pelling to hijack Andre's boat. They were to split Andre's money three ways, and Pelling was to keep the *SeaOx*," he answered. "Ladies, I really must ring off now, but before I do, could I have a private word with you, Marta?"

When Elspeth gave Marta a wink, she took the phone off speaker. Marta and Robert talked about when they would see each other again. "How about I fly to Paris early tomorrow morning, call you on the way, and give you my arrival time at Orly? Would you come and pick me up?"

"Absolutely! I'll await your call. If for some reason I'm unavailable, ask for Sergeant Alain Moline. He'll know where to find me. Before you hang up, can you tell me how Sylvie Bern is doing?"

"She seems to be doing quite well. She and Tice went into Amsterdam to shop for a present for her granny who will be eighty-five years old in a couple of weeks. They're staying at the downtown Hyatt for a few days, making plans for a trip together somewhere. It's great to see how much fun they're having together. When they call again, I'll tell them you asked about them. I'll see you tomorrow morning, Robert," Marta said.

"Yes, see you then. I'm looking forward to your visit," Robert answered and hung up.

Marta and Elspeth talked about her evolving relationship with Robert. Marta then turned more serious and wanted to know about her mother's relationship with Andre. "Tell me where you two are at, please? You haven't said two words to anyone about him until just now when you asked Robert about him. Did you guys quarrel?" Marta pressed her mother.

"No, nothing like that, dear, I think we both got a big dose of reality and decided we would go no further with our relationship just now. Sweetheart, I spent the night in Andre's bed before you flew him to Scheveningen to see to his sailboat. That was such a strange evening, very difficult to explain. We tried so hard to please each other that we ended up just holding hands. He was so preoccupied after I finally convinced him to accept the money we gave him. Poor Andre, he's been so devastated by not being able to prove conclusively he wasn't involved in my kidnapping that he became impotent and very distant. Anyway, we were both so glad to have escaped death that we cried and comforted each other as best we could. After a long discussion, we decided to accept the special week we had together as a lucky happening, and to stay in touch as good friends for now. Marta, Andre was so relieved I heard him sigh. And to tell the truth, I felt the same way.

"You know, when we first met we both felt a tremendous attraction. The chemistry between us just got stronger as we got to know each other that week in my apartment. We parted with so much anticipation, deciding to meet one month later. All that month we both looked forward to our upcoming rendezvous. The night you and Robert rescued him and brought him here we did have sex, but Andre was very troubled. He wondered how he could have gone from an innocent respectable guy in charge of his life to a key suspect in a conspiracy to kidnap and murder. Then when Sylvie got shot, he . . . he just couldn't seem to regain his self-esteem. So my dear, we decided we would stay friends and let time work its magic. We're both disappointed that we can't seem to get past the effects of our ordeal, but we realize all the stuff we went through is the reason." Elspeth smiled and took the beautiful, but sad, face of her daughter in her hands and kissed her teary eyes.

"Oh Marta, now don't look so sad. It really is for the best. Don't you worry about me; I'm going to be just fine."

* * *

Ruth Werner and Teddy Pelling returned to the hotel from the Royal Bank of Canada in Bordeaux, their mission accomplished. She had left the hotel earlier and walked to the bank, followed closely by Pelling in his old-man getup, complete with cane. He followed her into the bank and lined up behind her at the teller where she made her initial arrangements. She was asked to accompany the assistant manager who conducted the actual transfer of the balance of her account at his desk. The teller brought the eight cashier's cheques and handed them to the assistant manager, affecting the transfer. Ruth took the cheques from him, put them in her purse, and signed the slip for the transaction.

The old man in line waited patiently until the teller returned, then, using his cane, moved to her wicket and asked her to make change for a fifty US dollar bill. He asked her for five fives and twenty-five dollars' worth of French francs. After tucking the money into his inside coat pocket, he busied himself reading some of the pamphlets on retirement, while Ruth completed the transfer to her numbered account on Grand Cayman Island. When the assistant manager completed Ruth's e-mail money transfer, she signed something for him, thanked him, shook his hand, took one of his business cards, and left the bank. The old man dawdled off as well and followed her to their hotel. In their room, Pelling looked over the e-mailed transfer deposit slip, studying it for some time, which made Ruth very uncomfortable.

"Teddy dear, this disguise you're wearing is incredible. You looked and acted like you were in your eighties. You may not believe it, but I've always had a thing for much older men. Do you wanna play with me a little? I'll let you feel me anywhere you want to, mister. I bet I can make your thing big and hard, mister."

Pelling looked at Ruth sitting on the bedside taking off her blouse and wiggling out of her skirt. He looked again at the deposit slip showing the transfer of $10,052,000 to the Royal Bank of Canada in Georgetown and brightened. Ruth had just given him two million in cashier's cheques. *Hell, yes, I like little girls, especially ones built like this one.* He picked up his cane and tapped his hunched body over to where Ruth sat at the edge of the bed.

"How much of the ten million belongs to me, Ruth?"

"I owe you another $4,026,000, mister," Ruth answered as she undid his belt and zipper and reached for him.

After their sex play, Pelling put six of the cashier's cheques into the Gucci bag, which now held nearly $2.5 million dollars. The remaining two cashier's cheques were in his money belt, along with a hundred thousand in cash, and his real passport in the name of Edward Theodore Pelling. He wasn't overwhelmed by the amount of money he had at his fingertips. His thoughts concerned his new status with his former employer, the Basque ETA. Pelling knew as soon as Raoul spoke with his people that he and Ruth would have targets on their backs. His weapons were both probably in the hands of the police by now—the custom rifle in its case left at the farm, and the pistol with the silencer left in Turrin's apartment bathroom in the hand of Andre Laurent. He could not replace them at the same outlets because the ETA would definitely be covering those shops, but Ruth could obtain a permit for firearms and not arouse suspicion. It was something to think about, but not just now. He wanted to get this Gucci suitcase to a safe place. He left it with the bell captain, gave him a hundred-dollar tip, and asked him to look after it until he returned. Pelling purchased a newspaper and went back to their room.

Chapter 17
Andre Cleared, Ruth, and Assassin at Large

Andre Laurent left Robert's Sûreté office a free man, finally and conclusively proven innocent, and took a taxi directly to the Hotel de Lutèce. Upon his arrival, he received an unexpected welcome from the desk clerk who remembered him from his last stay with Ava Haas. Andre ordered a bottle of single malt Scotch and ginger ale for a mix, as well as a ham and cheese sandwich to be sent to his room. From his room, he dialled the rental agency he had previously dealt with and ordered a Jaguar Sovereign to be delivered to the hotel by 9:00 a.m. As soon as his room service order arrived, he tipped the attendant, bolted the door behind him, and began removing the clothes he had been wearing since he'd flown commercial to Paris from The Hague that morning.

Andre dumped the contents of the small bag he brought with him onto the bed. He then fixed himself half a glass of Scotch, added ice cubes, and filled it with ginger ale. He stood looking at the items on his bed as he took a long drink from the glass. A shirt, underwear, a pair of socks, forty-eight-hundred in US bills, a few French francs, and his wallet lay there. He unbuckled the money belt around his waist that held his passport, inserted four-thousand dollars of the cash in it, and threw it onto the bed. The Scotch was beginning to take effect as he finished eating his sandwich. The events of the day began to unravel, and he began to shiver.

Well, for a fellow who has been hijacked, drugged, almost murdered, rescued—but not entirely exonerated—you sure as hell took care of business today, mister! He knew he could have gotten himself killed again today. *That fucking Pelling seems to be bound and determined to frame my ass! I'd like to wire up the demented prick and throw him into a scalding shower. Listen to me . . . I'd need Green Berets with baseball bats to back me up, and I'd have to be holding a very big gun.*

That little snot Turrin had laughed at him when he accused him of setting him up. He knew he had to scare the shit out of him, so he slapped him senseless, threw him onto his stomach in front of his closet, and stood on him until he got the coat hangers wrapped around his arms and hands nice and tight. He'd ripped Turrin's shirt down to his belt, marched him into the bathroom, and turned the shower on hot. From the look of terror in his eyes, it definitely got his attention when Andre told him he was going to scald the truth out of him.

Andre threw him in, and Turrin told him everything he'd suspected. When he was about to turn off the hot water, he heard muffled shots and saw Turrin's face explode as he slid into the tub. As Andre turned, he felt a hard rap on his head and was knocked unconscious.

Have to have another pull on this Scotch, it's doing a job on me, Andre thought.

He was looking forward to seeing Ava tomorrow. She'd sounded enthusiastic on the phone. When Andre called to tell her he was going to Paris, she said, "I'll meet you there. I'll get a flight right away. Call me back in fifteen minutes." He did as she asked, and she said, "I've got to see you. I insist! I have a morning flight that will arrive there just before noon."

Well, friend, I can't wait to see you either. Andre kept thinking back to when he was trussed up on the *SeaOx*, drugged, unable to move much, and barely able to rationalize. *I thought I was going to die, but you must have been watching over me like a guardian angel, and I'm very interested in hearing what sent you into action. Hmmm . . . good drink! I wonder why people who have just escaped death feel the need to get plastered. I dunno, but I'm gonna!*

Andre stepped out of his underwear, fixed another glassful of Scotch and ginger ale, carried it into the bathroom, and pulled the sliding shower door open. Reaching in, he turned the shower to lukewarm. Drink in hand, he stepped into the stall and turned his back to the spray. He felt the shower begin to sooth him. He quaffed a mouthful from the drink and noticed the spray was diluting it, so he stepped out and put the glass on the toilet box before returning to the soothing water. Andre concentrated on soaping his body and rinsing it off. The booze was working on him now, getting him warm inside as well. He began to relax and empty the day's events from his head. The images of Turrin shrieking in pain and dancing in his shower kept flashing in his mind until those shower scenes turned into more pleasant images of Ava. Tomorrow when she arrived he would order frosty mugs of cold beer for their reunion. Frosty mugs, indeed!

* * *

When Pelling arrived back at his room, Ruth was hungry and wanted to go out to eat. "Yeah, sure, I could eat, but let's go out and walk or take a cab somewhere. I don't want to eat here in the dining room," Pelling said.

"Fine with me, sweetie, I'll be just a minute. By the way, am I having dinner with an older man or someone else?" she asked.

Pelling smiled, studied his reflection in the mirror, and made a decision. He made a few adjustments by removing his vest and bow tie, combing out his hairpiece, and donning a wine-coloured sweater vest over his shirt. He completed his outfit with his new shirt-like orange leather jacket. Looking in the mirror again, he was satisfied with his new look.

Ruth came out of the washroom and complimented him on his younger look. They left the room, walked down the stairs, exited the hotel unnoticed, and hailed a taxi. "Take us to the Seafood Shack at the city docks please, driver."

The ride took ten minutes, during which Pelling told Ruth he purposely chose this place because the marina had a Beneteau boat dealership. He told her that he had toured the company's factories here a month ago. He thought at the time he would like to own one of their very well made boats. After their meal, they walked the short distance to the dealership at Pier 6. Pelling became interested in a fifty-foot Sense offered for sale. It was three years old and completely outfitted with many extras. The asking price was just under two-hundred-thousand dollars. Pelling looked all through the boat, while Ruth sat on the cosy circular couch in the sailboat's dining area, listening to the questions Pelling asked and the sales agent's positive answers.

Ruth wondered, *is Teddy thinking of sailing offshore for a while until things cool down? This would be an awesome hideout, indeed! Too bad we missed out on the Bordeaux estate I was sure we could buy. I know I outbid the Canadian group who were interested. Damn, I thought that old buzzard got real close to letting me have the property when I indicated I'd give him a roll in the hay just to seal the deal. I even opened my blouse and let him see what he would be getting. He got real close, even felt me up, then abruptly ended the meeting by saying, 'Young lady, I can't thank you enough for the show, but I have to refuse both your offer to buy my estate and the . . . uh . . . err . . . other as well. My ill health, you understand.' I was steamed. I still feel that had I been able to get the old buzzard into bed, I'd have convinced him to sell to me. I can't remember the last time anyone refused me sexually.*

While she sat sipping a cup of tea, she listened to the conversation between the sales agent and Pelling. A deal was in the making. The questions Teddy asked were mostly about registering the boat and the guarantee that pertained to this particular model.

"So, you are certain this boat is in a sail-away condition as is?"

"Absolutely, sir. This is a list of items the yard has attended to prior to offering her for sale."

The agent handed over a typewritten page containing the work done, the cost of each item in hours, and the price extensions. The total came to fourteen-thousand dollars. While Pelling looked over the list the agent explained, "This boat was traded in on a seventy-five-foot custom model presently under construction in our Navale facility here in Bordeaux. The owner has kept this boat in first-class condition, and with the extra work done recently, the boat is offered at well below replacement cost."

Pelling looked at the agent and said, "I have been through your factories at St. Gilles and Navale. I've seen the construction process and was impressed. That's what brought me here today, actually. When I was at the Navale factory, one of your agents there mentioned some of these larger models get sailed across the ocean to Charleston, South Carolina, the closest marina to your US operation. He explained that the boats are hauled out over there and tuned up before delivery to US buyers. Is that still being done?" Pelling asked.

"Absolutely, sir. As a matter of fact, there are three boats leaving later this week from here for Charleston. Why do you ask?"

"If we buy this boat, would it be possible to join up with those three and tag along with them to South Carolina? Safety in numbers, you understand." Pelling smiled.

"I can call our factory to see if they have any objections. Would your purchase be conditional on being included in this little flotilla?" the agent asked.

"Yes, it would, and please ask for the planned route from here and all the details."

The agent made the call. He spoke to the manager of the factory, and came back smiling to announce that the delivery captain would welcome another Beneteau and her new owners into his little fleet. "Captain Petain says they plan to leave in two days at 6:00 a.m. He suggested you let us provision the boat with food and the extra seagoing gear you will need. You will need your passports for entry into other countries. His sail plan is to go first to the Azores, then to Bermuda, and finally to Charleston. From there, they plan to attend a reception at the Marion, South Carolina factory. From Charleston it's a drive of two-hundred-forty kilometres. Once you arrive at Charleston, the boats will remain there to be inspected by the company's pre-delivery crew. There is one other owner on the sail over. The other two boats will be sailed by our delivery crews. If this meets your satisfaction, let's complete the paperwork."

Pelling delayed the purchase for a minute to have a private word with Ruth. They walked up on deck, went toward the pulpit, and spoke in lowered voices. "I think this is probably the safest way to the United States. Sailing with these delivery people, I mean. You heard the agent say they will stop in the Azores, Bermuda, and then continue on to Charleston. If you want off for any reason, you could stay in the Azores or Bermuda, and then fly direct to the Cayman Islands from there. I'd prefer your company all the way for obvious reasons and . . . well . . . we both have pretty strong needs in that department, right? This is a real good way to obscure our trail. I know the ETA and the Sûreté will be looking for us. I'm going to make the deal for the boat and let him get it ready for the trip."

Ruth reached up, touched his face, and smiled at him saying, "I'm all for it, lover. We can shop for sailing clothes in the next two days before we leave. By the way, just a thought, but can you really sail this thing all by yourself?"

"I'm sure I can. By the time we get to the Azores, I should be totally clued in. Going with the group will simplify the navigation. Nah! I won't have any problem. And by the time we get to Charleston, I promise you we will both be in terrific shape."

"If you are right about the Sûreté having your fingerprints now and wanting me for questioning, we are both better off out of France for now," Ruth continued. "But I really don't see how they can connect Ruth Werner to any of this unless Raoul tells them what he knows about Ruth Meikle,— her description and all the millions she has."

"I think Raoul will keep you as a special target for the ETA, hoping to recover your money, right? The Sûreté will be trying very hard to find out just who this Ruth is that had connections to the ETA and hired me. Raoul could make the connection for them, and may! If they check the two banks you told Raoul about and find only pocket change, they could easily take it further and check all banks for any Ruth with a large amount of money. That's a bit of stretch, but a worry nevertheless. It's too bad we couldn't have purchased that vineyard in Bordeaux. That would have been a great place to hide, right under the noses of the authorities and the ETA."

"When Raoul started asking about you and what I'd done with the money you gave me over the years, I just strung him along for a while, but I immediately took precautions with our investments. I opened the numbered account in Grand Cayman through the Royal Bank of Canada. I had to show my Ruth Werner passport and get two other bank references. Those brokerage companies sent letters of reference to the Royal Bank, along with a list of our holdings showing the cost of acquisition and the present value. This was necessary to establish that the money was generated from legal sources over the past several years. The account was then opened and awaited a wire transfer when those assets were turned into cash.

"The actual transfer of the funds was easy. I do have to appear in person with my passport and account particulars at the Royal Bank in Georgetown whenever I want to take money out. I can also transfer funds from there to any other Royal Bank branch in the world. So if, or when, Raoul checks the two banks I told him held our investments and money, he will be shocked to find less than a hundred dollars in each one. He could bribe people in every other bank he may suspect holds our funds, but I doubt it. I just don't think the ETA or the Sûreté can connect me to anything," Ruth said, suddenly becoming animated, "Hell, I'm all psyched up now for a sea cruise. And, like you say, if by the time we get to the Azores I find I can't go the distance, I'll just stop, take a few days off, then fly over to Charleston and wait for you. C'mon, let's go buy this boat."

"Right, it will make the dude's day."

* * *

Marta Vander Riis landed at Orly Airport in her Lake Renegade and was directed to the Falcon Flying Club by ground control. After radioing the club on her arrival at their fuel pumps, they radioed her back. "Welcome to Orly again, Ms Vander Riis. Just leave the Lake at the pumps and do your shut down. An attendant will bring it into the hangar after he tops up the fuel. Do you require any help with your luggage, ma'am?"

"No thanks, I can manage. Lake Renegade, over and out."

Marta swung the plane parallel to the pumps and did her shut down. She smiled at the attendant waiting for her to step down from the cockpit after lifting her overnight case from the rear seat. She handed the ignition keys to him and walked the fifty yards to the office. Glancing at the cars parked close to the hangar, she didn't see anyone waiting for her. Marta didn't know what Robert would be driving, so she entered the office and signed her plane into their care. As she was about to ask if there were any messages for her, the door opened behind her and Robert appeared.

Marta smiled at him. Instead of rushing at him and kissing him, which she really wanted to do, she walked slowly toward him, put her arm around his waist, and hip checked him, saying, "Thanks for meeting me, Robert. I wasn't sure if you could get away after I spoke with your sergeant, even though he assured me he would relay my arrival time to you. I'm glad you made it and I can't wait to get you alone."

Robert had an ear-to-ear grin and a flushed face from the time of the sexy hip check until she waltzed him to his car. He carried her bag and pointed toward a late model black Mercedes. Once at the car, he set her bag down and felt in his suit coat side pocket for his car keys, withdrew them, and opened the passenger side door for her. Marta, however, wanted a proper welcome, so instead of entering the car, she pulled him close and kissed him full on the mouth. He responded, kissing her back enthusiastically, while enjoying her hands on his behind pulling him into her midsection. He backed away and helped her, reluctantly, into her seat. He closed the door, and made it around the car and into the driver's seat with only one thought in mind. He tried to pull his coat over the embarrassment in the front of his trousers, then thought, *oh what the hell!* He just smiled at her and blushed.

"If it was dark out, I bet I could have had you right there, right, Lieutenant? I know. I'm shameless, but I do like to tease you. Honestly, it makes me want you all the more. Where are we going right now?"

"We can go to my apartment if you like, or a hotel?"

"How far to your place from here?" Marta asked.

"Not too far, about twenty-five minutes."

"I have a better idea. It's only fifteen minutes from here to Mother's apartment. Let's go there. She suggested we use it if we wanted. Please say yes."

Robert smiled at her, blew her a kiss, and said, "I think I remember the address, but direct me, please."

"Okay, I'll behave, but only until I get there. Just stay in this lane until I tell you to pull over when we get close to our exit."

The black Mercedes pulled into the Vander Riis parking stall at their apartment building at 12:45 p.m. Good as her word, Marta stayed on her side of the front seat until they arrived and held hands going up in the elevator to the seventh floor. Eighteen minutes had elapsed, but it only took seconds after she locked the apartment door behind them to get to the master bedroom. They silently and slowly watched each other undress and met under the covers.

Later, after the welcoming sex had exhausted them, they showered together and discovered to their delight that they were not completely exhausted after all. Once they towelled each other dry, Marta suggested she show him the rest of the apartment, which consisted of the entire seventh floor. She found terry-cloth robes for each of them and led him into the huge living room. The east and north walls were floor-to-ceiling windows, offering a panoramic view of the Paris skyline. Standing and sipping brandy, they pointed out landmarks to each other.

"Are you hungry, darling?" Marta asked.

"Hmmm, not very. Are you?"

"Actually, I am. I just had a light breakfast and it's getting on to four o'clock."

"Well, I must check in with Sergeant Moline to let him know I'll be off duty until further notice. I intend to keep you under close surveillance until you leave."

"Oh, that will be just heavenly. Are you sure?"

"I have so much time off coming that it will be a big relief for the inspector if I take some."

He telephoned his office and spoke to the sergeant. "Any new developments I should know about, Sergeant?"

"The results of the fingerprinting of the farmhouse and barn have come back, but they don't match with any known criminals in our database, or that of Interpol. However, we have prints taken from the *SeaOx*, the hunting lodge on the Vander Riis estate, and Pierre Turrin's apartment that match."

"Were prints taken from the custom rifle in the case found at the farmhouse?"

"Yes, Lieutenant, the same person who handled the rifle and the cutting torch in the barn was also in the Vander Riis hunting lodge. We are in the process of comparing the bullets taken from the dead motorcycle patrolman's body, the murdered UPS driver, and those fired from the gun with the silencer found in the broker's bathroom."

"Good work, Sergeant. I'm going off duty for the next day or so, but I will check with you periodically for further results. I think it would be wise to take the fingerprint crew back to Turrin's apartment and go over it again. If we can place our suspect there, along with his gun, I would feel much better. Anything on the woman named Ruth?"

"We have a couple of possibilities, Lieutenant. Without a description of her it's difficult, but we'll keep at it."

"How many visitors has Raoul de Vascos had so far?"

"I checked the prison log just before you called, Lieutenant. He has had two visits with the same lawyer so far, that's all."

"I have a feeling our shooter, Pelling, is still in this area. I'm sure he has more to fear from the ETA at the moment than he has from us. He said he would send proof of Raoul's connection with the ETA. Has anything come in yet?"

"No sir, nothing."

"Very well, Sergeant," Robert said and looked over at Marta as he hung up the receiver.

"Robert, why don't you go have a hot tub and relax while I find us something to eat?"

"I think I will, that sounds like a good place to do some thinking."

"Think about us a little, too, while you soak, handsome. When the food is ready I'll come get you. And I mean that literally."

Marta called the Chez Basile and ordered a full dinner for two of roast duck with garden vegetables, plus two bottles of Sauterne, to be delivered within the hour. She had eaten at the quaint little sidewalk bistro two blocks away and had their food delivered to the apartment on many occasions. The food had always been well prepared, delivered on time, and reasonably priced.

After completing the order, Marta joined Robert in the hot tub. Settling beside him she said, "Dinner will be delivered in forty minutes, so we have time to relax."

Robert snuggled closer to Marta saying, "I was just thinking about how clever this Pelling is. He has created a heady turn of events, indeed, arranging to have de Vascos arrested and held on suspicion of committing every crime ever attributed to the ETA. And let's not forget his promise to provide further evidence of Raoul's link to the attempt on my life. I've wondered what evidence he could send me. If he actually does provide some connection to the ETA and the bombing of my car, it would seal de Vascos's fate. This event could be the single biggest break in our on-going anti-terrorism program and it has kind of thrown me for a loop. I should be hard on this guy's heels. Instead, here I am soaking in a tub with a beautiful companion, awaiting evidence from a very questionable source."

"I think there must have been a breakup between Pelling and de Vascos," Marta said. "Pelling insisted he was a high-ranking officer in the ETA, and guaranteed he would prove it. Seems to me these two know a lot about you, my dear. Why else did he use the one hook he knew would get you onto de Vascos immediately? And from what you told me, it worked. You had those helicopter squad teams in action so quickly they caught him on foot close to the farmhouse. Pelling wanted him in jail, and it appears he doesn't want him out on some technicality. I'd wager that you get this proof quickly."

"We'll see. In the meantime, I'm perfectly content to spend as much time here with you as you will allow."

"Silly fellow! I could keep you here forever, and very busy too," Marta said, "and, I liked your beautiful companion comment."

At that moment, a large brown envelope was delivered by courier to Sûreté headquarters in Paris, addressed to Lt. Robert Bizet.

Chapter 18

Andre, Ava, and Frosted Beer Mugs

Sergeant Moline opened the brown envelope, and after he went through the contents, telephoned Robert at the Vander Riis apartment to report the arrival of new evidence.

"Come back here when you can and tell me all about it," Marta insisted as he headed out the door to his office.

He was at his desk by six thirty that evening. His eyes became misty, fixed on the photographs of Marie-Claude. Anger began welling up inside him. He clenched his teeth, and in a barely audible voice said, "You murdering bastards! This picture proves you blew up my car knowing I was standing on the balcony."

The picture he held clearly showed his fiancé entering his car. There had definitely been no mistake. *You didn't care whether you killed Marie-Claude or me you bloody butchers. Sweet Jesus, Marie-Claude, they killed you as an object lesson for me.* Either the bomber or someone with them had taken the photos. Robert new it had to be a warning for him. Why else take the pictures? But why haven't they turned up before now? The only thing he could think of was that perhaps the bomber saw an opportunity to profit from blackmailing his superior in the future. Whatever the motive, this evidence would ensure that de Vascos would stay confined, and if the voiceprints on the tape were between Raoul and Pelling, it was more than enough proof for a conviction.

Marta may be right about a rift between Pelling and his control. De Vascos has, no doubt, set his other killers onto you, Pelling. There are just too many people looking, for you not to be found. But because you have money, nerve, and other identities, you may stay hidden. Because you'll eliminate anyone who gets in your way, you do have the advantage. Where in the blazes are you?

* * *

After a hello hug and bag retrieval at the luggage reptile, Andre rolled Ava Haas's suitcase out to the rental Jaguar, turned to face her, and grinned as he opened his arms inviting her to him. They hugged until sobs died in her throat.

Andre spoke softly into her hair, "Thank you. Thank you, Ava, thank you for looking for me. You helped save my life."

Ava looked into his eyes and said, "I'm so glad you are safe, Andre."

He kissed her, and she kissed him back until some of the passers-by started to slow down to watch. "We had better get in the car before we get arrested," Andre said, opening the door for her.

Ava reached over and unlocked the driver's door for him, and he slid in behind the steering wheel. Andre asked in a serious tone, "Will we go straight to the de Lutèce? Or is there somewhere you need to go first?"

"I need to be real close to you, Andre, to show you how glad I am you are alive and well. I will cry, but only because I'm glad to be with you, and not wondering where you are and if you're okay. Can we go to the hotel now?"

"Of course, Ava! I want you to sail with me, and I don't really care where we go, as long as you're with me. I have a pressing need to tell you everything that happened after I mailed that audiotape to you, and I feel it can best be told aboard the *SeaOx*.

"I hoped you would ask me to sail with you again, but is everything all right with the boat? I was afraid you would not want to sail her again because of what happened," Ava said. "Everything is now different for me, Andre. I sold my share of the Hamburg Marina to my partner and I have someone renting my home on a permanent basis. I thought if you didn't want the *SeaOx* anymore, I would buy her from you."

"I have no intentions of selling the *SeaOx*, Ava. But I remember my promise to give you the first choice to purchase her if ever I do sell."

"Good! Do you have something to drink at your room?"

"Some good Scotch and some wine. What would you prefer?"

"You could ask the kitchen to send us some beer and two frosty mugs," she answered with a broad smile. "I have brought a few special cigarettes to make us relax, if you like."

"Perfect! When we get there, I'll arrange with room service to send us something to snack on, as well as beer and frosty mugs."

The mention of frosty beer mugs and the image of Ava came back to him as if he'd pushed the play button on a VCR in his head. There had been much to learn about the *SeaOx* and Andre was delighted that Ava had accepted the job of teaching him the boat. He had kept focused, especially during the first couple of weeks from Hamburg to Oostende and when crossing the channel to London. But on the return trip from London to Le Havre, Andre lost his concentration.

They had just finished a sail change, adding the Genoa. Andre was at the inside steering position, watching Ava make adjustments to the downhaul. It was warm, and she wore only ragged shorts and a halter-top. Tanned from the wind and sun, Ava was agile and able, and seamanship seemed to come second nature to her. He had seen her attend to all manner of things on the trip. The fact that she was an extremely desirable woman didn't distract him from his focus of learning everything he could from her about the boat. She glanced in his direction, noticed him watching her, waved, and came nimbly into the pilothouse, and then disappeared down the stairs into the galley. Minutes later, she slowly made her way up the steps carrying two icy mugs of foaming beer. Andre noticed how carefully she approached with the mugs held to her chest, trying to avoid spilling the contents. She handed a mug to him, which he nearly dropped along with his chin, as he caught a full frontal view of Ava's breasts and the effect caused by the cold mugs.

"Something to cool you off," she said as she smiled at him.

"Thanks, I needed this," Andre said with a leer, "now more than ever."

She stood at her full height, slightly arching her back. "Really? Why? Does this bother you, Andre?" she asked, pirouetting in front of him.

"Hmmm, of course it bothers me. I'm human, for Pete's sake!"

"I was beginning to wonder if anything other than the *SeaOx* could interest you? You don't seem to get any of my signals. So I thought, 'what kind of guy is this? Maybe he likes men better than women.'"

Andre gulped a mouthful of the cool, foamy liquid, and felt awkward at her suggestion he might be gay. He kept his eyes on hers, thinking, *me gay? Yeah, right. Maybe I have been preoccupied. But, what signals?*

"I know I'm an employee, but I thought by now we would be friends. It wouldn't hurt anyone I know if we become close friends." She smiled at him. "Would it hurt someone for you?"

Andre put his mug on the marble ledge in front of the wheel, took her beer, and placed it beside his. Reaching for her, he gathered her to his bare chest. He felt her snuggling to his neck, kissing him hungrily while she moved her lower body tighter against him. She felt marvellous in his arms, moving erotically against him, as he inhaled the scent of her hair. There was no mistaking her signals now. Ava's teasing nudity, passionate kissing, and sexy closeness meant just one thing, *take me to bed, now!*

* * *

Marta had been alone in her mother's Paris apartment since Robert returned to his office four hours ago. It was now ten o'clock. Why hadn't he called? *I insisted he go to his office, examine the evidence that came in, and do whatever he needed to do. So, why am I wandering around in a semi-snit because he hasn't called me? Just cool it, girl. He's busy trying to catch the bad guys.* The telephone rang, bringing an end to her speculating.

"Marta, it's Robert, would you like to meet me downtown for a drink?"

"That's very thoughtful and sweet of you. It sounds like you have more work to do, but you must need a break. Otherwise, you would come home, right lover?"

"Yeah, something like that. If I came home to you now, I wouldn't want to leave, and I must make some arrangements before I leave here tonight. Meet me at the Crepery across the street from my building. I will see you there in thirty minutes."

"Okay, I'll put on something comfy and meet you in half an hour.

Marta hung up and called down to the doorman to order her a taxi, saying she would be down in fifteen minutes. She picked out tailored slacks and a black satin long-sleeved blouse from her mother's closet, pulling the slacks on over the black pantyhose she was wearing. She slipped into a pair of high-heeled black pumps and stood in front of the mirror while she adjusted the thin belt on the slacks. Smiling at her reflection, she blew her image a kiss of approval. She put on the metallic blue raincoat her mother had bought for her, selected a black umbrella from the assortment in the large standing bowl, felt for her keys, closed the door after her, and locked it. She thanked the doorman, stepped into the waiting taxi, and gave the driver instructions.

During the taxi ride to her rendezvous with Robert, Marta examined her feelings about her policeman who was driven by his work. Would he share this new evidence about the car bombing of his fiancé, or would it be far too personal? Marta decided she would trust her own feelings about Lieutenant Robert Bizet and wait and see what happened. The taxi pulled up in front of the Crepery. Marta paid the fare before stepping out onto the wet sidewalk and made her way inside. Robert stood up as she entered. She went to him and kissed him. He helped her out of her coat and hung it on a rack close by. He looked at her for what seemed a long time before speaking.

"Marta, thank you for coming. I must tell you how much you have come to mean to me in the short time we've been together. I've been preoccupied with my work over the years, as you no doubt have noticed. The reason has been personal and my work habits are those of a compulsive. I was obsessed with finding the person, or people, responsible for the murder of my fiancé. Tonight, when I examined the evidence Pelling sent, it was as if a heavy weight of guilt was lifted from my shoulders. I want you to see these photographs and understand, as I do now, how they prove the bomber knew exactly what he was doing. He exploded my car with Marie-Claude inside in front of me as an object lesson to break my will. Just look at these pictures, Marta. See, I'm on the balcony, waving to her as she is getting into my car. Now look at the next photo. It's the same photo, except the car is reduced to a pile of smoking rubble, and I'm still on the balcony staring in disbelief at what I just witnessed."

"My God, Robert, it's so . . . horrible. I'm so sorry." Marta reached for his hand as the tears rolled down her cheeks.

"There's more: a tape of Raoul de Vascos giving instructions to Pelling on different ETA assignments. Raoul's ETA code name is Sergeant, and Pelling's is Corporal. We confirmed by voiceprint match who they are. Your mother was right to pay this creature off. My assessment of him is that he's pure evil. As long as he is free and has money, he may well stay away from all of you, but should his circumstances change to desperate, there is no way of knowing what he might do."

"Robert, you are beginning to frighten me. What are you going to do now?"

"I intend to keep my promise to your mother," he said. "However, I plan to continue my police work as well. Thank you again for coming here to meet me. I just had to tell you about all of this."

"My darling, I'm so glad you confided in me. Now, I'm going to order a couple of stiff drinks, sit for a while, and just think about us."

"I'll have one of those drinks with you," Robert said. "Then I'm going back to the office. I have to advise the next shift of the plans I'm setting in motion. After that, I'm coming straight home to the prettiest young lady in Paris."

Marta wiped away her remaining tears and said, "In that case, Lieutenant, I'd say I'm the luckiest young lady in Paris."

When the waiter arrived with their drinks, he brought the sandwich in a bag Robert had ordered prior to her arrival. After he finished his drink, Robert stood, stooped to kiss Marta, and left.

Marta sipped her drink while watching Robert depart. He strode purposely across the intersection, swinging his lunch bag, and entered the building that housed the Sûreté. Marta was relieved. He had shared the pictures of his fiancé's murder with her and expressed how he felt about it. She knew he must really be over grieving for her. Robert was handed Raoul de Vascos gift-wrapped. Pelling had to implicate himself in providing Robert with this new evidence. *What arrogance this Pelling has shown. He appears to be waving a red flag at my lieutenant, daring Robert to try and catch him. Why?*

She decided she had to speak with her mother again to hear what really happened on the *SeaOx* when she was held hostage. She seemed so certain that if they even try to help the authorities, Pelling would find a way to murder all of them. She finished her drink, took a taxi back to the apartment, and called her mother while she waited for her handsome lieutenant to come home.

"Hello, Marta dear! What are you up to?" Elspeth asked her daughter.

Marta related how Robert had shared the new evidence of his fiancé's murder and de Vascos and Pelling's involvement. "My heavens that's just awful. That poor young woman! Robert must be shaken to the core. And Pelling was the bomber, on orders from this Raoul person. Tell me, dear, how is Robert managing?"

"He is back at work. After sharing all this with me, he said a great burden of guilt had been lifted from his shoulders. He has Raoul de Vascos under lock and key, and now a tape recording, which proves he gave the order for the murder of his fiancé. You know Robert will not stop hunting for Pelling until he captures him. He thinks Pelling is an evil, arrogant stone-cold killer who may well not bother any of us as long as he is free and has money." Marta said. She then asked, "When you were on the *SeaOx*, what went on between you and this monster, Pelling? Did he rape you? And why in heaven's name are you so sure he will stay out of our lives from now on?"

"No, I wasn't raped. Although, I sensed he was purposely restraining himself. How can I explain? I felt that he expected me to come on to him. That's how arrogant he is. One thing for sure, this ransom money is very important to him, and even though I am bargaining with the devil, I intend to keep my part of it—and for some unknown reason I feel he will keep his. I can't explain it."

"Well, I'm with Robert. Nothing I learn about this murdering bastard inspires me with any confidence in him whatsoever! Quite the opposite, I'm afraid. Have you heard from Tice and Sylvie?"

"Yes, Tice called from Amsterdam to tell me they will be checking out of their hotel in the morning to come to the chateau to pick up different clothes. They're planning a trip together. Marta, they are having so much fun. They left their number for you to call before they check out."

"I'll call them as soon as we hang up."

"Well, I'm glad you and Robert are now on solid ground. His willingness to share his deepest feelings indicates a wonderful relationship in the making for both of you. Kiss Robert for me. I'm planning a trip of my own. After Tice and Sylvie leave, I'm going shopping in New York."

"New York, really? Now that sounds interesting!"

"Yes, well, once I get my plans finalized I'll tell you about them. Bye for now, dear. Please call your brother."

* * *

At the Bastille in Paris where the priority criminals are sometimes held, Raoul de Vascos lay on his bunk staring up at the bare light bulb encased in wire mesh. The light was always on. *Why in the hell did I think I could trust Ruth to do as I told her? I guess I turned her off when I made up that bit about having to hand over five million of her money to the ETA council.* He knew if the council got wind of this deal they would take all the money for themselves and wipe him, Ruth, and Pelling off the face of the earth. He figured Ruth must have freed Pelling, and no doubt he put the Sûreté on his ass. Two helicopters had dropped out of the sky and their teams surrounded him in seconds. Now his ETA lawyer says he can't get him out on bail.

Shit! Well, they have set out a net for the elusive corporal, and if I found him through Ruth, so can the Sûreté and the ETA. My only chance of getting out of here is if I arrange my own kidnapping. If, not, I may just be able to arrange some sort of deal by turning over to the Sûreté everything I know about the ETA and their operation.

Raoul de Vascos rose to a sitting position on his sparse bunk as two guards entered his cell, handcuffed his wrists behind his back, and led him to an interview room. Robert and Sergeant Moline sat across a big metal table and remained silent until the terrorist was seated opposite them.

"I am Lieutenant Robert Bizet and this is Sergeant Moline. We are from the Paris Sûreté and are here to inform you that we have received evidence that identifies you as the person giving orders to an operative under your control to assassinate Pierre Turrin, me, and others. We have also received photographs of the bombing of my car, which killed my fiancé. We are charging you for ordering the murder of Marie-Claude Proulx. We are hoping for a speedy trial and your quick execution."

"I'm sure you will go over all this so-called proof with my lawyers, if you haven't already. Frankly, gentlemen I think you must have me confused with someone else."

Sergeant Moline said, "No, we have you dead to rights. We know your connection as the nephew of one of the major fundraisers of the Basque ETA ruling council."

"I have nothing to do with my uncle's business. I suggest you talk with my lawyers. I have nothing more to say to you."

"We intend to speak with your lawyers, but we wanted to confront you with this damning evidence that will convict you of murder," Robert said. "There is a slight possibility you may get a stay of execution if you tell us everything you know about the terrorist ETA organization. This is your only hope of staying alive."

"I've heard enough! You have no reason to hold me!"

Robert and Sergeant Moline rose from the table and left the room. The two guards came for de Vascos and returned him to his cell.

The two policemen discussed Raoul's options. They agreed that when the ETA lawyers understood the airtight evidence, they would point out to him just how hopeless his situation was. Robert knew that Raoul would try to work out a plan of escape when he realized he would be found guilty and sentenced to death. Or, he could decide to tell the Sûreté everything he knew about the ETA operation, hoping for a more lenient sentence. They decided they would wait him out. Under no circumstances would they move their prisoner, which could give the ETA an opening for a rescue attempt. Given his family connections, both Sûreté policemen thought such an attempt was a real possibility.

They also understood how precarious their own safety had become. Their growing celebrity with the press had made them ETA targets. Since this group of terrorists had already targeted Robert, he recognized the risks they faced. Between them, they agreed on a plan to take extra precautions. They would now use many different vehicles. They would not post or announce their meetings in advance, and would communicate by fax and e-mail. They already felt the ETA was watching them.

"My main concern right now, Sergeant, is the safety of Marta Vander Riis." Robert said. "I'm staying with her in her mother's apartment. Pelling took her mother, Elspeth, captive from this apartment. I suspect Pelling was working with Turrin and his elusive friend, Ruth, and not the ETA. But I can't be sure, so I have to get her the hell out of there and to someplace safe. It won't be easy to follow her in her airplane once we decide on a destination. And that's a consolation."

The telephone on the Robert's desk rang. "Lieutenant Bizet speaking."

"Hello Robert, Andre Laurent speaking. I'm calling from the Scheveningen Marina at The Hague. The yard found an electronic device stuck to the metal brace under the bowsprit on the *SeaOx*. It attaches magnetically, so anyone could have walked by on the jetty and stuck it where it was found. Ava Haas is staying with me and was busy fussing about below deck while I was shopping in the marina chandlery. The authorities that have been checking the *SeaOx* scanned the boat after I got back and found it. It's a locator. The marina manager said the scanner went ballistic when the technical guys went close to the bowsprit.

"Just to bring you up to date, Ava and I plan to sail the *SeaOx* down the coast to Le Havre, then head farther south along the coast for sightseeing. By the way, Ava says hello."

"Hi to Ava, and thank you for calling, Andre. I'd like our lab people to examine that device so we know what we're dealing with. Then I suggest you put it back in the position you found it. I'll get the device looked at this morning, so it shouldn't delay you very long. I want to know the range of this thing and just how close Pelling has to be to track you."

"Okay, we'll stay put until the technicians are through and you have your report. You should know I've buttoned up the *SeaOx,* making it much safer. I've installed a satellite telephone and global maritime distress safety system with satellite and digital communication technology. I'm comfortable knowing that if I punch a certain button the coast guard will board us via helicopter. When we are sailing along our course, I'll give you a call on my sat phone to see how it works."

"Okay, I'll send the lab techs over to the *SeaOx* ASAP. Do you have a fax on the boat?"

"Yes, the number is 011-55-71001. Please fax me the report on the device and then I'll call you again so we can discuss it. I just wish I knew what this mad bastard has up his sleeve."

"It may have been so he could easily locate the *SeaOx* in a busy marina at some point for whatever reason. I'll be in touch."

Andre turned toward Ava who had been listening closely to his side of the telephone conversation. "You heard that the lieutenant is having local police lab technicians take the device back to their shop and analyse it, then put it back on the bowsprit. He will fax us the report and then call us back." Andre said.

"They have not caught your hijacker, or he would have said so, am I right?" Ava asked.

Within the hour, two uniformed police arrived with a suitcase, extracted the electronic device, packed it in a case, and left. It was quiet on the *SeaOx,* which was gently rocking in a lazy motion on the incoming tide. Ava, busy at the chart table with an intended route in mind, did the navigation, supposing a trip of two-thousand-three kilometres. If the winds held favourable, they could expect to average between five and six knots, which would move them between two-hundred-fifty to two-hundred-sixty-five kilometres in a twenty-four hour run. It would take seven or eight days to do that distance. Ava knew it would take them more like two weeks if they stopped in two or three places on the way, and was anxious to be at sea behind the wheel of her favourite sailboat.

A smile came across her face as she recalled the past few days. She had spent a good deal of her first night just holding him. Those marijuana cigarettes were a big help in relieving Andre of pent-up anxieties, but they hadn't done a lot for their lovemaking. They couldn't seem to rekindle their previous passion, either in the shower together or later under the covers. Andre, sensing her tension and arousal, had easily satisfied her with his fingers. *But when I got my hands on him, I couldn't get him hard, and I needed him hard. So I got my mouth on him and sucked him to a state of hard-enoughness, but he didn't seem to want to be inside me, so I continued giving him pleasure, finishing what I started.*

Ava squeezed her knees together remembering how he groaned in ecstasy and how fast he retreated into sleep. The chattering of the fax brought her back to the moment, and she turned her head toward the machine. Her wristwatch told her it had been two hours since the police techs left with the little passenger. Ava rose and went to the forward berth to awaken Andre. She wondered if there was enough time before the lab techs arrived. They didn't need to enter the boat anyway.

She looked down at Andre, who was sound asleep. Ava felt for him through the front of his sailing shorts, undid his zipper, and brought him out through the slit in his boxers. She slowly squeezed his enlarging member until she had it erect. Andre started to stir, so she brought her mouth onto it and began her specialty. Andre looked up at what was happening then reached for the back of her head. He let her complete him again by holding her head to her task. Ava wondered why Andre hadn't wanted intercourse, yet he would let her fellate him whenever she cared to. She backed away from

Andre, who was now wide awake, and said, "There is a fax coming through on your machine."

They huddled over the machine while it chattered out the last of two pages. They read:

Andre,

The lab investigation report is attached. This device is strictly for location and has a broadcast range of about five kilometres. It is usually attached to a car, which can then be followed from a distance with a radio frequency device. This transmitter broadcasts a blip every ten seconds and has a long life cycle. When Pelling installed it is just speculation. It is easy to do: just spot a bit of metal and slap it on. It attaches by magnetism like a limpid mine. Why he needed this locator is further speculation, but it would make it easy if he wanted to locate the SeaOx in a busy marina. He would just switch on his tracking apparatus and, if he got a blip, he would know the boat is there.

The telephone rang. It was Lieutenant Bizet. "Hello again, Andre and Ava, have you read the fax I sent?"

"Yes, we have, and if Pelling steps on my boat again I'll shoot out his knees, hands, and ankles. You can interrogate what's left of him."

"Good, I think I would do the same. I'm glad to hear you are armed. Be alert, you two, and have a pleasant voyage."

"We are leaving the marina this afternoon and will sail southwest along the coast to Brest, across the Bay of Biscay to the tip of Spain, and then continue down that coast. Not sure where we'll end up or if we'll stop along the way. Ava wants as much sea time as possible. How about I call you along the way? And, Robert, it's reassuring knowing you are on the job. Good hunting."

"Ava, you take good care of our Canadian friend, will you?" Robert asked.

"He will not be out of my sight, Lieutenant," Ava replied.

At 5:30 p.m., the *SeaOx* chugged slowly away from her berth and made for deeper water on the ebb tide. One hour later, they had the main and the jenny up, both drawing nicely. The boat was speeding along at a surging six and a half knots. Andre and Ava moved into the inside steering position of the pilothouse and enjoyed a pre-supper brandy. She put her snifter on the window ledge and hugged him for all she was worth. Andre let go of the wheel and hugged her back, giving her a lingering kiss as well. They were once again as one with the sea.

Chapter 19

Andre and Ava Sail to Portugal, Ruth and Pelling Plan Their Escape

Teddy Pelling, using his Rolf Erik Studer passport, purchased the fifty-foot Beneteau sailboat at their marina sales office in Bordeaux. He gave the sales agent a cashier's cheque for two-hundred-fifty-thousand dollars and received a cashier's cheque for the forty-seven-thousand-five-hundred dollar difference. The agent listed all the offshore tackle and gear that had been installed, as per Captain Petain's requirements. The sailboat kept her original name, *Bijou*, as Pelling did not wish to fool with the laws of sea lore, which said it was very bad luck to change a boat's name. So, the *Bijou* was made ready for sea.

Teddy had brought all his belongings, stored in the VW van, aboard that morning. He was dressed as the old chap when he claimed his Gucci bag from the hotel concierge and gave him another hundred-dollar tip for his trouble. He drove the van to a shopping centre parking lot, and after changing and stowing his disguise in a backpack, he walked to a bus stop as a casually dressed young man. He took the bus back to the marina and settled in on the *Bijou*.

Ruth was getting into the swing of the offshore adventure and shopped for new sailing attire at the chandlery, including foul-weather gear. Pelling had done likewise in the marina store. Along with his new sailing togs, he purchased safety harnesses and a hand held GPS. The *Bijou* did include a Davis sextant, sight-reduction tables, and a few texts on celestial navigation, but Teddy purchased a how-to book for the journey as a resource. The *Bijou* was equipped with just about every navigational aid you could want: a Dell personal computer with Internet capability, an Internet cellular telephone, Loran radar, a weather fax, and a complete software package of charts.

Teddy was anxious to leave, and when he was offloading his stuff from his van he lamented the fact he didn't have his weapons. He felt incomplete without the pistol with the suppressor he planted on Laurent in the broker's bathroom, and the high-powered custom rifle with the scope and silencer that Raoul de Vascos took from him. *I wiped the pistol and its silencer very carefully. They won't find my prints on either. But, my rifle is another story, being as Raoul took it from me after he woke me that morning in the barn. My prints are on the rifle for sure.* He knew if they found the shell casing that he failed to find after he took the shot at Elspeth's estate, then he was a wanted man. They also would have his description from Elspeth, her son, the marina manager, Andre Laurent, *and very likely Raoul, if and when he talks. The Sûreté will no doubt interview our landlord, Louis Huot, whenever he returns from abroad. He will give a good description of Ruth, who signed the rental agreement. I never met the guy. Man, how plans change. Originally I planned to be in Switzerland, the United States, or at our new estate in Bordeaux by now.*

The Beneteau fifty-footer was bigger than the *SeaOx* but not quite as homey. Pelling preferred the polished darker teak and mahogany of the *SeaOx* to the lighter holly in the *Bijou's* interior. He was looking forward to the journey very much. It wouldn't be a chore for him to tag along with the other three Beneteau sailboats being delivered to Charleston, and it would allow them to slip out of Europe without being discovered by the authorities or the ETA.

Pelling imagined Lieutenant Robert Bizet alerting Interpol and all the police down the coast to be on the lookout for him and Ruth. The ETA had a special reason to capture him alive—money, but that was only if Raoul told his superiors how much he was suspected of having. He would eventually have to give Ruth up as well, but they only knew her as Ruth Meikle. It may not be that easy to make the connection to her real identity since she was presently traveling under her real name and passport. She had sidestepped Raoul's grab at their money by having it wire transferred from Paris. Pelling supposed Bizet would be especially motivated to find him now because of the evidence package he sent him. Bizet would know for certain that Raoul ordered him sanctioned, and he would see that Pelling had killed Bizet's lady in front of him.

I thought for sure it would destroy his will. It didn't, and he kept up the heat with his on-going vendetta against the organization, and for his dogged police work he got promoted to lieutenant—very impressive, indeed. I'm sure it has become personal with the lieutenant. He'll want to settle the score. I'll be on my guard.

Captain Petain, the Beneteau delivery person, came aboard the *Bijou* and outlined the route the four sailboats would follow on their way to South Carolina. They would tie up for forty-eight hours at Lisbon, Portugal, their first stop. Their next destination was the Azores, where they would stay for three days before leaving for their final destination, Charleston. Captain Petain handed over two charts with the course lines drawn in. He also demonstrated for them how to keep in touch with his lead boat while under way. Lifting the mic off the hook on the ship-to-shore radio, he tuned it to channel eighteen and asked for his own boat, *Bosun's Pipe*. A crewmember on the boat answered and a brief conversation took place. After Captain Petain signed off and replaced the mic, he went over a few of his rules: Leave the radio on channel eighteen at all times, stay in sight of one another, and relay speed and position every two hours. Captain Petain assured them that these rules would see them safely to their first stop in Lisbon, where they would all have plenty of time to go over plans for the next leg to the Azores.

"Let's just concentrate on getting safely to Lisbon. I figure the sail should be five days if we average six knots, and so far the weather looks cooperative. Incidentally, I've gone aboard the *Pancho,* which is owned and skippered by Don Paul Nolan, and gave him the same on-board instruction as we just went through. We'll leave together tomorrow at 6:00 a.m. I'll lead us out of the marina in *Bosun's Pipe.* She's the fifty-five-foot Beneteau with the red hull. You can't miss her. The *Pancho,* a white fifty-footer, will follow, and then the *Jacqueline*, a new fifty-footer with a black hull skippered by my associate, Captain Felix, whom you will follow out.

"We'll continue motoring up the Gironde until we come to the Bay of Biscay when I'll call everyone on the radio and give the order to hoist sail and steer two-hundred-fifty degrees, any questions, folks? None? Fine! Oh, one more thing. I have one crewman aboard and Captain Felix has two, so if the trip gets too tiring and you want one of my experienced hands to take over for an eight-hour shift anywhere along our course, get on the radio, let us know, and we'll put someone on the *Bijou* so you can get some solid sack time. The food you requested was stored last in, first out on your boat this afternoon, so as we progress you can easily access your daily menu goods."

"That's very thoughtful and comforting, Captain. We'll see how it goes. I think you've covered everything. We will be ready to sail at six in the morning."

"Good to have you along, Studer, and you too, ma'am. Sleep well!" With a smile and a wave, the burly delivery captain, barrel-chested and easily six-foot four, bounded up the stairway like a teenaged athlete, and stepped off the *Bijou* into the night.

"Man, he certainly exudes confidence, doesn't he, Teddy?"

"He's probably only done this trip about a hundred times or more. Just look at the condition of these charts he left. They've been rolled up and unrolled so often they're like cloth. We'll each have to do eight-hour shifts from here to Lisbon. Five days sailing is one-hundred-twenty hours divided by eight. That's fifteen shifts. So, how about the first couple days you can watch what I do on my shift so you'll know what to do on yours. I'll catnap during your first few shifts to see how you get on, just until you get the hang of it. I'll do the first shift from 6:00 a.m. until 2:00 p.m., and then watch you from 2:00 p.m. until 10:00 p.m., when I'll take over until 6:00 a.m. As you know, Ruthie, I don't require much sleep anyway. We'll be fine, and if we get pooped we'll ask Petain to put one of his extra crew on-board to give us a break so we can crash and charge our batteries. Hell, I'm pumped! I could do the five days by myself, no sweat."

"Well, sailor man, I'm excited about this trip too! So, what say we jump into our brand new ocean-going pad and give it a good old-fashioned christening?"

"I'll go up on deck for a last look around, then I'll lock up for the night and come right back."

Pelling stepped off the *Bijou*, walked along the jetty to the bow, and then back to the stern. He tugged at the spring lines as well as the mooring ropes. Satisfied all lines were secure, he stepped aboard the sleek sailboat, closed and latched the hatchway covers behind him, and then went down the stairway and into the master stateroom. Ruth lay naked on top of the covers. He took his time undressing, watching her watching him as she slowly dialled a circle around her right nipple with her index finger.

"Did you ever get serious with any of your lovers or clients, Ruthie?"

"Now this is a first, sweetie. I mean the very first time you ever asked about my lovers or clients. But, yes . . . yes I did. Twice, actually."

"Tell me about them."

"Well, the first one was thirty years old when I was seventeen. We met at a summer camp where I worked my last year of high school. I was with my friend Ida, who I've told you about. He was the camp doctor. I remember when we first saw each other. The chemistry was so strong we both began a campaign on each other. Ida wanted him just as bad as I did, but I managed to persuade her that I should have him first.

"I've told you about some of our escapades, but did I ever tell you I shared my first lover with her? My cousin Bruno must have thought he was born under a lucky star. After talking him into teaching me how to take care of him sexually when I was fifteen, I convinced him to show Ida the ropes as well. God, I thought I was bad, but Ida was always so horny, and she's seven months younger than me. After I arranged her deflowering, Ida was my buddy for life. That summer we were quite the threesome. We used to take a train into the city and stay for the weekend at a place that belonged to Bruno's college chum and really get it on. Man, we were crazy wild. We would change partners, and well . . . you name it and we did it. That was in our second and third year of high school.

"In our final year, Ida and I got kitchen work at the summer camp. We were given free board and room and a little spending money. That poor doctor didn't stand a chance. To this day he probably thinks he seduced me. There was something special about him, though, and I guess I thought I was in love with him. However, when he asked me to marry him, my feelings toward him began to change. Thinking back, it was because I had a very different slant on our relationship than he did. My thinking was that we could just live together as special friends. He'd help me get situated in Paris, and when I finished the financial planning courses, I would start my own business and he would be my first client. I guess I wanted him to be my benefactor. You know . . . my sugar daddy. I'm sure I told you this part before."

Pelling smiled, but shook his head.

"I didn't? Well, after the initiation to sex, the summer I was fifteen, it occurred to me I could use sex to make a good living if I was smart about it and took some business training. Hell, I felt I wouldn't have any trouble getting wealthy clients and establishing an influential list. So, when the doctor got all smarmy and possessive and practically insisted we get married, I had to extricate myself from the relationship, and quickly. Enter Ida. I picked a fight with the dear doctor, left for the weekend in a huff, and left Ida conveniently available to comfort and ball the brains out of the poor heartbroken guy. Ida played with him for the rest of that summer, totally enjoying his attentions, but she never got a marriage proposal. I left for France at the end of that summer, and Ida went to work in a bank in Boston."

Teddy had stripped to his underwear, walked to the chart table for Captain Petain's charts, and examined them during Ruth's story. Other than the odd *hmmm* and *uh huh*, he hadn't really said anything while she spoke. "You mentioned two times. Who was the second?"

"Now really, this is something, lover! I mean this sudden interest in my sex life. Are you really interested, or do you just want to hear sexy stories for their erotic effect?"

"Where is Ida now?"

"Why Teddy, did I hit a nerve? Or are we still on the same topic? Actually, I spoke with her three weeks ago. She is living in Atlanta, Georgia, still with the same bank, living with a radio personality, but thinking about making a change. Ida has visited me in Paris twice a year since that last summer, and we've partied with some of my regulars. Sweetie, we always hoped that you would get in touch when she was in town, but it never happened. You seemed to always appear with a 'delivery' after she left, or Ida would get in touch after you left. Did I ever mention that we look alike? We've often been mistaken for twins. Oh, sweetie is that it? You want to try us together, or is it just her?"

"So, who was your other love interest?"

"It was Ida, silly. Does that surprise you?"

"Interesting."

Teddy came to bed to cuddle with her for a while until they needed to be joined. They took pleasure from each other as they had in the past. Ruth would begin by saying the same things to him she had said years ago in Greece when she first took him into her bed. "My, my . . . what yummy muscles you have, and so handsome. Are you sure you're only seventeen?"

Then, when they began making love he would hear her say the same familiar words, "You're making me so hot, lover . . . such a big boy. Do you like it when I squeeze you like this?" He never answered her that first time, or any time since. He would just keep at her until she lost it, telling himself, *that's what she wants . . . that's what they all want.*

Ruth knew from that first time they had sex that he was special. And what an apt pupil he was. She taught him early on in their relationship how to give her the ultimate pleasure of multiple orgasms. She was aware that he got lots of practice with prostitutes, not wanting to complicate his life with normal relationships, when he wasn't with her. Teddy quickly became an experienced lover, enjoying all her sexual talents. He imagined it was the reason her special clients kept on coming back. Teddy could always take her to that level of ultimate sexual pleasure, and once in that zone Ruth would regress to her teen years, crying out "Bruno" until her spasms quieted. She told Teddy she had only been able to get off with him, ever since Bruno, her first lover. She explained that while she enjoyed herself very much with all her clients, none of them took her over the edge like he could.

Ruth had known Teddy Pelling since that summer he spent in Mykonos with her brother, Oscar. Oscar was in love with Teddy and had brought him to Greece because of the tragic drowning of both his parents. Oscar was Teddy's high school gym coach and all around confidant who thought an idyllic holiday in Greece away from inquiring eyes would be just the place to continue his quest of the young Adonis. Oscar convinced Teddy he needed expert financial advice on what to do with his inheritance, and who better to look after his money than his sister, Ruth, a certified financial planner living in Paris. So, the three arranged to meet in Mykonos.

Oscar confided in Ruth that his sexual advances toward Teddy had been rebuffed and, rather than sulk, had made Teddy his co-beneficiary with Ruth. She could tell Oscar was smitten and would do anything for the lad. Ruth told Oscar she was gaga over the well-built youngster herself and planned to take a run at him. That's when a tiff broke out between them. The tension in their idyllic summer household was immediately evident, so Teddy took it upon himself to rectify the situation.

A few days later, Oscar drowned when he apparently ventured too far out to sea on a routine swim. Teddy was scuba diving in the area at the time, but not close enough to offer assistance to his friend and mentor. The athletic youngster did, however, manage to console Ruth, the voluptuous grieving sister. When he was told he was the co-beneficiary with Ruth of Oscar's estate, Teddy appeared pleased but worried. No longer encumbered by Oscar's presence, the two became lovers and friends. Ruth handled all matters concerning the settling of Oscar's estate, the net of which was four-hundred-thousand US dollars. Teddy gave her his share, plus his own inheritance, which totalled four-hundred-thousand dollars. He kept ten-thousand dollars for his own personal use. Ruth was to invest his money wherever she saw opportunity.

Teddy then dropped a bombshell, telling her he felt he needed some specialized training for the future he had planned. Ruth suggested he enrol in a private military college, He could afford to choose even the most prestigious one. He convinced Ruth that he needed to start a new life away from everything. He didn't explain why, but he was feeling anxious about his recent history and, in particular, the drowning of his parents and his friend, Oscar. He convinced Ruth that the best place for him for the next five years was a hitch in the French Foreign Legion.

Teddy Pelling was accepted into the Legion on his eighteenth birthday, December 7, 1995. His enlistment papers showed he had no family, but named Ruth Anna Werner of Paris, France as his beneficiary and executrix. Ruth spent a weekend with him every year on his birthday until his honourable discharge as a corporal at the age of twenty-three. She noticed a gradual change in the handsome lad as he matured into a bigger, harder version of himself. He didn't talk much about the training he had undergone during his tour of duty with the Legion, but she gathered from the little he did tell her that he was an armament and demolition specialist.

Ruth received a twenty-five-thousand-dollar T-bill in the mail from him a month prior to his discharge. What was Teddy up to, she wondered? She pressed him for information, and he reluctantly advised he was working for an organization that hired him as a security advisor because of his training. Teddy's job took him all over the world. He would disappear for months at a time. He brought her large amounts of US currency three times a year, some years more often. She invested his money, along with her own, in the deals she would garner from pillow talk with her upscale clients, some of whom insisted she put some money in this or that stock.

She had done very well with their money. Ruth smiled, recalling how Teddy would hand her a suitcase, or sometimes a bag with a warm baguette sticking out of it, the bottom stuffed with cash, and say, "There's two-hundred-thousand dollars in here, which makes a total of $1.2 million I've given you to date, correct?"

Ruth would confirm the total and he would continue, "I said it before and I'll say it again, Ruth. I don't care how you invest my money, nor do I care about the return *on* my money. I only care about the return *of* my money when I want it."

And was she ever right about Teddy Pelling! He had easily been her best client, bringing her gobs of money on a regular basis. Using information from her special clients and trading discreetly through two banks, she had made some great gains in the markets. Their combined contributions had been just over three million, over three-quarters of that provided by Teddy. She wasn't a greedy person, but she felt she was due half of the total because she had been the one to work that amount up to millions. On the off chance that he did ask for his money, Ruth kept three million in T-bills.

I did the right thing rescuing Teddy from Raoul. I've made up my mind to go along with him come hell or high water. Actually, I haven't really done anything illegal. If the authorities do catch us, Teddy says he'll say he forced me to tag along with him. The real fright is the ETA catching us. Don't like to think about that . . . at all! But like Teddy says, I'll find out that he's not that easy to kill. He honestly thinks of us as a couple, buying this boat and putting it in both our names. And now this thing about Ida, well I can't blame him for wanting to get it on with both of us. Why not? The three of us could get pretty steamy!

Teddy Pelling never failed to amaze her with what he could do, or what he learned how to do. She remembered when he called and asked her to fly to Bordeaux for a pickup, the code that he had another two hundred grand for her. She hadn't heard from him for five months. When he met her at the Bordeaux airport, he whisked her into a taxi that went to a flying club at the end of the airfield. When she'd asked where they were going he answered, 'For a short flight.' They left their bags in the flight school office, and he waited while she visited the washroom. He then led her to a little four-seat airplane and began walking around it, wiggling the wing flaps, looking under the caps, and under the engine hood. Then he finally stepped onto the wing, opened the cabin door, and got into the pilot's seat.

He motioned her to get in. Once she was seated, he smiled at her concerned look, reached behind her head, and pulled a lever to close and lock the door. When they'd buckled their seatbelts, he began his checklist, talking to himself out loud as if she wasn't even there. The engine chugged, the propeller began to spin, and they began to move.

He'd spoken into the microphone he was holding, "V3LAN Piper Arrow requesting taxi instructions to active runway."

"V3LAN Piper Arrow, proceed on A-21 until you reach active runway 27, then switch to the tower at 220."

"Roger ground control. V3LAN out."

She remembered moments later when they arrived at the end of a runway and turned facing its length as a very large airplane flew over and landed in front of them down the runway. *Holy crap, that had shaken me up!*

Teddy turned the tiny knob on the radio until the numbers showed 220 and he spoke into the microphone again. "V3LAN Piper Arrow ready for take-off. Please activate my flight plan for St. Jean du Lux, Tower."

"V3LAN, you are cleared for take-off as soon as the traffic ahead of you clears the runway. When you are airborne we will open your flight plan to St. Jean du Lux. Have a pleasant flight. Tower out."

"Roger that, tower." Just as soon as he replaced the mic, he pushed the throttle forward, causing the engine to roar and the plane to move down the runway. As he eased back on the steering wheel, they lifted off. He kept it in a gentle climb and turned south. That's when he finally decided he would acknowledge she was there. He'd looked over and patted her leg in what he must have thought was a gesture of reassurance. It wasn't.

"Where in blazes did you learn how to fly an airplane?" she asked.

"In the past four months, I got my license and I've been practicing. I have over two hundred hours now. This is the first chance I've had to take you on a little trip. We'll fly down the coast about a hundred-sixty kilometres to the resort town of St Jean du Lux, land, and look around. Then we'll fly back to Bordeaux. So, just relax and enjoy the scenery."

And that's just how Teddy Pelling is, a very clever guy. It won't surprise me one damn bit if he can sail this boat himself.

After thoroughly pleasuring each other, Teddy got out of the tangled bed sheets for a drink of water and said, "When we get to Lisbon, I'd like you to call Ida and have her meet us in Bermuda. Send her ten-thousand dollars via courier for her expenses."

Ruth smiled at her lover and revisited her earlier thoughts about the three of them in bed together. "Aren't I enough for you, lover? Or are you wanting to experiment a bit? Ida will come running when she sees the money and learns it's you we are going to play with. *Mmmm* . . . the three of us sounds just yummy."

"Good night, Ruth."

Chapter 20
Lisbon Marina, Where Old Enemies Meet

Ava looked content at the steering position in the pilothouse of the *SeaOx* when Andre came up the stairs carrying a nautical chart to announce, "We're making very good time. We're still off the coast of France, the western-most tip, actually. It's 3:00 a.m., and we've been underway sixty-three hours and made over eight-hundred kilometres. So, we're averaging close to seven knots. Not bad, eh? How are you holding up? If you want a break, we could pull into Brest and have a good rest."

Ava looked at him with concern. "Andre, I have come to sail, and for me it's more enjoyable to be at sea than to dock. Besides, the forecast is more fine weather, so let's just sail the next leg across the mouth of the Bay of Biscay. We will be across in three days at this speed. Okay with you?"

"I'd hoped you would say that," Andre said. "We'll stay on this heading until we enter the bay, past the tip of the mainland over there." Andre pointed toward the end of the landmass. "You can see the glow of the lights on the headland."

Ava smiled at him. "We will notice the boat's motion change once we are out in the unprotected waters. I say it's at least another three hours before we start southing a little."

"All right then, if you are sure you're okay. I'll nap for an hour or so then make us some breakfast before I take the wheel."

"Make me a mug of hot water with lemon juice, please," she asked. "That will be good for me until breakfast."

While Andre slept below, Ava sipped at her tepid drink and wondered about him. She thought he was beginning to seem more like the Andre she knew when they first sailed together, although at times he seemed to be concentrating on some problem. Though, something had definitely changed about him. Perhaps he was just more worried about his safety. *God, but this is a fabulous sailboat. The money he spent on the electronic devices on board, just to keep in touch with the authorities, seems like a lot.*

If someone came aboard the boat now, Andre would be alerted immediately by the new motion alarm system. He could easily signal the coast guard to board the *SeaOx* for a security check just by pushing a button on the ship-to-shore microphone. *Andre really believes he will be safe from now on and capable of protecting himself. If that Pelling isn't found soon, Andre will stay jumpy. But when I joined him in the shower we made better sex together. We are good for each other in the shower, mmmm.*

The sudden change in the motion of the *SeaOx* brought Ava out of her reverie. They were now well into the Bay of Biscay and out of the wind shadow of the headland. She knew the motion would wake Andre. No sooner did she consider this than he appeared, coming up the stairway into the pilothouse.

"Good morning again. Getting a bit rougher, I see."

"Yes, because the wave patterns are different in the bay, but she holds the speed between six and a half and seven knots."

"All right, I'll get breakfast started and call you when it's ready. Put her on auto then and come eat, okay?" Andre said as he disappeared down into the galley.

"Aye, aye, Captain," she yelled after him.

* * *

On the fifth day at sea, the flotilla of four Beneteau sailboats were passing just west of the Berlengas Islands off

Cape Carvoeiro, Portugal at 6:15 a.m. on a bright sunny morning. They had, so far, experienced only one twenty-minute rain shower. That happened two days ago while they were in the Bay of Biscay making for the tip of Spain. The light crackle of the ship-to-shore radio alerted Pelling to an announcement. He put the *Bijou* on autopilot and went to hear the radio.

"Bosun's Pipe to *Bijou*, Captain Studer. Come in, please."

"Bijou to *Bosun's Pipe*. Good morning, Captain Petain, this is Captain Studer, over," Pelling said.

"Good morning to you, Studer, lovely morning indeed. The lights you see due east are the Berlengas. I've called the others individually to ask them to change course now to one-hundred-seventy degrees from one-hundred-eighty. We're about a hundred and five kilometres from Lisbon, and at our current speed of just over six knots it will take about eight hours to get to the marina Rocho Do Conde De Orbidos. It's the maritime station for the ferries to and from Madeira Island. We should arrive around 2:30 p.m. I'll call everyone again for the next course change at 11:00 a.m. If there aren't any questions, I'll say over and out for now."

"No questions, Captain, *Bijou* over and out."

Pelling hung up the microphone and went to look in on Ruth. She lay sprawled on the bed with only a single sheet partially covering her naked body. *How fabulous she looks, not a care in the world and sleeps the sleep of the innocent. She has been the closest thing to a pal that I've ever had. The way she picked up sailing this boat is just great, standing almost as many watches as I have. Of all the different ladies I've had since I've known her, only a few could fuck me like she does. But, no matter how I analyse her turnabout with Raoul, I just can't get passed it. Other than our money and the sex, our bond of friendship and trust is about as strong as a cobweb.*

He knew they'd be safe from the ETA and police in the company of this little fleet, at least while they were at sea. He wasn't sure what might happen in Lisbon. He wanted to be careful not to attract attention, but figured they ought to be inconspicuous while mingling with their present company. *I don't have my weapons so I won't be able to get out of a tight situation. So, I'll avoid them.*

He looked back at Ruth and wondered what was going on in her head. She could slip away to the Caymans with her passport and banking information and pick up all their money for herself, and then to hell with Teddy Pelling. There was no sense being stupid about this. He'd keep her close and involved until they get to the Cayman bank. Then he'd decide. *At that time, I can change my appearance and look for an estate in wine country, doesn't have to be the South of France or Italy—— maybe Australia or South Africa . . . lots of choices, actually.* In the meantime, the greedy, merciless Raoul was exactly where he planned to put him, locked up awaiting execution.

Pelling reached out and brushed her hair away from her face. She woke instantly, moved her head to kiss his open hand, which led her next to sucking his index finger deep into her mouth. The force of her suction indented her cheeks and began to excite him.

"Good morning. Why don't you hold that thought? Better still, why not bring it up on deck while I go and adjust our course."

He took the wheel and changed his heading to one-hundred-seventy degrees as requested. Ruth came up the stairway into the pilothouse wearing only binoculars around her neck. Teddy left to change the sails. He made the adjustments on the winches, easing off the main and Genoa to sail a broad reach from the beam reach they had been on since the last course change.

Ruth scanned the three other boats just ahead of them, stating, "Nobody else seems too interested in us from what I can see, sweetie, so why not just keep us on course while I help myself to the sexiest sailor on the ocean."

She set the binoculars down, took a cushion from the bench, dropped it onto the teak floorboards, and knelt on it while she dropped his shorts. He stepped out of them and moved back, offering himself to her. She smiled, then took him so deep that her lips were kissing his pubic hair. Both her hands had a firm hold on the cheeks of his ass. She had taught him well, so he knew not to thrust, but rather to let her finish him her way. He felt the hot air from her nostrils on his pubic hair as she continued. She had told him many times in the past just how much she liked oral sex. Today, she was very much into it and thrust her chest out, so he could see her extended nipples. Teddy stroked her face then her breasts, straining to remain still. She felt he was close and kept at him until his knees buckled and she finished him.

She removed him from her mouth and said, "Teddy, that little session got me so randy. Can you come to bed with me right now?"

Pelling did as asked and followed her to their bed in the master stateroom below. She stretched out on the bed and put both hands at her pubic area. Teddy watched. She groaned as her fingers found her wetness. He got between her open legs and began to lick her through her fingers. Ruth withdrew her fingers in favour of his tongue. He tongued her to ecstasy, as it became a writhing demon sending her over the edge. She couldn't help noticing he had become ready again and put her mouth on him quickly, administering her specialty. She stopped, remembering he liked to take her front-on at this point in their sex play. He smiled at her, lifted her legs up under his muscular arms, and pulled her closer to him.

He stayed on his knees, entered her, and took her to that level of pleasure where she became multi-orgasmic, going back to her teens and moaning, "Oh, Bruno . . . sugar . . . God, Brunooohh." Teddy always climaxed when she called out Bruno's name. He held her, impaled, until her shuddering stilled.

Ruth came out of her trance, saying, "Honey, I swear to God, nobody since Bruno can make me feel the way you can."

Hmm... no, I don't think it's a well-acted bit at all. I've screwed enough women to know I can get them to an almost delirious state when they start getting off. Always, a turn-on for me when the ladies howl with their pleasure, and that's when I really get after them. Can't figure out why I can't ever feel any kind of a bond with a woman!

He guessed it was because he never really got over his mother. He'd finally just told her that he'd drowned her useless husband, the cripple, so they could be together. When they finally lay down side by side, she thought he was grief stricken the way she pretended to be, saying they just needed to just hold each other. *Yeah, right! I had to rip her bra and panties off in order to get at her. What an act she put on. Fought like a bloody hellcat, screaming that I was raping her! When I started to love her real good, that's when I knew how she really felt. I was getting to her real fine when she wrapped those gorgeous legs around me, started crying, and began to love me back, taking it real good and letting me get her off... so... awesome! God damn it! Why did she run out, jump in that fucking river, and drown herself?*

The only woman since his mother that had stirred up the same feelings was that feisty widow, Elspeth Vander Riis. She looked at him the exact same way his mother had. *She was daring me to take her to bed, putting on the very same act as you, pretending outrage, with that phony look of contempt. I know damned well she would have fought, too, just like you did. But once I got at her, she'd have loved me good, exactly like you did, Mother dear. God damn you!*

Teddy Pelling looked down at the sexy behind of Ruth Werner, as she turned onto her stomach to present it to him. He put a pillow under her tummy to keep her rear up and positioned for him. He let her place him where she wanted him this time. After a few careful thrusts, Ruth adjusted to the intrusion and the rhythm. He held her by her hair while he continued. In his mind, he was driving hard into a squirming, moaning widow. This image changed quickly to one of his mother. Ruth boiled over when she felt him finish. She turned over, smiled into his staring eyes, and said, "After I tell Ida just how good you are, lover, she will be on her way here in a New York minute."

* * *

Andre Laurent, sitting at the chart table, looked again at the chart in front of him and said, "Ava, that's the fishing village of Galas on the shore to our left. I show we've come nearly two-thousand kilometres and averaged just over six and a half knots. You can see the bridge over the inlet that separates the Costa de Caprica and the south coast of Portugal. We're booked at the Rocha dos Conde de Orbitos Marina, which is just under that bridge over on the port side. You'll see the ferryboats docked at the Martima Gare, which go back and forth to some of the outer islands, but mostly to the Isle of Madeira. I figure it's another twelve kilometres straight ahead."

"Aye, aye, Captain. We're making over five knots on this reach, Andre. I can't remember when I enjoyed a trip more unless it was the first one when I was the skipper, teaching you this fabulous sailboat."

"It's been great having you sail with me on the *SeaOx* again, Ava. I'm very lucky to have you back in my life."

"Andre my dear, I was never out of your life," Ava said, frowning at him. "After I heard the tape you sent me, I was determined to speak with you. I heard between the lines, you had obviously met someone else and only had room for one relationship at a time. So, shit happens! I figured my Andre still had some wild oats to sow. But, I'm a realist. I wanted to see you in person and tell you I wished you well. Hell, I even allowed myself to hope that perhaps Andre's new love hated the sea and boats, and then you would sell the *SeaOx* to me.

"When I couldn't find you, I checked your float plan, which you hadn't cancelled at La Havre. You didn't keep your appointment with the Furano shop, and when the marina manager told me you had sold the *SeaOx* to a Theo Pelling, I got damned good and mad. Soon I became frightened for you because of your strange behaviour. I just knew you were in trouble! Thank God, Lieutenant Bizet listened to my concerns and started to look for you and the *SeaOx*. Believe me, Andre, if he hadn't I would have gone looking for you myself."

Ava's eyes searched his. Andre smiled as he walked into a welcoming hug. They kissed. He came up for air and said, "Making and mailing that tape to you was the luckiest damn thing I ever did. I owe you my life, Ava Haas."

"Okay, Captain Andre, why don't you take over while I go below and freshen up? I'll come back up to give you a hand when we dock."

Andre watched her disappear down the stairway. *She sure is a beauty, and full of surprises. She is one hell of a sailor. When she is at the wheel, she reverts to her rank of captain, kind of funny to watch. Nevertheless, I'm glad she's a good friend.* He was pretty sure she had a hidden agenda, though. Andre just couldn't put his finger on what it was. She told him she was as free as a bird, and had all the money she will ever need, but wouldn't elaborate. He knew her lovely hillside home in Hamburg was well rented on a long-term lease. She received a monthly income from it, which was collected into an account with international branches. *She calls herself independent and self-sufficient, and isn't that just mighty fine. Yes indeed, yet something lurks below her surface . . . but what a surface!*

After a quick check in all directions and finding only two other boats moving across their wake a long way back, Andre put the *SeaOx* on autopilot and went below to Ava. She lay on her back on the berth, naked, except for her panties.

"Is everything all right up there?" she asked.

"Yes, everything is just fine up on deck," Andre said, "But we have some urgent business to take care of down here."

Ava lifted her midsection so Andre could remove her panties, and they spent the next twenty minutes taking care of business. When he withdrew after the latest torrent of excitement quieted inside her and she had exhausted him to her satisfaction, Andre sensed this lusty bout had a different undertone. Andre knew this wasn't love. It was just pure lust. Something had been taken from him before he had a chance to offer it. Hell, not just taken but bloody well yanked from him. Ava got all the cookies at this tea party.

"This was almost too much, but very delicious, —yes, very delicious."

"We should run this sailboat responsibly and that means from topside. Come on deck when you're ready, and bring the lunch with you. I'm starving!" Andre said.

* * *

Ruth and Pelling spent twenty minutes with Captain Petain and the others on the jetty after tying up the four Beneteau sailboats and hooking up water and electricity. The captain suggested they all meet at a place on the docks called the Promenade Bistro for their late afternoon meal. He said he would be there at 4:00 p.m., hoisting a few, if anyone cared to join him.

"Petain says there are public telephone stalls in the Maritima Gare," Pelling told Ruth. "It's a short walk from here. You can call Ida from there. I'm going to rent a car for the two days we're here."

"Should I ask Ida to meet us in Bermuda in two weeks or sooner?"

"Ask her to come to Bermuda a week from today. Tell her we will UPS some expense cash today. We will make the hotel reservations where we'll stay and let her know."

"Okay, but isn't it going to take us longer to sail to Bermuda?" Ruth asked, looking puzzled.

"It would, yes, but we may end our trip in the Azores. It depends on a number of things. I might even stay and fly from here. I haven't made up my mind yet. Besides, it shouldn't matter to Ida when we arrive in Bermuda. She will have the money we sent her and can wait a few days if our arrival is delayed."

"Fine with me, lover, doesn't matter a tick to me."

"Good! We can find a travel agency in the Maritima Gare and see where we should stay in Bermuda, then book it for two or three weeks beginning next Sunday. Phone Ida, tell her to expect a package via courier, and confirm she'll meet us. Then we can decide what we do next, and how we get to Bermuda. I'll slip into the washroom and take enough cash from my belt so you can send her ten-thousand dollars, and still have some handy for tickets and expenses. I want to get some passport pictures taken in my old-man getup."

As they began their walk, Pelling looked over across the marina and saw something unexpected. *"I don't believe this! What are the fucking odds of this happening? That boat looks like the SeaOx, for Christ's sake! Can't get a good enough look through these binoculars to tell if it's Laurent, but the lady at the wheel is sensational. Ah, the mainsail is coming down now. She must be stopping here. Yes, she's turning in, and a guy who is tall enough to be Laurent is coming up on deck. I can't read the name on the boat at this angle.*

"Ruth, I've been watching that sailboat with the dark green hull coming into dock at the marina," Pelling explained.

"What about it, sweetie? Someone you know?"

"Can't say for certain, but it looks like the boat I stole from the Canadian sailor in Brest. I'll keep these binoculars on him until I can confirm. He's coming up on deck again. Yes, it is Laurent all right. What in the hell is he doing here? Good taste in women, though. First, the widow, now this one." Pelling said.

"Is there a problem?"

"Don't know yet, but let's get what we have to do done, and then get back on the boat. Later, I'm going to pay a visit to the *SeaOx* and take care of some unfinished business," Pelling said as they entered the Maritima Gare.

* * *

After they had the *SeaOx* temporarily tied at the arrival dock, Andre presented the ship's papers to the marina manager who assigned a slip away from the core population of boats. After they had snugged the *SeaOx* at her birth they connected water and electricity. They were all set to take a few days off to explore Lisbon before leaving on the return trip to Le Havre.

"Let's walk around the marina, look at the boats, and get the feel of the place. I really would like to stretch my legs."

"Sounds good to me," Ava said. "It's warm out, so we can go as we are. It's nearly three thirty so we could find a place to have some shore food."

Later, after their investigative walk around the marina, they ended up at the Promenade Bistro and were shown to a table against the wall. They were within viewing distance of the main throng of tables where a boisterous group was celebrating and paying the band to play another polka. In that group, Pelling still nursed the same beer he had ordered with his meal of red snapper. Ruth was on her second Scotch and soda, but he never worried about her and booze. She was always a sensible drinker, never an embarrassment on a date. Captain Petain, however, was well into his cups after having consumed much of the beer continually delivered to the table in foaming pitchers.

It was now 6:00 p.m. and the band was singing a Portuguese ballad of bravery. Andre turned toward the lead singer and his eye caught a glimpse of Pelling. *My God, it's him! Pelling is with that noisy table by the bandstand. Jesus, it is him, or it's his twin brother. Got to stay clear of his line of sight and make doubly certain before I contact the lieutenant. Better tell Ava.*

"Andre, are you okay? You were looking across the room and your face went all strange. What is it?"

"Sorry, but I just got a flashback from when I was tied up on the *SeaOx*. It's just unreal. Take a look over toward the table where the big red-faced, white-haired sailor and his friends are sitting. See them?"

"Yes. What about them?" Ava said.

"Do you see the muscular guy in the blue short-sleeve shirt with the skull-cut blond hair?"

"You mean the good looking guy sitting next to the sexy blond lady?" Ava asked.

"Yes, that's him. He is the vilest bastard that ever lived! Ava, that son of a bitch is Pelling, my kidnapper. We have to leave here unnoticed. Follow close to me; I've got to get word to Lieutenant Bizet."

Quickly, they made their way back to the boat, and Andre went straight for his sat phone. "Hello Robert, Andre Laurent calling aboard the *SeaOx* in a marina in Lisbon. Do you read me?"

"Yes, Andre, I read you loud and clear. How are you both doing?"

"Robert, I'm absolutely positive Teddy Pelling is here at this same marina. I noticed him with a small group having lunch on the breakwater. A little while ago I followed him to a fifty-foot Beneteau sailboat called the *Bijou*, out of Bordeaux. Ava checked with the marina office and found out the *Bijou* is registered jointly to Rolf Studer and R. Anna Werner, who are in a small group of four Beneteaus being delivered to Charleston in the United States via the Azores and Bermuda. How quickly can you arrange to have them arrested?"

"Andre, is there any chance Pelling may have spotted you?" asked Robert.

"They arrived two hours before us and could have seen us coming in. He certainly would know the *SeaOx*. So, I suppose it's possible." Andre said.

"I'd like you both to leave the *SeaOx* immediately for a nice safe hotel room without being spotted," Robert said.

"I guess so, sure Lieutenant. It's a short walk to the Maritima Gare where we can make a hotel booking and get a taxi."

"Better to be on the safe side until we check further and arrange to bring this Studer and Werner in for questioning," Robert said.

Moments after they hung up, Ava quickly packed for an overnight stay at a hotel. Andre took his cash and passports from the safe and a change of clothes, and put them into a shoulder bag. His .22 calibre Hornet Python pistol went into the side pocket of the bag. They left the key to the *SeaOx* under the floor mat, where the lieutenant suggested, and walked quickly to the Maritima Gare. They encountered an older fellow who'd had too much to drink and looked lost. Nearer the station, three young men were singing loud harmony off key. Inside the building, Ava picked up the telephone to the Harbourside Hotel at the kiosk where hotels were advertised. She made a reservation for a suite and was asked to stay put, as the hotel shuttle would be along to pick them up in ten minutes.

Outside the building, Ava and Andre waited anxiously. Ava snuggled closer and whispered into his ear. "I'm beginning to feel nervous. I can't wait until we lock ourselves in our hotel room."

"It's spooky for me, too, seeing that creep Pelling again. The lieutenant wants us to call him after we check in. He said he'd know when we called how long it would take to get the local police to make this arrest."

Later, after they had checked in to the Harbourside, Andre called the lieutenant back. "I have been assured by Lisbon that an arrest is in progress," he was told. "You and Ava get a good night's sleep and I'll see you tomorrow morning. I'm going to fly to Lisbon in the morning."

After an hour in the hotel room, Ava was asleep, but not Andre, who decided to go watch the arrest at the *Bijou*. He slipped out of the room with his shoulder bag and called a taxi to take him close to the slip where the *Bijou* was tied up. He squatted behind the pillar that held the utility connections for the boat. Andre could see through the porthole into the main dining area and saw them scurrying about the boat, putting things into a small suitcase. Both were stripped to their underwear. Pelling wore a leather vest with pockets, which looked like it had been sewn together by someone who failed leather craft. Andre was now certain it was his kidnapper. There was no mistaking that build. He next appeared wearing a sport shirt and tan slacks. The woman wore fashion overalls over a skimpy top.

Damn! They're about to leave. I'm sure the local police aren't in place yet. Hell, it's only one thirty. I can't chance letting them get away. I wonder where Pelling parked that Mercedes sport car I saw him with earlier. Cripes, I've got to stop them somehow.

* * *

Robert hung up the phone after arranging the arrest of one Rolf Studer, alias Theo Pelling, ETA agent wanted for murder, and his companion R. Anna Werner, a person of interest wanted for questioning. He advised that he would be in Lisbon in the morning, and would appreciate it if the detective in charge of this arrest would please meet him at the airport. He would send details of his arrival.

He then turned his thoughts to the recent phone call from his staff member at the Bastille who reported that Raoul de Vascos had spent almost an hour with the ETA lawyer who visited him every morning and evening. Robert had granted the visits in the hope that the lawyers would convince Raoul his fate was sealed. He knew the ETA leader would have ordered his network to search and capture his agent, Theo Pelling, and his companion, who both were responsible for his incarceration. De Vascos would work every angle to get free. He wondered if they could be planning a hostage taking and a swap for him?

The hair on the back of Robert's head stood up. Shivers ran the length of his spine. Images appeared on his mind's screen and sent him into action. He shook his head to clear the disturbing scenes and reached for the telephone. "Hi, Marta, what are you up to?"

"Robert, I wasn't expecting you to call until later! Are you coming home soon?"

"I'm going to make a hotel reservation for us and have their limo come by in an hour to pick you up. Turn your fax machine on, please. I'll send you the details of our evening."

"This sounds exciting, but also a bit scary. Should I pack a few things?"

"For me a shirt, underwear and socks, and a few things for yourself."

"I'm intrigued, handsome. I'll pack and wait by the fax machine."

"See you later at the hotel," Robert said.

As soon as he hung up, he dialled the Hotel de Lutèce, booked a suite, and arranged for their limo to pick up Ms Marta Vander Riis at her apartment. The driver was to ask the doorman to call up to the apartment and say the code name "derriere". The manager of the hotel read the instructions back and said the limo would be sent. He estimated forty-five minutes until it arrived for the pickup. He thanked the manager and said he looked forward to meeting him later that evening. Robert then wrote a fax by hand and sent it to Marta at her apartment.

Marta, darling,

Be ready to leave in forty minutes. The doorman will call up and say "derriere," which is the code word to go down and get in the limo. The driver will take you to a hotel where we are registered. Don't, under any circumstances, stop along the way. When you get to the hotel, just ask for your key, and go to our room. I'll see you there shortly when I'll explain everything.

Robert

The fax machine in the Vander Riis apartment dinged, Marta read the arriving message, and went to pack. She first packed the things Robert requested, added his razor and toiletry items, and then what she thought she would need. It all went into a carry bag. Marta dressed in new undies and a bra, slipped into a straight-cut spaghetti stringed black shift, brushed her hair, and stepped into black pumps. She took the bag to the door along with her purse. She reread the fax and stuffed it into her purse. She was ready when the telephone rang moments later.

The familiar voice of the doorman, Louis, said, "Evening, Miss Vander Riis. Excuse me, but . . . err . . . derriere."

"Thank you, Louis. I will be right down."

Minutes later, Marta said good night to the doorman and stepped into the waiting limo. "Which hotel are you taking me to driver?" she asked.

"My instructions are to drive you straight to the Hotel de Lutèce, ma'am."

"Where is the hotel located?"

"Along the Seine on the Isle de St. Louis, right downtown, ma'am"

"Thank you, driver." Marta said as she watched the "city of light" whizz by.

Robert requested an unmarked vehicle be waiting in the basement carpool for his use. He made himself comfortable in the late model Citroen, buckled up, and drove out into the Paris evening. The drive took nearly half an hour, in the busier-than-usual traffic, to reach the Hotel Lutèce. He'd chosen the hotel after hearing Andre Laurent speak of its charm.

He surrendered the car to the valet and introduced himself at the small front desk. "Ah, Lieutenant Bizet, it is a pleasure to meet you. I have read about you in the papers and how you captured the Basque terrorist, Raoul. Welcome to the Hotel de Lutèce. Your party has arrived, Lieutenant, and gone up to your suite. If there is anything you wish, please phone down."

"Thank you, we will. Good evening."

At his suite door, he knocked and Marta let him in. He glanced quickly around the room, and then looked into her beautiful, but troubled, eyes as he took in the svelte beauty before him. Marta knew this ritual well. She lifted her arms up over her head and arched her back, beckoning him closer with her eyes, and then dropped her arms over his shoulders and tousled his hair with her fingers. She had to stand on her tiptoes as he held her tightly in his embrace.

"Now what is this really all about, sweetheart? Code name derriere, really Robert! Poor Louis was still blushing when I went out the front door. What is it, darling?"

"In a minute; first, just let me drink you in. God, you smell marvellous. Okay, let's just call this a practice run for getting away quickly," Robert said.

"Hmm, let me guess! You got thinking about my safety and you cooked this little mystery date up to see how fast you could sweep me away and into your arms—right, Lieutenant?"

"That's very close, very close indeed. Do you believe in premonitions, Marta?" Robert asked.

"Darn right I do! You had one, huh?"

"I was thinking about Raoul de Vascos, who has been in a cell for more than a week now, having two visits a day like clockwork. Doing what? Running his business as usual? I don't think so. Searching for Pelling, who put him there? Absolutely. They have put out the nets for him and his friend, Ruth. Raoul must realize we won't move him until his trial. So what is he busy planning? That's when I got it and the movie started playing in my mind—the ETA taking you hostage, and then attempting to exchange you for his freedom. I dropped everything and called you, and . . . well . . . you know the rest," Robert said.

"Oh, honey, if you don't think I'm safe at Mother's apartment, we can stay in different hotels if you like. As long as we're together," Marta said, "I don't care where we are."

"Well, maybe I'm just paranoid, but there is no mistaking that premonition," Robert said. "By the way, I got a call from Andre Laurent. He called from the *SeaOx*. They're docked at a marina in Lisbon. He's positive he saw Pelling in the company of a sexy blonde on a sailboat at the same marina. I have asked the Lisbon police to take them into custody immediately and hold them overnight. I'll interview them myself in the morning. Sergeant Moline will call me first thing and tell me my flight details. Andre and his friend, Ava Haas, have moved from the *SeaOx* to a nearby hotel until we know more about these two suspects. Andre is adamant that it's Pelling. Wouldn't that be a huge stroke of luck?"

"Well at least we will have the time together before you leave in the morning," Marta teased.

Robert agreed.

* * *

Andre Laurent had his gun in hand as he arrived at the cockpit of the *Bijou*. He had stepped lightly onto the big sailboat so as not to cause an abrupt dip, which would alert them. Andre could hear Pelling hurrying the blonde. He watched from the top of the hatchway, out of their line of sight. Finally, Pelling stepped onto the first step leading up to the cockpit. When he got to the third step, his right hand on the railing, Andre moved into the cockpit doorway, held his gun steady in both hands, aimed, and shot Pelling in the right wrist and again in the left knee. The shock sent Pelling reeling backward, crushing the blonde onto the salon deck. Andre moved down the steps slowly, watching Pelling trying to get up. The woman was out cold.

"Don't move or the next bullet goes through your brain, and I do the world a big favour," Andre said.

"Well, I'll be damned, if it isn't my old sailing buddy, Laurent. Why in the hell didn't I kill you when I had the chance, do you suppose? Because you got set up and I felt you deserved a chance, so I let you live. Now, mate, I ought to be entitled to the same consideration, don't you agree?"

"Stay down and turn over slowly. Keep your hands where I can see them," Andre said.

"As you can see, I'm unarmed, hobbled pretty good, and bleeding a lot!"

Andre lifted Pelling's shirt with his free hand, checked him for a weapon, and found none. "I'm going to assure your safe delivery to the authorities by putting a few more bullet holes in you," Andre said.

"Whoa! Just tie me up for God's sake. I'm in no condition to resist or escape."

"Just lie quiet and don't tempt me, or the next shots will destroy your other hand and your remaining good leg. Where do you keep that syringe with the crap you pumped into me and Elspeth?"

"In that small black case in the chart table drawer," Pelling answered.

Andre found the case containing the half-full syringe, and noticed the blonde beginning to stir. He sniffed the familiar odour of the drug, which reminded him of freshly mown lawn.

Pelling spoke up, "Be careful with that stuff. There's enough there to put us both out for twelve hours or more."

Andre leaned over the blonde, jabbed the needle into her buttock, and injected half the liquid. "Turn over onto your stomach, Pelling. I really want to fire more bullets into your evil hide first, but let's just see how you handle this shit you pumped into us."

"For God's sake, Laurent, I'll bleed to death while I'm unconscious if you do." Andre jabbed the needle hard into the back of Pelling's leg and injected the rest of the drug. "Be a sport, Laurent, and do me a favour before you leave—put tourniquets above my bleeding knee and wrist. You'll find sail ties in the forward sail locker. Thanks, buddy, that will even us up," Pelling said as his head drooped to the side.

Andre slapped him hard across the face but got no reaction. He was unconscious. With only the thought of all this coming to nothing if Pelling bled to death, Andre hurried to the sail locker, found the sail ties, returned to tie two around Pelling's leg above the bleeding knee, and two above the slower bleeding hole in his right wrist. The blonde began to snore, drooling on the teak floorboards.

Andre rolled the terrorist over on his side and opened a pocket of a crudely made money belt, extracted four two-hundred-fifty-thousand-dollar cashier's cheques, and whistled appreciatively. He probed another pocket of the belt and took a total of twenty-thousand US dollars in cash. Andre, not at all curious about what he might find in the other pockets, noted the time was now 1:50 a.m.

He was sure both Pelling and his blonde girlfriend were secure, but he still checked to make sure. He tied Pelling's wrists behind him with sail ties, and then bound his feet at the ankles. Andre tied the blonde's hands behind her back and left the sailboat. When he reached the end of the jetty and stepped onto the pier, he saw Ava hurrying toward him. Andre's stomach began to knot up and he bent over until the dry heaves and nausea passed. Finally, his face twisted into a grin as he looked up at her.

"Are you all right, Andre? When I woke and you were gone I just knew you would come here. I was worried. What happened?"

They walked to the Maritima Gare to hire a taxi, while Andre told her what he had done. Ava listened anxiously, putting her hand to her face as Andre's story unfolded. Ava noticed Andre's usually serious eyes were alive with excitement. When they were back in their hotel room, Andre made a decision. No reason to bother the lieutenant at this time of night to report what had just happened on the *Bijou*. Pelling and his blonde friend aren't going anywhere. It was now 2:35 a.m. and the local police should have them in custody. *I'll explain their condition to the lieutenant when he arrives in the morning. All in all, it's been quite a day. I'm ashamed of the bloody joy I felt shooting that bastard, Pelling. He's toast, Ava. Thank God we've heard the last of him.*

* * *

4:45 a.m. Lisbon Airport

A line of passengers waited impatiently in the cool morning air until pre-boarded passengers had been seated on the

Air France jumbo jet leaving for Bermuda. A flight attendant pushed an elderly man in a wheelchair toward the airliner. Near the head of the line-up, an attractive redhead watched as the wheelchair approached and proceeded up the ramp and into the jet.

* * *

At ten the following morning, Robert landed at Lisbon's Portela Airport. After making his way through the busy terminal, he was greeted at the curb entrance by two plainclothes officers who ushered him into a waiting police van. After introductions, he asked Lieutenant Juarez of the Special Tactical Force what they had found at the marina.

"Our special squad went aboard the Beneteau sailboat *Bijou* at exactly four thirty this morning and found no one on board. The team leader reported he could smell cordite in the cabin. There was also quite a bit of blood on the stairs, as well as the floorboards—obviously signs of a struggle, but nothing more. The team found an empty syringe, which our lab will analyse and send me a report. We've taken fingerprints from the cabin and should have those results later this morning. We have interviewed the auto rental agencies in the Maritima Gare and learned that Hertz rented a new Mercedes to a 'yachty' named Studer. He was to return the car late this afternoon. We've put out an APB on the car. I guess that's about it, Lieutenant."

"It appears we missed our terrorist by the narrowest of margins, gentlemen," Robert said, unable to keep the sarcasm from his voice. "Drop me off at the Harbourside Hotel near the marina, if you please. And Lieutenant Juarez, please keep the *Bijou* quarantined until further notice. I will be claiming it for the Sûreté as confiscated goods. I would appreciate it if you would call me at the Harbourside as soon as results of the prints and blood types are available. I am also interested in what was in that syringe."

When the police van pulled up to the front door of the Harbourside Hotel to let Robert out, he went to a house phone, called Andre Laurent's room, and was asked up to room 517. On the way up in the elevator, he felt a wave of anger surge through him. *Four and a half goddamn hours from the time of my call from Paris until these lazy bastards finally boarded the Bijou. They refused to take any responsibility for their snails-pace response, stating they had to have proper legal search papers in order to arrest anyone who wasn't a citizen of Portugal.*

After greeting both Ava and Andre, Robert had calmed back down to his objective self. Andre asked, "Do you have them in custody, Robert?"

"The Lisbon Special Force boarded the *Bijou* at four thirty this morning and found nobody aboard. They smelled cordite and found signs of a struggle and blood. I can't believe we came this close and missed them."

This revelation caused both Ava and Andre to look at one another in astonishment. "When we spoke on the telephone, Robert, you indicated it would probably be a couple of hours before the local police would act on your directive to arrest Pelling. Anyway, I started to stew about it and imagined them slipping away. So, I went to watch the arrest. I was close enough to see into the *Bijou* and, by God; they were getting ready to leave. That's when I took it upon myself to make sure they bloody well stayed put until the police arrived."

Andre then related the details of shooting and drugging his kidnapper and tying the two of them up. "I can't believe how stupid I am!" he said. "Pelling conned me good, Robert! He said, 'be careful with the needle, there's enough dope in the syringe to keep us out for twelve hours or more.' And I believed the son of a bitch! Having first-hand knowledge of the stuff, right? I can't for the life of me think how they managed to get away. Damn! I should have stayed and kept watch until the police got there."

"It was dangerous to have done what you did, Andre, but it may yet work in our favour. We'll check all flights to the Azores, Bermuda, and the southeast coast of the United

States. This time they are only a couple of hours ahead of us."

"There is something else. After Pelling passed out from the injection I gave him, I opened his rather elaborate money belt. I took these from one pocket; four quarter of a million US cashier's cheques. I helped myself to some of the cash from another pocket. I took twenty thousand, about what I think the son of a bitch has cost me since I was unlucky enough to cross his path. I'd like you to return a million dollars to Elspeth unless, of course, you capture him and turn up enough money to repay the ransom he took from her. In which case, I would like you to keep the money and put it with the other funds you are accumulating in that special fund to eradicate this sort of scum."

"I would rather you keep the money for the time being. This way, I won't have to make out a report. If we do recover more money when we arrest Pelling, we can do the bookkeeping at that time. I think you both realize that you have now become of special interest to Pelling. And I warn you again, Andre, from here on he has more than a passing interest in you."

"Pelling told me he had spared my life on a number of occasions, and I should reciprocate by applying tourniquets to his knee and his wrist so that he wouldn't bleed to death while he was drugged. He really conned me, damn it!"

"Well, I suggest we just wait and see what the lab reports say was actually in the syringe," Robert said. "If it is a knockout drug, then we have to consider they got away with the assistance of a third party, and that would be worrisome."

Chapter 21

Trapping the Assassin

Robert, using an office in the Lisbon police building, hung up the phone after talking at length with Sergeant Moline at the Sûreté in Paris. The sergeant updated him with the latest reports from the Interpol Notice Program, which is responsible for the transmission of international All Points Bulletins to and from the 176 member nations. Robert had circulated the descriptions of Teddy Pelling/Studer and his blonde companion in APBs throughout Interpol Zone Two, which included most of the cities on the west coast of the Netherlands, Belgium, France, and Spain. The response to these APBs would come directly from Interpol headquarters located in Lyon, France, but so far no sightings had been reported.

It was now evident to Robert that Pelling was a man of many names and faces. The Sûreté had so far matched his description with three identities, Edward (Teddy) Pelling, Rolf Studer, and Klaus Bergen. Andre Laurent had wounded him in the left knee and the right wrist, thinking those wounds would incapacitate the terrorist until the Lisbon police arrived at the *Bijou* to arrest him. Not only did Laurent admit shooting Pelling, he had described how he had injected him and the blonde with the same drug Pelling had used on him and Elspeth.

* * *

The 5:00 a.m., the Air France flight from Lisbon to Bermuda was seven hours along its course when the call came from the Lisbon dispatcher asking the crew to unobtrusively check their passengers for a couple in their early thirties—a well-built man travelling with an attractive blonde. The co-pilot left the cockpit, walked to the last occupied seats, and then slowly made his way back to the front of the jet. He noticed two possible matches. He asked the chief flight attendant to scan the passengers and compare suspects with him. She returned with only one possibility, a young couple that was one of the co-pilot's choices. She didn't agree with his other choice. "Too old," she argued.

Meanwhile, a husky elderly man sitting across from his attractive redheaded niece had to make a trip to the washroom and needed assistance. The redhead managed to walk him the short distance with his arm over her shoulder and her arm encircling his waist. The chief flight attendant opened the washroom door for them and the redhead left her uncle standing, bracing himself with his left arm straight out, and his hand flat against the bulkhead above the toilet.

The chief attendant smiled and said, "He seems to be able to manage pretty well by himself."

"Yes, he is doing remarkably well after his knee operation," the redhead said.

The door reopened and the elderly gent stepped through the doorway, put his arm over the redhead's shoulder, as she drew him closer with his right arm snugly around his waist. Three or four steps more and they were back in their seats.

* * *

So, how in the name of blazes was Pelling able to escape? Robert wondered. Andre told him that he was certain he left both of them "out like lights" around two in the morning, but when the Lisbon swat team went on-board two and a half hours later, they didn't find anybody, just evidence of a struggle. So now they had Pelling's blood type, presently being analysed along with the contents of the syringe at the Lisbon police laboratory. Also, a couple matching the description of

Pelling and friend were arrested when the flight from Lisbon landed in Bermuda.

Robert figured the Lisbon flight to Bermuda, which left at 5:00 a.m., would have been Pelling's best bet to escape. They had ample time to make that flight. No sightings of the couple were reported on the Lisbon to New York flight, which left at 7:00 a.m., and nothing positive from security at the Maritima Gare who was checking the passengers on the three departing ferries that morning. Nothing in this case had been easy. *But why choose Bermuda? Arresting Pelling would have been a major coup in the net we have out for him. We have to capture him before the ETA does, or we will be dealing with another homicide.*

The airline dispatcher, when asking the flight crew to check the passengers for Pelling and his blonde companion, neglected to mention that Pelling had been shot in the left knee and right wrist. Had the crew been told this, I'm sure they would have made a different choice instead of the look-a-like young couple that was arrested at the baggage claim area and taken into custody in handcuffs. They'd protested their innocence all the way to the police van, and why wouldn't they?

When Robert spoke to the Bermuda police, the first thing he asked was how bad the gunshot wounds were. "What gunshot wounds?" came the answer, and because no gunshot wounds were found, the shaken young couple was immediately released with an apology from the police and the airline, which quickly offered them compensation—a free open ticket to fly anywhere the airline went. *No doubt the Sûreté will hear from the airline about this fiasco. But I double-checked, and my directive to the airline did indicate wounds to the left knee and right wrist of the suspect. So, it's their omission and it's on them.*

During his telephone conversation with his sergeant in Paris, they discussed every possible way out of Lisbon available to the fleeing couple. Both he and the sergeant agreed they had covered all possibilities. Pelling had given them the slip. Could a third party have come to the rescue? If so, they could still be in Lisbon, or they may have split up. The Sûreté had only the description given by Andre Laurent and confirmed by the yacht salesman in Bordeaux to go on.

Whoa, just a minute! Back up a bit. Why couldn't Pelling be in some sort of disguise? He would have had to have assistance walking because of the gunshot to his knee.

"Damn it!" Robert shouted, jumping up and grabbing the phone. "Sergeant, it's Lieutenant Bizet. I'd like you to go back over the passenger list on that 5:00 a.m. Lisbon flight to Bermuda. This time, make a note of all the passengers who needed assistance pre-boarding and deplaning in Bermuda. Get their passport particulars, or as much info as you can. Also, get the names, addresses, and schedules of the aircrew on that flight. Find out when they are due back here in Lisbon. I would like to interview them. Get back to me with this information ASAP. Oh, one other item, please send paperwork to the Lisbon Special Squad, attention Detective Juarez, and claim the fifty-foot Beneteau sailboat, *Bijou*, tied up at slip 11 at the Lisbon Marina by the Maritima Gare. Claim it for our Special Force at the Paris Sûreté as confiscated property used in a terrorist operation."

"Okay, Lieutenant. I'll get right to it. Anything else?"

"No, that's all for now, Sergeant."

Robert walked out the front of the police building and requested a ride back to the marina where the *Bijou* and *SeaOx* were tied up. Upon arrival, he asked the constable assigned to him to wait while he spoke with the staff at the marina office. He was back within the hour and had to awaken his sleeping driver with a loud rap on his window.

"Please take me to the Harbourside Hotel. I think I'll call it a night, Constable."

Inside his hotel room, Robert readied for bed. He mixed a Scotch and soda over ice, sat on the side of the bed, took a good swig from his drink, and reached for the telephone.

"Ah, Marta, I'm glad you're still up. I miss you very much. I can't say how long this investigation is going to take here.

It depends on what Sergeant Moline turns up in Paris for me. What have you been up to?"

"Oh, not very much, sweetie. A little shopping, but it's kind of spooky. I'm always looking over my shoulder. I miss you terribly, Robert. Can I fly down to Lisbon? Or would I be in your way? God . . . listen to me. I sound like a shrewish wife, don't I?"

"Just as soon as I hear from Sergeant Moline and I know more, I promise to call you back and let you know. I do think it wise if you stayed out of sight at the de Lutèce until I get back or make other arrangements for you."

"Are you getting closer to Pelling?"

"Actually, he appears to have disappeared off the face of the planet, but only because I think we are looking for a description of someone who has changed his appearance and is using another passport. The sergeant is checking on this possibility. After we hang up, I'll call him and see what he has turned up."

"All right, lover, I won't keep you. I'll stay right here in my hotel room until I hear from you. Good luck, good hunting, and be careful," Marta said and hung up.

Robert drank the last of his Scotch, and as he put the empty glass down the telephone rang.

"Sergeant Moline calling, Lieutenant. I spoke with the airline and they faxed me a list of the crew and passengers. The crew returns to Lisbon tomorrow morning. On the passenger list, there is an asterisk beside four names of passengers that required assistance pre-boarding Flight 299. The flight attendants doing this task were also responsible for picking out the suspect couple that was arrested and later released. The names of the four passengers requiring assistance are listed, along with their ailments. I'm afraid none match the description of Pelling, but I did make arrangements with the airline for you to meet with the two flight attendants when they land at 6:15 p.m."

"Good work, Sergeant. Please fax that information to my office here."

* * *

The following afternoon, the interview with the airline attendants went quickly. Robert got the information he wanted from the head flight attendant. He couldn't help but smile as he left for his hotel room to pack for his return to Paris. The other flight attendant was a flagrant flirt, obviously taken with the handsome young lieutenant.

The theory must be correct, Robert thought. *When you are in love with a woman, the opportunities with other women come at you from all directions. I'm going to fly home this afternoon to be with Marta. That flight attendant got me feeling randy.*

He decided to send Sergeant Moline to Bermuda to pick up the trail of Pelling and investigate R. Anna Werner and her uncle, Linus Svensen. He had a hunch about them. But he decided his first stop would be to say good-bye to Andre Laurent and Ava Haas, who advised they were leaving in the morning and sailing the *SeaOx* back to Bordeaux.

* * *

Pelling put his chair back in the upright position in preparation for landing at Wade International Airport in Bermuda. The back of his left knee was numb, and his bandaged right wrist was throbbing like an aching tooth just from unzipping and zipping his fly while relieving himself. Nevertheless, he felt confident they would not be noticed in their disguises.

They'd had no problem getting on the plane in Lisbon, and he was sure they wouldn't have a problem after landing either. It was a stroke of luck that they had only been out of it for about an hour on the boat. *I misjudged Laurent big time. Never thought for a second he would come after me and shoot me. He deliberately wounded me to incapacitate me. That worthless bloody Valium mix he shot into Ruth and me must have deteriorated considerably.*

Ruth had managed to wake and untie him. She'd done a quick bandage on his wrist and knee, helped him into his old-man disguise, and put on a red wig that changed her appearance completely. At the airport, Ruth made arrangements for them to pre-board, telling the airline her uncle had trouble walking after his recent knee operation. His Linus Svensen passport, which showed his age as sixty-one, passed through without problem, thanks to the photo he had taken in the disguise. Ruth's picture had been taken when she was a blonde, but the ticket agent never even questioned it. *I guess women don't need new passports whenever they change their hair colour.*

Pelling still had his authentic passport, which he figured he could turn into a new identity when they reached Bermuda. It would be simple enough to change the old man to a younger Linus by altering the age and changing the picture. After all, he'd learned the art of passport altering from a real master, Raoul de Vascos. *We'll set up in a nice spot, which will accommodate the three of us while I get well.*

It had been either dumb luck or fine shooting by Laurent. The bullet just nicked the top part of the knee and creased Pelling's calf. The other bullet went clear through the wrist, but didn't seem to have smashed anything up too much. It still hurt like hell when he moved it, though.

Laurent wanted me disabled. My guess is he called the cops and was waiting in the cockpit until they arrived. He probably panicked when he saw us leaving. He tied us up pretty good and drugged us, thinking we'd be out for a while. Good thing for us he didn't hang around and start shooting again when we got loose.

The righteous bastard had taken four of his cashiers' cheques and twenty grand in cash. He'd be a bloody hero again and return the ransom sum to the widow. What will Elspeth think then? *She will likely hide her twins in her cellar.*

Yeah, Laurent, what you did to me will heal quick enough, but the damage I've done to you will be with you for as long as I'm alive. I wonder who the good-looking lady is that is sailing with you now? There is something familiar about her. Can't do much about the money you took from me, Laurent, but I'll come up with something special for you and yours, my friend, in case our paths ever cross again.